MANHATTAN
MANGO

Published by
FiNGERPRINT!
An imprint of Prakash Books India Pvt. Ltd.

113/A, Darya Ganj, New Delhi-110 002,
Tel: (011) 2324 7062 – 65, Fax: (011) 2324 6975
Email: info@prakashbooks.com/sales@prakashbooks.com

facebook www.facebook.com/fingerprintpublishing
twitter www.twitter.com/FingerprintP, www.fingerprintpublishing.com
For manuscript submissions, e-mail: fingerprintsubmissions@gmail.com

ISBN: 978 81 7234 512 9

Processed & printed in India by HT Media Ltd., Noida

MANHATTAN MANGO

MADHURI IYER

FiNGERPRINT!

For Suresh.
Thirty years and counting . . .

1

The microwave bleated a warning, but it was too late. Sticky, scalding coffee brimmed over the rim of the mug in muddy rivulets.

"Shit! Shit! Shit!" Neel cursed under his breath. He kept it low, because he also happened to be long distance with his immediate boss in Hong Kong. He dashed towards the micro and pulled out his mug of coffee to rescue what was drinkable. Very little was. *Son of a bitch*, Neel fumed, puckering his lathered face. He had been prepping for his morning shave when the call came and disrupted his morning routine. His coffee was ruined, and now he'd have to brew a fresh cup.

In his stylish loft in Chelsea, Manhattan, Neel's work day had already begun, at five in the morning. "Yeah, no sweat, I got it," he assured his superior at the other end of the world. In Hong Kong, the markets were buzzing and Neel, as always, was chasing the money. He'd follow the money anywhere it took him, even if it meant landing on Mars to get to it! The reason he chose to live in New York City, the epicentre of the financial world, was because that was where the big boys played the big bucks. And Neel was determined to have his own stake in that rarified circle.

Intelligent, immensely ambitious, and enviably good-looking, "Wall Street poster boy" was Neel's calling card. He had realised early on that in America, even in investment banking, a handsome face and a charming manner were assets that could be put to work. Sometimes he couldn't help feeling that the external packaging almost compensated for actual experience. All he'd needed was a healthy infusion of the larger-than-life New York attitude, and after four years of living in the Big Apple, he had acquired it. In fact, he'd practically cloned himself into a Gordon Gekko in the making.

"Right chief," he signed off, "I'll have that update out for you by noon . . ." He disconnected the overseas call and turned his attention to *The Wall Street Journal* on the kitchen counter. Gold up, dollar down. He glanced through the trading sections, as he shook out the last crumbs of spelt cereal flakes, and splashed the remaining milk into a ceramic bowl. The groceries needed to be topped up, he noted, a trip to Whole Foods was overdue. Maybe the new cleaning lady could help out with the shopping. The last one had left in a huff, because he'd thrown a minor tantrum about his laundry pick-up being delayed. The fallout was that his kitchen was now perpetually running on empty.

Neel had another crazy week ahead of him, which, according to him, was as it should be. But he was certainly not an all-work-and-no-play guy. Neel liked to party, and party hard. Regrettably, his last hectic work spell had taken a toll on his social life. He'd had to pass up his weekly get-togethers with the Ganpat Gang, or the G Gang, as they called themselves.

The other two G Gang members, Shanks Subramanian, and Shrikant Godbole, were Neel's buddies from his Mumbai college days. They were also his closest friends on planet earth.

Back in 2007, they'd all watched *Shootout at Lokhandwala* together at the PVR in Juhu. The pithy "Aye Ganpat" score had been all the rage at the time, and the song had struck an instant chord with the three buddies. It encapsulated their innermost feelings and desires, which was why they adopted it as their theme song. So when the G Gang bro-hood shifted base, from Mumbai to Manhattan, the song got transported too, like a piece of baggage.

Even after moving to Manhattan, they continued to share the song, and each other's lives, with a cliquish intensity. Apart from looking out for each other, they were one another's conscience-keepers as well. They also kept a close watch for any "breaking news" within the tightly knit circle, particularly if a girl was involved. Of late, Neel's buddies were totally convinced he'd hooked up with the hot Latina from his condo building. His friends were hoping to get a heads up on the developing story. But the truth was, there *was* no story. All Neel had shared with the sexy Latina was an occasional cab, when taxis were in short supply. Basically, his love life had hit the pause button because work had played spoilsport. A pathetic state of affairs, Neel had to admit to himself, *pathetic!*

He found he couldn't spare the time or the emotional bandwidth required for a serious relationship. He had decided, early on, that instead of wasting his time wooing women, one-night stands were more suited to his hectic schedule. When time was money, he preferred to account for every waking hour with something to show for it. So, in his opinion, networking over an evening scotch was smarter than making small talk with a girl who wanted to "take things slowly."

Two blocks west on 27th Street, in the heart of Chelsea, Shankar Subramanian, Shanks to friends, was having his own New York morning. He was also brewing coffee, albeit in a more organised manner. His coffee-making ritual, practiced by many generations of South Indian coffee-worshipping ancestors, was quite as structured as the Japanese tea ceremony.

Shanks liked his coffee made from scratch, which was why he used a manual decoction filter to brew it. Once the decoction was ready, he poured it into a saucepan, and added the requisite hot milk and sugar. Next, using excellent hand-eye coordination, he rapidly transferred the milky brew from one saucepan to another, raising the dispensing pan sky high, and whipping up the tall column of steaming hot coffee with a ferocious frenzy. The result was a strong, zesty mug of coffee, with a crest of froth that would have done his ancestors proud. And given any cappuccino machine a run for its money!

Then, he helped himself to some Wonder Bread slices, and slathered each slice with a bright pink mixed-fruit jam. Coffee mug in one hand, and his plate of jam and bread in the other, Shanks made his way to the well-worn leather sofa in his living room. On the sofa, lay his Macbook Air.

This was his *me* time. First, with a marked lack of enthusiasm, he checked out the local weather forecast. It was going to be a rainy spring day. So what's new, Shanks told himself. Then, in a state of anticipation, he turned his attention to the daily horoscope forecast. On this particular day, the boss was going to finally realise his true worth, and offer him a long overdue promotion. He was also going to meet a potential life partner, quite by accident. However, it was important that he wear orange and vibe to the number six.

"Bullshit," muttered Shanks to himself. But he knew he'd come back the next day, and the day after that, because he always wanted a fix on the future. It was sheer force of habit. It sort of set him up for the day.

As he worked his way through the jam and bread, followed

by a toasted bagel, three cheese singles, two bananas, and the rest of the coffee, it was a wonder that his lean brown frame and sculpted jawline remained unaffected by such excesses. Fortunately for him, the vegetarian genes seemed to be holding up!

At twenty-seven years of age, Shanks was the quintessential new generation "Tam Brahm," tall, dark, and handsome. His smile was easily his best feature, revealing a set of even white teeth. He smiled easily, and often, and displayed an open, inclusive manner that endeared him to one and all. Another big point in his favour was his guilelessness. Shanks was as uncomplicated as the Wonder Bread he had just consumed.

Shrikant Godbole, the third member of the G Gang, did not need morning coffee. The up-and-coming banker was buoyant from the moment he woke up. So, unlike most New Yorkers, who carried their branded caffeine fix along the busy city sidewalks, he was unencumbered by any such handicap. "Coffee's crap," he'd joke in the office. "Do your yoga, and you don't need coffee, you'll be full of beans anyway . . . ha ha!" By then, many bleary-eyed co-workers would have been happy to put a gun to his head. His routine of thirty-six *suryanamaskars*, followed by a glass of fresh-made veggie juice, obviously had a lot to do with his sociable but suicidal morning bonhomie. His not-so-health-conscious buddies often poked fun at his super-disciplined lifestyle, but Shri told them to stop carping, and try almond milk, or shoulder stands. Or just get a life.

Originally from Pune, he often reminisced about his boyhood breakfasts. And he planned his mornings to replicate those happy memories. Whenever he was home from boarding school, for the summer holidays, his mom would serve up Maharashtrian staples like *pohe*, or *sanza*, with freshly grated coconut and freshly squeezed lime juice on top. The breakfast was accompanied by *tak*, homemade buttermilk. During the winter break, the *tak* was substituted with masala milk, or hot chocolate.

He had continued the breakfast tradition and tweaked it to the need of the hour, depending on what his fridge had in stock. So if *batatia cha kees* morphed into potato latkes—Jewish-style pancakes made with grated potato—he was merely Manhattanising an old favourite!

This morning, he was doing made-from-scratch latkes. "Go, Godbole!" he exulted as he expertly flipped his pancake onto a plate. As he sat down to eat, he topped the pancakes with sour cream and chives. Shri's breakfasts invariably ended up looking like food-porn in glossy magazines, because often that was where he sourced his fancy recipes from. However, if time was a constraint, he avoided the kitchen and picked up a working breakfast to eat at his desk.

Breakfast done, Shri glanced at the digital display on his micro. Seven o'clock. Time to shower and head out. He quickly defrosted some chicken for his evening meal and started stacking the dishes into the dishwasher. His friends often vied with one another to receive a dinner invitation at his place, but Shri was picky about whom he chose to have over. Neel and Shanks, of course, were the privileged ones. They had open access to his tiny studio apartment, at any time of the day or night.

Shri and Neel had known each other from their boarding school days in Kodaikanal. Shanks had made his appearance later, when they were in college in Mumbai. None of them had brothers, so they'd ended up being more like brothers than most brothers. Although they were very different people, with diverse interests, their bonding was based on their common backgrounds and, more importantly, identical life goals.

Their nuclear family background and upper-middle-class circumstances gave them a comfortable lifestyle, but not an entitled one. Unlike some of their other college friends, they had no family fortune to fall back on. The rich kids, with their inherited wealth, were bound by their geography and had to stay rooted to family-owned businesses in India. But the G Gang could afford to burn up the air miles as they charted the course of their careers. Going places was, quite literally, what they had in mind.

During their more intense discussions, they'd concluded that being middle-class came with its plus points. And the biggest upside was freedom. So when it came to career choices, they decided unanimously that an H-1B was the way to go. They knew it wouldn't come easy. Working in the US meant competing with millions of equally talented professionals, from hundreds of other nations. But it was still the ultimate destination for ambitious young professionals who wanted to work in an international environment and play the big league.

It had been inspiring for their generation, Gen Y, to witness the rise of so many iconic CEOs of Indian origin. In the top echelons of economics, finance, academia, politics, and corporate life, Indian names were now becoming commonplace. Men like Vikram Pandit and Vinod Khosla, women like Indra Nooyi and Sunita Williams were idolised and accorded cult status by the G Gang. The end game, therefore, was to emulate these hallowed icons, and follow in their footsteps, chasing dreams that only the very young dare.

The three of them had found different paths to converge at the same point. Neel had worked with a firm in Mumbai for two years, and had then winged his way to Manhattan. He'd gotten his first break with an American bank, and then moved on to a more impressive portfolio, with a multi-billion dollar hedge fund based out of Hong Kong. Shanks had started off as a techie in Syracuse and, with the help of Neel's contacts, had subsequently secured a job as a systems analyst with TD Bank, Manhattan.

Shri had gotten just plain lucky. His father had come into the US on a UN deputation, and after a period of time, this had allowed his dad H-1B status. Shri was past the age of getting citizenship, but he'd used the opportunity to finish his MBA from Wharton. And even before completing his programme, he had been hired on campus by Citibank.

Ghoom phirke, as Shri often stated, all three of them had ended up in Manhattan, and that too, within walking distance of each other. Shanks insisted it was destiny. Shri argued it was all about working hard. Whatever the rationale, the fact was, it had happened. They were together again. The reunion had led to many happy, inebriated evenings in each other's company, where they reminisced about the past, plotted the future, and generally had a great time.

While there were constant additions and subtractions to their casual circle, the core G Gang continued to remain tightknit. Not because they were closed-minded, but because they didn't want to dilute what they had. Neel had once expressed it for them all, when he had been under the influence. "*Single malt mein paani milake mazaa nahi aata, yaar.*"

By filtering out extraneous company, they could also hark back to old times without having to explain things to the uninitiated. How could you share Santa Banta jokes with someone who'd never been to India? Or debate the merits of the biryani at Delhi Durbar, Colaba, over Jaffar Bhai's, at Mahim? Anyone who hadn't burnt their fingers having charcoal-roasted *makkai* on the *phootpaths* of Mumbai in pelting monsoon rain had never been properly baptised! Those poor souls would always have to be a work-in-progress. It was a pure snob mentality—what the G Gang called their Mumbai Quotient—and the cut off to qualify was pretty high.

But the adage "change is the only constant" was soon going to be put to the test. The G Gang had no idea that their cosy little club was about to be rocked with an off-chance encounter that no one could have anticipated. The world as they knew it was never going to be the same again!

Shefali Bhansali, new to New York, was as far removed from the G Gang prototype as you could get. She was neither driven nor ambitious. And she certainly wasn't middle-class. Mundane pursuits, like making morning coffee or making ends meet, were not for her. She had a breakfast tray laid out for her, usually around noon. Midday was when her morning started, because Baby Ben liked to have her breakfast in bed. Of course, after a really late night, Baby Ben felt justified sleeping in well past the lunch hour. In that case, breakfast was scrapped and, instead a sushi brunch or a fruit platter with cheese was ordered from the deli downstairs.

At present, Shefali was between jobs. Her diamond merchant father, based in Antwerp, wanted her with him, helping with jewellery design. Shefali, however, found shaping and setting gemstones too arduous, and Antwerp too boring. She loved London, but her ex lived in London, and the city just wasn't big enough for the both of them. Paris was great, but her French was not. So, soon after her break-up with her boyfriend, she decided to test new waters. Flying across the pond, to the other side of the Atlantic, seemed like the perfect solution.

"Pappa, I want my space," she announced to her dad. "I'm moving to Manhattan." Her father took her quite literally and bought her a luxury co-op apartment in the city that never sleeps. But Shefali was doing a lot of sleeping in her Manhattan apartment and still had to get down to looking for a job. And although she'd qualified in fashion design from Europe, she preferred to *write* about fashion rather than get into the nitty-gritty of the business.

Nothing was super urgent though. Right now, she was content to just laze about and do nothing. She could afford to. Stretching languorously, with graceful, feline movements, Shefali leaned back into her goose down pillows. She sipped her iced tea, as she browsed through her SMS messages.

While her dancer's body did turn heads, her most attractive physical attribute was her heart-shaped face and expressive almond eyes. Often her eyes did the speaking for her. She could draw people close, with a sidelong glance and a come-hither look, or keep them at a distance, with a cold stare. It was all part of the on-going Shefali drama!

Once she'd finished a leisurely brunch and had a long shower, her post-noon schedule kicked in. Her afternoon was starting out with an appointment at a fancy new hair salon, and after that, she was meeting friends to check out a gallery opening in Soho. These were just casual hang-out friends she had met at charity galas and fashion events in the city and not her immediate circle of close friends, who were still mostly in London.

From her humungous walk-in closet, Shefali picked a semi-formal outfit, just in case the art event was followed by dinner plans. She liked to be sartorially prepared, so a Cashmere dress, matched with a belt and a printed silk scarf, seemed appropriate. There was nothing tackier than dining at an upscale establishment looking slightly sketchy, she reflected. Then, she stepped into her designer heels and walked out of her front door.

But despite being dressed to her satisfaction and stepping out in style, her day was turning out to be anything but satisfactory. At the salon, after almost two hours of cutting, colouring, and curling, Shefali's teeth were on edge. The hairstyle was not what she had in mind at all. She thought it made her look like an aging sixties sitcom star, with her hair all poufy and plastic.

If that wasn't enough, she emerged from the salon to find it was peak rush hour, something she'd been hoping to avoid. It was also beginning to drizzle. Finding a taxi in Manhattan during the rush hour was like hunting a prize catch in an over-fished ocean. Shefali was just one of the many commuters trying to get lucky. And the worst of it was that her expensively coiffed hair was already clumping in thready strands over her face.

Just when she was losing hope, she spied a taxi approaching. It stopped right in front of her disbelieving eyes. The occupant was getting out, so there was not a second to be lost. Shefali sprang forward, waited for the passenger to get past her, and jumped right in. As she slid in thankfully, she was taken aback to find a man easing himself into her taxi from the other side. They stared at each other, speechless. Shefali found her voice. "Sorry, this is my taxi."

The young man was calm, almost smiling. "I got in first," he said.

For Shefali, this was a surreal moment. Here she was, dripping and desperate, and this smiling oaf was actually trying to hijack her taxi. "I'm in a rush," Shefali told him, "so if you could just get out, I—"

"I'm in a rush too. Why don't we share the ride?" he asked.

The taxi driver was getting restive. His taxi was blocking an entire lane and the cars behind were honking. He twisted around and, with exaggerated politeness, raised his eyebrows. "So. Which one of you gets out?"

Shefali wasn't taking any chances. Having a bad hair day was sucky enough; all she needed now was to walk all the way home. She mentally kicked herself for not having had the foresight to order a limo service. However, it was too late for that. Any car would need at least half an hour to make its way through the traffic. So she turned frostily to her fellow passenger. "Okay, I'll drop you off, just tell the driver where."

The stranger really had the most angelic smile. "Why don't I drop you off first?"

Behind them, the honking was reaching a crescendo. Shefali was fast losing her cool. "Just tell him where, *now!*" she hissed.

Looking alarmed, the guy turned hastily to the driver. "21st and 3rd, south side." Then, he reverted his attention to Shefali. "Hi, I'm Shrikant, you can call me Shri."

Here, Shefali used one of her many social skills—the art of tossing her head disdainfully. It was not easy, with all those slimy strands weighing her down, but she managed a fairly creditable head toss. "Shefali. Hi."

Then she turned her head away, towards her rain-splattered window. She had known from his accent that this guy was Indian. Not that she cared. Surely there was no need to get pally in cabs just because you happened to belong to the same country.

However, she couldn't help noticing, even in the brief encounter, that behind his rimless glasses, he had the most humorous grey eyes. And a friendly if slightly aggressive manner. He was extremely well dressed too, and had that soft-spoken, sing-song accent of the urban convent-educated Indian from India. Mumbai, she guessed, her sensitive ears picking up the unmistakable intonation. Sure, he was rolling his r's about a bit, but that was a recent affectation, just like the way "dance" and "chance" were pronounced by newbies who wanted to blend in.

As a child Shefali had loved to single out Indians in public places. It had been her hobby. At international airports, or restaurants in Europe, it was fun to spot the well-oiled heads and polished black leather shoes with blue jeans. Many carried their own snacks around too, in plastic *dabbas*.

Increasingly though, *desis* were blending in. Her generation was so mainstream, that Indian-spotting was no longer a diverting pastime. She observed that the second-gen kids, born and bred outside India, were so whitewashed that they were truly global citizens. Even their names were whitewashed. Being introduced to a Nick usually meant the guy's name was Nikhil, and Samir invariably turned *gora* as Sam. Moreover, many weren't even born in India, like her teenage crush actor Imran Khan, who, she had heard, was born in the USA. Or like Katrina Kaif, who happened to be of mixed parentage.

But Shrikant, aka Shri, clearly did not fit that category. He was still very Indian in his mannerisms and in the way he spoke. He had even demoed the classic yes-but-it-could-mean-no headshake, which meant he was from India, *proper!* While trying not to appear too interested in her new acquaintance, Shefali couldn't help being intrigued. He resembled someone she knew back in London. The same buzz cut and very fair skin, which, with the slightest stubble, tinted green.

In a social situation, at a function, or a party, she might have sought him out. However, the tiff in the taxi had got her a bit miffed, and now she wasn't sure she wanted to start a conversation. But the cab was crawling along, and, like it or not, she was going to be stuck with him for a while. She might as well make the best of a bad situation. She turned towards him, and there he was again, smiling that beguiling smile.

"You know, even before you told me your name, I knew you *had* to be Indian," he said when she looked in his direction.

Although she was trying to slot him into a stereotype, Shefali was annoyed that *he* was doing the same thing with *her!* She tilted her chin up. "I'm *not* Indian. I'm a British citizen."

"You know what I mean," he said.

She sighed. She knew exactly what he meant. It might be smarter to just give in. And start a conversation. "So . . . you work in the city?"

He smiled. "Yep, *at* Citi actually, head office!"

That made her smile too. "Hah. Banker."

"What's 'hah' about bankers?"

"Really?" Shefali raised her eyebrows. "Like you had no idea! You guys continue to fleece the world and we are all supposed to stand by and watch! Seriously, I totally supported Occupy Wall Street!"

"You don't strike me as the Occupy Wall Street type yourself, so you can hardly blame bankers for all the world's ills." He smiled. "I mean, think about it, you're the one percent those poor people were protesting about!" He pointed to her Hermès bag and bejewelled fingers. And made a mental note that she had no wedding ring.

Shefali bristled. "So what are you expecting me to *do,* exactly? Hold up an official banner, announcing I'm against bankers who've helped themselves to cash that isn't theirs? Stand in Battery Park, shouting slogans about—"

"Zuccotti Park."

"What?"

"Not Battery Park. It was Zuccotti Park."

"Oh, whatever." Shefali rolled her eyes. "It was a while back, and really, do I have to know every park in this city?"

Shri smiled to himself. He suspected he'd won round one. He glanced at her to check if she was sulking. He thought not. She was busy checking out something on her cell phone. Suddenly, he had an idea. "Hey," he said, "why don't I show you how nice bankers can be? I'm headed out to meet my banker friends in the East Village. How about you join us?"

Shefali was amused. "Seriously? *More* bankers? No way!" she said, and turned her attention back to her cell phone. Her friends had called off the gallery-opening plan. Apparently, nobody wanted to commute in the pouring rain.

"Actually," Shri clarified, "they're not *bankers bankers*. One's a hedge fund guy and the other's a techie who happens to work in a bank. Does that work?"

"God, I'm not allergic to bankers or anything, so don't make me sound like a weirdo!"

"Is that a yes?" Shri wanted to know.

With the gallery plan cancelled, Shefali figured that she had limited life choices. Her options were a solo evening at home, or an evening out, with some random Indian bankers. She sized Shri up once more. Then, like most of her decisions, this one was quick. "Okay, you know what . . . I'm on!"

She regretted it the moment she had accepted, but it looked like a done deal. He was already texting his friends to let them know. She made up her mind that if the evening got too unbearable, she'd plead a headache and make a quick exit. Well-timed entries and exits, like the famous head toss, were very much a part of Ms. Bhansali's social repertoire.

So the cabbie ended up getting just one single fare. The squabbling lady and sanguine gentleman got out together and made their way towards a popular lounge, with a long line-up outside. The pelting rain, or the fact that it was a weekday, did not seem to dampen the New York spirit in any way.

2

The lounge was packed, and there was barely any space to stand. Shri negotiated his way through the crowded interior, towards a section that had reserved seating. Shefali followed close behind him. As her eyes adjusted to the dim light, she spotted Shri's two friends, occupying a cluster of bar stools in a far corner. She had no idea that, at that very moment, the friends were eyeing her approach with open dismay. Luckily for her, it was too dark to see that far.

Shri's two best buddies were, in fact, directing expletives at him, and not sparing the language. By dragging a girl to their sacred once-a-week boys' night, Shri had broken their gentleman's code of honour. Apart from totally ruining the evening, of course.

There was an unspoken understanding that every Thursday night, regardless of work pressures, regardless of other social commitments, regardless of wind and weather, it was bro time. The time to booze and bond in each other's company. The three of them revelled in letting their hair down, and letting it all hang out. If a psychiatrist had been listening in, he'd have been amazed at how much these friendly powwow sessions saved in shrink's fees.

This week, they'd had to ditch their usual Thursday night in favour of Tuesday, because Neel had to be travelling on Thursday. It was one of those rare, unavoidable aberrations. But that was a minor glitch compared to this! What could have possessed Shri to show up with some unknown girl, and that too at short notice? Now, their sacred boys' night was going to morph into a be-polite-to-the-girl affair, which was *so* not happening. Really, Shri deserved to be lynched!

However, when faced with the inevitable—in this case, Shefali—the Gang was quick to adapt. As Shri and Shefali came nearer, and they got a closer look, their natural curiosity got the better of them. If their friend was actually escorting a girl, something he'd never done before, this one might be worth the ruined evening. Even Neel had to admit, she looked pretty hot, at least from a distance.

"You think he's like, dating-shating?" Shanks asked Neel, who was the undisputed expert in such matters.

"Doesn't look like it, the body language is all wrong." Neel didn't bother to mention that Shefali had already made eye contact with him. And it wasn't a casual checking-him-out kind of glance either. He knew enough about female admiration to see that.

He had been right. Shefali *was* riveted to his amazing good looks. Her glance had passed swiftly by Shanks, the dark and reedy one, and shifted over to Neel. The one with the aquiline nose, chiselled cheekbones, and haunting eyes caught her attention, and kept it there. She had always bemoaned the lack of good-looking Indian men, but this guy's drool-worthy quotient was on top of the scale, even by international standards. Quite unconsciously, she flicked back her wet hair and held her chin high. She figured the evening might turn out to be fun, after all.

Aware that he had broken the accepted code of ethics, Shri

decided to brazen it out. "Hey, wassup guys?" He turned to Shefali. "Meet Shankar—Shanks—and Neel, my buddies from Mumbai." He turned to Shanks and Neel. "And guys, this is Shefali."

The moment he made the introduction, Shefali's suspicions were confirmed. "Oh my God, Shri, this is one of those boys' night thingies, isn't it! Oh my God what am I doing here!"

"So who said a boys' night has to exclude girls!" Shri turned to his friends, hoping for a confirmation of his bizarre theory. But his friends turned away shiftily, and refused to meet his eyes.

By then, Shefali wanted to curl up under her bar stool, and stay there. When Neel turned to her with a dutiful smile, and asked, "Tell me, what can I get you to drink," she felt even more like a trespasser. However, since crawling under the bar stool was *not* an option, she smiled at Neel, peeled off her sodden jacket, and said, "Umm, a scotch please. On the rocks."

Shri, who was still standing, touched Neel's arm. "I'll go, bro. You keep sitting . . ."

"And a Jack for me," Shanks called, addressing his turned back.

With Shri absent, she felt it was important to set the record straight. She didn't want the girlfriend tag attached to her, not with Neel around! "Shri and I," she explained, "we just met . . . we shared a taxi . . . and he invited me to join you guys."

Was she imagining it, or did they both look slightly disappointed?

All the while, Shanks had been eyeing Shefali with unconcealed interest, and now, the time had come to engage her in conversation. He smiled encouragingly. "So . . . you work in Manhattan?" he asked.

"I don't work."

"Oh, laid off?" That was Shanks, again.

"No, no, I just came, about a month back, from London. Antwerp, too."

"Oh, *looking* for a job!" That was Shanks, yet again.

"Well, not really, not right now, at least." Shefali smiled serenely up at him.

Shanks continued to stare at her. He failed to notice Neel glaring at him and trying to catch his eye. But then, Shanks was not looking in that direction. Shanks, as always, was focused on getting answers. "Oh, so how come you're staying here, in Manhattan, when you're not—"

At that very moment Shri reappeared with the drinks. Neel let out a sigh of relief.

Shanks had been going into what his friends called "The Inquisition." He would keep asking questions till he was satisfied with the answers, and if he was not, he felt it was his duty to continue the interrogation. If the answers confused Shanks, which often was the case, he felt the need to clarify. Not once did it occur to him that he was being impolite, or intrusive, or just plain irritating.

However, Shanks was distracted with the arrival of the drinks and turned to pick up the Jack Daniel's that Shri had refreshed for him. The Inquisition was on pause, the interrogator was taking a break.

Over the raised glasses, Shefali's eyes met Neel's for a long moment. She was glad she'd been sitting, because the heady sensation she felt had nothing to do the alcohol. Her scotch-on-the-rocks was still waiting to be sipped.

Shri saw the attraction between them right away. Through their early teens, it was a familiar old pattern. Girl meets boy. Girl falls for boy. Boy falls for girl. Within a short timespan, boy tempted by another girl. Boy and girl break up. Girl finds shoulder to cry on. Since it was often *his* shoulder the girl found,

Shri had a feeling of déjà vu about the Neel-Shefali encounter. Of course, he could be entirely wrong, and in fact, he hoped he was. He liked Shefali. She was very attractive, and pretty smart too, he figured, from the little he had spoken to her.

The evening turned out to be a boys' night after all. Shefali was surprisingly adept at being one of the boys. She could outwit Shri in the *desi* jokes department, outdo Shanks on cricket trivia, and out-drink them all. Neel was intrigued by her. While she seemed friendly and approachable, there seemed to be some mystery, some hidden, lurking secret that he could not quite fathom. Shanks, in his free and easy way, had asked her a couple of questions, and she had instantly clammed up.

In fact, through much of the evening, she seemed evasive and on her guard. When her cell phone rang, she had excused herself, and disappeared to the ladies' room. She'd returned just as she was concluding her call, so obviously, it was a conversation she wanted to keep private.

Shortly after the first call, Shefali got a second call. That was when she announced she had to leave, then and there. She'd just ordered her fourth drink, but it did not seem to bother her.

"Hey, not fair! Remember our deal in the taxi . . . I'm supposed to drop you home!" Shri reminded her. "And seriously, I thought we just got started!"

Shefali glanced around, apologetic. "Guys, I know, it's been fun, but really, I have to go, I . . . just lost track of time. This was, honestly . . . this was so much fun." She fumbled inside her purse and pulled out a couple of business cards. "My contact," she said. "And, oh! My contribution for the evening." This time, she produced a crisp hundred-dollar bill and stuck it on the table. As she turned to leave, her eyes were on Neel. "See you around, people."

They were all quite taken aback at this sudden turn of events!

Neel was the first one to react. He stood up, and reached out to touch her shoulder lightly. "Hey, let me walk you to a cab, I don't think you should—"

Shefali flashed him a reassuring smile. "No no, please, no need, really, I'll be fine! Thanks again, all, for a wonderful evening! Bye-eee." They watched as she purposefully made her way towards the door and let herself out.

More out of concern than curiosity, Neel and Shri went after her, towards the exit. It was still drizzling, and they were worried whether she'd be able to find a taxi on the rain-soaked streets. Just as they swung the lounge door open, they saw a uniformed chauffeur ushering her into a waiting limo. Neel quickly pulled Shri back inside and released the door. "She didn't want us to see her." They stared at each other, flummoxed. True to form, Shefali's exit had been as dramatic as her entry!

Shri glanced at his watch. "Two minutes to twelve, exact. Wow." As they walked back to their table, Shri let out a chuckle. "This whole thing's pretty weird if you ask me! I'd say the poor gal's got a midnight phobia . . . a Cinderella Syndrome or something like that! I mean, think about it. Just before the clock strikes twelve, her magic carriage appears," he waved his hands about, re-creating a vivid scenario, "the liveried footman ushers her in, then she zips off mysteriously, like a shadow, into the dark, rainy night . . . I can't help thinking—"

"*I* can't help thinking I need another drink," interrupted Neel impatiently. They made their way towards the bar, where Shanks had settled himself, and already ordered replenishments. The crowd had thinned a bit, so they found three spare bar stools and perched on those. Neel turned his attention to Shefali's business card. "Fashion consultant." He looked up, eyebrows raised. "Really?"

"She looked very fashionable to me," said Shanks.

"She looked *expensive*," Neel clarified. "There's a difference between fashionable and expensive. Expensive is, Hermès bag, Dior watch, I think her shoes were—"

"Blahnik. I particularly noticed in the cab," said Shri, who was the most fashion forward of the three. "What I don't understand is why she—" Suddenly, Shri broke off, and his jaw dropped.

Neel, who had just taken a deep swig of his newly arrived Scotch, stared up at Shri. "You don't suppose . . ." he began, but the thought was too awful to articulate.

Shanks stared at them, not catching the drift. "You mean, she's a con artist . . . something like that? I saw her pull out that C-note from a whole pile of notes. Maybe she's—"

But Shri and Neel weren't listening to him. Shri turned to Neel, wide-eyed. "Oh my God, it's the only likely explanation!"

"Yeah, the clothes, the call, the car, it makes sense! Everything makes sense!" Neel exclaimed.

Shanks, while very brilliant in his field as a systems security analyst, was slow in daily life. "Okay, so is she on some kind of watch list? Female terrorist? Drugs? Embezzlement? Fake notes? Hello? Hello? Is anyone here going to tell me what the story is?"

Shri leaned forward conspiratorially. "Not con girl dude. Call girl."

Shanks recoiled. "No!" He stared. "Can't be! I don't believe it! And she wasn't wearing red patent leather, they always wear red patent leather!"

Neel smiled. "Only in the movies, dude. The top-end girls, they're actually very well dressed, they're like any other working girl you see in the city, in fact, very much like . . . like Shefali."

Shanks did not look convinced. But he also knew it was no use arguing. Man-of-the-world Neel would have a better idea of how these things worked. It was an open secret that Wall Street used high-end escort services all the time—a win-win business model for all parties. Then, Shanks had another question for Neel. "You speak from experience, I take it?"

Vastly amused, Neel shook his head. "I'd have mentioned it, bro."

Shanks chewed his lip, still trying to make sense of the whole evening. He couldn't help wondering, if Shefali was who she was, why she'd choose to hang out with them in the first place. But when he asked his friends about this, they were not very forthcoming.

"Maybe she thought three bankers were a hot prospect, who knows?" Shri said.

"Not hot enough, obviously," Neel joked, trying to ignore his bruised ego. But, at that moment, there were more pressing matters to occupy him. He raised his glass. "Refills, anyone?"

3

Shanks was working in crisis mode. In his line of work, problems arose 24/7, but this one was a disaster-in-the-making. He was at home, on call with the department's virus analyst, Vivian-with-a-Chinese surname. His eyes were glued to his laptop screen, and at the other end, in her East Village apartment, Vivian was similarly occupied. They had to crack the problem before business hours the next day, so it was going to be an all-nighter.

Shanks was finding it hard to keep himself awake, and his hyper-caffeinated system was surviving on the java. Taking a breather, he got up to refresh his mug of coffee. Soon, he was back, slumped in front of the computer again, patiently coding and recoding crucial data. They were hoping, quite optimistically, to solve the problem before sunrise. Shanks knew this Vivian girl was good. He had worked with her once before, and had found her highly professional. He also found her highly attractive.

They had stepped out for a celebratory drink after finishing that first project together. He had enjoyed the evening very much. However, it couldn't be called a date, because through the entire evening, all they had discussed was work.

That was almost six months back. Since then, they had exchanged occasional pleasantries in the office and shared data files from time to time. However, Shanks often thought about Vivian-with-the-Chinese-surname. She was tall and willowy, with a translucent skin and a soft-spoken, lilting accent. Maybe after this project, they could go out again. Only this time, he'd make a conscious effort to talk to her and ask her about her life. He also resolved to ask how exactly her surname was pronounced.

But, Shanks never got a chance to ask Vivian out, because she asked him first. And it wasn't after their project was complete, it was at four o'clock that very morning, over the phone. They were trying to map a particularly nerve-wracking set of interaction scenarios to different architectures.

"Okay, Mr. Slavedriver Subramanian," she said, yawning, "how much longer do we keep at this?"

"Till we crack it," Shanks replied.

"Oh, well, I'll just leave you to it then and go catch some sleep."

"Vivian! Another half an hour, and we should be done, please." Shanks pleaded. It *was* her job to work with him, but it was really his responsibility to see the whole thing through.

"Okay, half an hour max, but after this is done, Mr. Slavedriver, you are so taking me out for a drink!"

Shanks couldn't believe his luck. It looked like the planets were on a roll and his stars were aligning favourably in his seventh house, the house that mattered. The girl was succumbing to her astrological compulsions and inviting him out!

So, the very next evening, he was proudly escorting Vivian to a pan-Asian organic vegetarian restaurant that used an organic laundry to clean their table linen (or so they had advertised). They settled down at their table, decorated with an ikebana flower arrangement, and scented candles. Shanks checked out the menu. It seemed to offer every imaginable vegetarian choice in the plant kingdom—the dishes had soya beans, sprouts, mushrooms, various kinds of seaweed, algae, and lots of other stuff he'd never heard of in his life.

He shifted uncomfortably. "You know, I'm not sure it was a good idea, coming here."

"Oh? You didn't want to hang out?" She had dimples, he just noticed.

"No! My God, no, not that way," Shanks was a bumbling mess. "I m-mean, it's vegetarian. Very boring for you. If you like, we can—"

"Hey relax, I like it here. Vegetarian is good sometimes, you know, a change. Tomorrow, I'll go right back to my carnivorous existence."

He smiled at that. "So what'll you drink?"

They settled for a pot of warm sake. It was the perfect drink for the cold, rainy spring evening. Soon, they got chatting, and this time, it wasn't just shop talk. Shanks finally got his chance to ask the question that had been on his mind for so many months. Her surname, he discovered, was originally Cho-Hsien. It had been shortened to Hsien and was pronounced *shian*. Her family had its ancestral roots in Taiwan. But now, the family was based in Hong Kong. Her younger brother was still a student, in university, and both her parents were teachers.

"What a coincidence!" Shanks exclaimed. "My mother was a teacher too! She used to be a history professor in Madras. Oh well, it's Chennai now."

"Like Peking and Beijing!" Vivian smiled.

Perhaps it was their common Asian background that made them discuss their families and home life. They spoke about parents' ailments, sibling problems, and the difficulty of bridging the generation gap with their elders. When Shanks brought up his early struggles with vegetarian food in the US, and the monotony of eating bread for breakfast, lunch, and dinner, he found a fellow sympathiser in Vivian. Likewise, when she articulated her warm and fuzzy feelings for rice on her plate, Shanks was practically moved to tears. Now here was a girl after his own heart!

The food arrived a little later and, seeing her dexterity with the chopsticks, he self-consciously stuck to his fork. When Vivian with-the-now-pronounceable-surname-Hsien gently teased him about it, Shanks felt he had to explain. "Okay, I confess, when my friends taught me how to use chopsticks, I just couldn't handle the rice! I mean, I was picking up two grains at a time, man, it was totally frustrating! At home we eat, like, huge amounts," he indicated a little mountain with his hands, "so now I feel embarrassed trying with chopsticks again. I . . ." He broke off, all a-blush.

After their first evening out, Shanks was not sure how the friendship would develop (if it developed at all). Their working relationship in the office had to continue, that was a given. But any extra-curricular meetings would have to be kept strictly outside office hours. So initially, after a few lunch dates, they preferred to meet in the evenings, after work. The dinners soon began to stretch over several hours, to romantic nightcaps at various bars around the city. Increasingly, Shanks was finding himself completely sleep-deprived. Despite his morning coffee fix, he was reporting to work listless and bleary-eyed.

But like his coffee, his brewing romance was yielding highly satisfactory results. (And, also like his coffee, he was savouring every moment of it.) The first time Vivian had held his hand, Shanks wasn't sure if it had been an accident. The second time around, even Shanks knew it couldn't be a coincidence. And the third time—he didn't wait for a third time. He was so emboldened that *he* initiated the move!

From there, the relationship progressed smoothly to the next level. Without a specific eureka moment, Shanks and Vivian found themselves romantically involved. "I'm in love with you, I know I am," Shanks declared after a few weeks. Vivian smiled. "Umm, I think I am too!" He wanted to kiss her, and, with some encouragement, he did. Their physical intimacy was tentative, not something either of them wanted to rush. But by then Shanks was sure that Vivian was the girl he wanted to share his life with. The sex was a mere formality.

Their first night together, a Friday night at his place, was magical. They'd ended up spending the entire weekend in bed and ordered out for pizza whenever they needed to eat. Just like their compatibility at work or at the dinner table, their sex life too had a made-for-each-other theme about it.

Almost immediately after the first date, Shanks had let his buddies in on the budding relationship. Neel and Shri were delirious. This was the first time Shanks had sounded so serious. Although they had been impatient to see things move quickly, they knew romance required a wait-and-watch approach. A real life love story, unlike a reel life one, couldn't be pressed to "fast forward"!

When Shanks was finally ready to go official and formally introduce his new girlfriend, they couldn't wait to welcome Vivian into the fold. So, the first available free evening was blocked off and an invitation was extended to the new couple. Since Neel had the largest, most impressive apartment, it was the default setting for any important get-together. And Shri was always the default cook, because Shanks had limited cooking skills, and Neel none at all.

The menu was up for major debate. Shanks wanted to do Thai. "A sort of combination of Indian and Chinese, you know."

Neel, however, was keen on a South Indian menu, to introduce Vivian to the staples of the Tamil kitchen. The argument would have continued but Shri, as the cook, got to make the final call. "I say we do something different. A Kerala-style menu, with a couple of interesting curries and fish . . ."

After the details of the menu were finalised, came the "guest list." So far, Vivian was the only invitee. One girl and three guys. Shri liked the idea of balanced gender representation, especially since Vivian was being invited for the first time. Neel had no current girlfriend, so it suddenly struck him that—"Hey," he said, "how about calling Shefali?"

He got a blank look from Neel. "Calling *who*?"

"Shefali," Shri repeated. "You know Shefali? The girl at our boys' night? She'll be great company for Vivian, and besides—"

"We're not calling Shefali," Neel cut in. "No way this hooker gets invited to our—"

"You keep calling her that!" Shanks was getting all heated up. He had *liked* Shefali. "I don't know why you should assume—"

Shri raised his hands. "Okay, chill guys. Chill." He turned to Neel thoughtfully. "Boss, I'd go with Shanks on this one. Sure, we can keep speculating about the possibilities, but we don't know for sure, right?" They'd made some wild assumptions about her that night, but they had no actual proof. And he wasn't prepared to brand Shefali without a fair trial, it simply wasn't kosher. So this became an opportunity to get to know her a little better.

But what Shri had failed to mention during the entire argument was that he had another, completely different reason for having Shefali over. And it was not purely an altruistic one. On the evening of the dinner in question, the IIFA Awards were showing live. He liked the idea of having someone like-minded around, to discuss the outfits and speculate on potential winners.

He knew Neel found the entire thing a dead bore and for

Shanks too, it was one big yawn. Vivian, of course, didn't count. But if Shefali was around, she could be relied upon to spice up the evening with her acerbic and incisive observations, her supposed "reputation" notwithstanding.

Finally Neel had to succumb to peer pressure. The Gang usually put contentious issues to vote, and the decision always went in favour of the majority. Shanks and Shri had already opted to include Shefali, so a vote was pretty pointless. He was clearly in the minority, out-voted two to one. So much for democracy!

When Shri called Shefali to invite her, he wasn't sure if she'd accept. If she actually *was* a hooker, their dinner invitation might be quite a dull proposition—she'd probably have other fish to fry! But to his surprise, she accepted right away and seemed quite enthusiastic about meeting them all again. He couldn't help suspecting, though, that the prospect of meeting Neel again was the *real* draw!

That evening, the doorbell rang at 7 p.m. sharp, just as Shri, the officiating cook, was giving finishing touches to his Kerala-style fish moilee. A Malayali stew was simmering on the stove, and the home-delivered appams were sitting in their foil packing. Neel had designated himself bartender and was all set to demo his bartending skills with the ladies.

When they saw Vivian, attractive and understated in a floral print dress, her make-up fresh and natural, they knew Shanks had gotten lucky. Very very classy, was the immediate verdict. Pretty too, Neel thought, with the kind of face that had hidden facets, a face that took its time to reveal its real beauty.

Behind her was Shanks, looming large, and looking uncomfortable in tailored khakis and a formal shirt. It was a departure from his usual jeans style. Even more incongruously, he carried two pots of beautiful magenta orchids, one in each hand. "Guys," Shanks said, "these are from Vivian, for you." As he awkwardly handed over the flowers, they tried to keep straight faces. Seeing Shanks in love was a pretty entertaining prospect!

He was so overwhelmed, in fact, that he forgot to introduce them to Vivian. So they introduced themselves. Then Shri ushered her towards the sofa and Neel stepped forward to acquaint her with the beverage selection. Shanks, basically, was left to fend for himself.

Not that he was complaining. He was delighted with the way his buddies were laying out the red carpet for the new love in his life. Shri was passing her the masala shrimp canapés, when the bell rang again. Neel got up, and headed for the door. "That'll be Shefali."

It was Shefali. They had not seen her with completely dry hair, so she looked a little different. She leaned forward to kiss Neel lightly, first on the left cheek and then the right, French style. Shri and Shanks were next in line. The guys were all trying to stay unbiased and not think about her profession. She was dressed in a turquoise-blue halter kaftan, and hoop earrings, and looked absolutely stunning.

"I love your dress!" Vivian said to Shefali, as they settled down next to each other on the sofa. It never ceased to amaze the guys how two women, completely unknown to each other, could get so chatty, so soon.

"Oh thanks, I got it on special, great price, at Neiman Marcus," Shefali confided.

"Umm, you know, I found the most amazing online deals recently, on Bluefly . . ."

When the topic shifted to summer dress lengths and new trends in hats, Shri decided it was time to cut in. He needed to take the drinks orders. Everyone wanted frozen margaritas, so Neel went into the kitchen to get the ice crushed. As he got to mixing the tequila and lime juice, Shefali appeared at his elbow.

"Any help needed here?"

"Umm, sure, I'm getting the frozen cocktail done, so if you could get the salt rims going, that would be great."

She nodded and deftly set about lining the margarita glasses with lime juice, and then turning them upside down in the little heap of salt. Neel, meanwhile, was frowning into the cocktail blend he'd just mixed. "Syrup tad too much, you think?" He extended a sample spoonful towards Shefali.

She leaned forward and sipped the cocktail. "Umm, it's good," Shefali said, wiping her lips with a finger. "Sugar's just perfect, actually."

She started handing over the salt-rimmed glasses for him to fill. As he spooned out the pale lemon-coloured ice, she smiled. "Wow, that's practically gelato." Their fingers had brushed a few times and she knew Neel was not averse to the physical contact. He looked hotter than ever, Shefali thought, glancing sideways, admiring how his super toned chest and shoulders moulded his black linen shirt.

Neel placed the glasses on a tray. "I'll take these out. So if you'll just grab your drink and step ahead . . . I'll follow . . ."

When they joined the others in the living room, Broadway shows were the topic of discussion. No one could decide which one was better—*Wicked* or *The Book of Mormon*. The debate appeared to be evenly poised. After a bit, Shefali turned to Neel. "Umm, I'd like to use the washroom, if you could tell me where . . ."

Neel rose and asked her to follow him. Guessing that she wanted him alone, he couldn't help feeling a little chuffed. She was very attractive, and her attention was flattering. As he led her down the little hallway, he said, "The apartment's kind of small, you know, but it suits my bachelor lifestyle." This quickly established what he wanted to convey—that there was no significant other in his life, and he was therefore quite at liberty to escort random women into his bedroom.

Since the bathroom was ensuite, they had to get to the bedroom first. His bedroom was a pocket-sized piece of real estate with a queen-size bed and assorted storage units. Shefali moved in sideways, to avoid bumping into him. As she was squeezing past, she tripped against the bedside table. He held out his arm to steady her. Here, Neel, predator of beautiful women, was in familiar territory. He was holding a gorgeous girl captive in the privacy of his very own bedroom. Too seasoned a player to allow such an opportunity to slip out of his hands, Neel was on high alert, his hunting instincts aroused. (And consequences be damned!)

So when he looked down into her eyes and saw what he expected to see—a mirror image of his own desire—he leaned forward. She instantly melted into his arms, and they kissed with a pent-up passion that had been simmering since their first meeting. But just as things were getting hot and steamy, there was a throttled sound from the doorway.

They jumped apart, and saw Shri at the door, looking like he'd just had cold water thrown at him. "Oh, oh my God! Sorry guys, I didn't know—"

"Stop apologising, it's okay," Shefali told him. Then she turned to Neel. "Oh 'xcuse me, the washroom . . ." He stepped aside to allow her to pass.

Once she'd disappeared inside, Shri turned to Neel. "Dude, what the *hell* are you doing!" he whispered fiercely. "First, you didn't want her here because of who she is! And now? Now, you're busy making out with her!"

Neel held up his hands in a stop-right-now gesture. "Chill, *yaar!*" He was quite annoyed with the interruption and a sermon was the last thing he needed. "With you around monitoring my sex life . . . you'll make sure I couldn't even actually seduce a . . . a pole!" Neel ripped his fingers through his hair, distraught. "You know dude, you're worse than the friggin' Indian Censor Board. I mean, even *they* allow kissing now, it's family viewing! Seriously dude, those guys should *hire* you to—"

"*So* not funny!" Shri cut him short.

"The joke's on me, if you ask me!" Neel said. Then, he looked at Shri's anxious visage, and his tone softened. "Hey, relax, okay, I was only directing her to the loo!"

"Yeah right!" It was not easy to shout and whisper at the same time, but Shri managed it. "In the *bedroom!*"

Neel was beginning to smile. "Hey, the loo just happens to be ensuite, through the *bedroom*, not much I can do about that." He adroitly shepherded Shri towards the hallway. "And tell me *why* are you even here, you should be out watching the awards."

Shri wasn't a happy camper, but he allowed himself to be nudged into the living room. "Oh," he said, "we're waiting, the ads are on right now, like, a gazillion ads, all showcasing deliriously happy homemakers frying puris and feeding their husbands and powdering their babies and cleaning their kitchens and—"

A few minutes later, they were all seated in front of Neel's enormous plasma TV. As Shri had foreseen, Shefali was quite happy to watch the Bollywood A-listers lining up on the red carpet. "Umm, Deepika's wearing a nice off-shoulder silk. Valentino, I think." At that very moment, the star announced she was in a Valentino gown.

Shri smiled. "Wow, you're good. Now tell me, Sonam's in—?"

Shefali frowned. "Some Indian designer? Manish probably?" She was right again.

The guessing game continued, with Shri and Shefali as the sole participants. From time to time, Shefali briefed Vivian on the more eminent luminaries from the Bollywood pantheon. Shanks and Neel were bored out of their skulls but they were trying, desperately, to keep awake. More than once, there came a suspicious snoring sound from Shanks' direction.

It was Vivian's trip to the washroom, half an hour later, that gave the party its second wind. She'd barely been gone a few seconds, when suddenly, she reappeared, quite breathless. She was holding up a sparkling bracelet, studded with outsize diamonds, the biggest anyone had ever seen. She held it at an arm's length, like a snake that might bite.

"Oh my God, look, I-I found this on the bathroom floor! I . . . is this real?"

All eyes swivelled towards Shefali. She took a deep breath. "Thanks Vivian, it, er, must have fallen out of my kaftan pocket." She looked around. "I suppose it's time to tell you guys . . . I mean, it had to come out, sooner or later, that I—"

"You don't have to tell us," Shri said hurriedly.

"Oh, absolutely, I mean, stuff like this . . . how you get it, it's *your* business," added Neel.

Shefali knitted her brows. "My *business*? What's with you guys? What, you think I stole it or something?"

Shanks was wide awake now. "No! No one thinks that!"

Vivian had placed the bracelet on the coffee table. Shri, hypnotised by its brilliance, couldn't resist picking it up. He slid the stones between his fingers. "It's very beautiful. And very real." He looked up at Shefali. "Must be worth . . . several thousands. You really are in the big league."

Shefali was shaking her head, completely perplexed. "Am I missing something here?"

Before anyone could stop him, Shanks took charge. "You know, honestly, *I* don't think so, but they think you are an escort."

Shefali drew her breath in so audibly it could be heard over the cacophony of the TV commercial break. She sprang to her feet. "They think—what!" A pause, as it sank in. "*What!*"

Everyone froze. Shefali's eyes were flashing, quite as brightly as her diamonds. "I thought you guys were different! Decent guys I could be friends with! But no! No! You guys? Crappy as the rest of 'em!" Her voice broke. "Do I *look* like an escort? Do I *behave* like a—" She shook her head in disbelief, and flopped onto the sofa.

To really rub it in, she leaned back, took a deep breath, shut her eyes, and started massaging her temples with both hands. If the idea was to graphically convey the acuteness of her pain and suffering, she succeeded. Vivian put her arm around her, made soothing noises, and, at the same time, gave the three miscreants a particularly dirty look.

They had had enough. They quickly retreated into the bedroom and threw themselves on Neel's bed, shaken. There were a few seconds of silence.

Then, Shri turned to Neel. "Harishchandra rides again!"

He referred to the ancient Hindu King, Harishchandra, a legendary monarch, famous for his honesty and integrity. The parallel was often used for Shanks, who was frequently more forthright than was required. As a result, his buddies often had to bear the brunt of his free-spoken ways.

Neel was grinding his teeth. "Harishchandra needs to have his head examined, that's what! 'I honestly don't think, but *they* think—'" he imitated Shanks. "Who gives a *fuck* about what he thinks. I say, quit thinking, moron!"

They spoke to each other as if Shanks did not exist. Shanks, wedged between the two of them, was very much the elephant in the room. He said, "Dude, I had to say something, you know."

Neel shuddered. "Why, dude, why? Dude, would it hurt too much to just shut up?"

Shanks squirmed under his gaze. "Okay, so I didn't think she'll be so upset."

Neel rolled his eyes heavenward and Shri slumped, face down, into the nearest pillow. It was going to be a long night.

Vivian single-handedly managed the turnaround. In her understated way, she calmed Shefali down by explaining that Shanks was honest, sometimes brutally so, but that he never meant any harm. She had also heard from Shanks that Shefali had been a little secretive about her life, so maybe that was why they'd all jumped to the wrong conclusion. Well, not all of them, because Shanks thought no such thing.

Then, Vivian offered to make some jasmine tea. Nothing like a soothing cup of tea, she told Shefali, to transform all human suffering into a zen-like state of equanimity.

The tea and sympathy worked like a charm. When the guys looked in, about ten minutes later, Shefali was sitting up on the sofa, feet crossed, head held high, regally sipping on her tea. She had the air of one who expects total obeisance. And she got it. Even Vivian had to hide a smile as they filed in, one by one, looking very chastised. Shri went down on his knees before her and held her hand. Neel sat next to her, mumbling apologies. Shanks simply hovered about, looking guilty.

While Shefali could be highly tantrum-prone, she was not without a sense of humour. The entire episode had its funny side. A tiny smile appeared at the corner of her mouth. "God, if I had any sense, I'd walk right out of this place, forget ever *meeting* you guys!"

That broke the tension and everyone lightened up immediately. But they wanted answers. "Where did you go off in such hurry that night? And the *limo*? What was with with the limo, I mean, what were we supposed to *think*?" Shri demanded.

"Guys, not a big deal, my ex texted, he was in town, okay,

not my ex, but my ex ex, Karan." She took a deep breath. "He lives in LA, and was stopping by in New York, it was one of those unscheduled trips. So I ordered a limo and went to meet him."

Shanks was shocked by the extravagance of it all, but that still didn't explain the bracelet. "And the bracelet?"

Shefali lowered her eyes demurely. "Oh yes, the bracelet. I had worn that bracelet when I came here, then in the lift, I decided to take it out and put it in my pocket because . . . because I didn't want you guys to know."

"Know what, honey?" Vivian whispered.

Shefali took a deep breath. "My dad's very wealthy. He's among the hundred richest persons in the UK." She looked around. "Sorry, guys."

There was a pin-drop silence, as the Gang, Vivian included, tried to imagine what it must feel like to be so very loaded. No wonder Shefali didn't need to work! No wonder she ordered limos! No wonder she casually carried around priceless jewellery that could buy a small house! And yet, reflected Vivian, when she discussed buying dresses at discounted prices, she attempted to blend in. Like the rest of them, she too, needed friends, and needed to be loved.

Finally Shanks broke the silence. "Hey, people, I thought we were invited here for dinner. I'm starving!"

That's when the two hosts remembered they had guests to feed. The on-going drama had put dinner on the back burner. With a little help from the girls, they set about laying out the spread. If the idea had been to impress Vivian, they certainly succeeded. She told them she had never had a home-cooked meal this good, except when her mom got into the kitchen, in Hong Kong.

By the end of the evening, Shefali and Vivian had passed the

Gang's stringent specs, albeit on slightly different entry criteria. They now qualified as legit Gang members, new entrants into the hallowed circle. Shanks sank back into the sofa and put his arm around Vivian, smiling in contentment. The Gang smiled too.

A new chapter had begun.

4

Like all highly eligible Indian men, the Gang had a part-time calling—the task of keeping their parents on pause when the next "eligible girl" was in the pipeline. But of late, their irate parents were in no mood to listen. They told their progeny to stop dragging their feet, now, because the best girls were being spirited away by more nimble-footed competition.

Shanks, at twenty-seven, was already under severe duress. His mother had started "showing" him girls six years back. Tall girls, small girls, fair girls, wheatish-coloured girls, plump girls, thin girls, working girls, home-loving girls. The single common feature all these girls shared was that they belonged to the Iyer community. Like most Iyer mothers, Mrs. Revathi had a life mission. And that mission was getting her son married to a nice girl from their very own caste, thereby ensuring she had her very own pure-bred Iyer grandchildren. Being a widow, she felt a double-duty responsibility about seeing her only son settle down and start a family.

He had been born after a wait of sixteen years. As a result, he had grown up as the apple of his mother's eye, the miracle baby who had arrived after they had given up hope. To think they might never have had a son to carry the name forward! But his mom was proud that they had managed to maintain the family line of succession. Now, it was up to their Sankar to keep the Subramanian glory alive and kicking—no pun intended—for future generations.

Shanks had an elder sister, Ramya, who had been married before she was twenty, and Mrs. Revathi loved reminding Shanks about it. "You don't want a girl who is too set in her ways. She must be able to adjust, like Ramya." Shanks sometimes wanted to ask why he shouldn't adapt a little bit too. His adjusting sister Ramya belonged to an obsolete generation, like a defunct piece of technology. He identified more with Priya, her daughter and his niece. Priya was closer to him in age, and attitude.

Lately, his mom's favourite refrain had been, "What would your father say!" The interesting part was that his father had very little to say when he was alive, because he was never given a chance. But seemingly, he had become quite voluble after he had passed on. There were daily strictures, on Skype or via email, on what his father would have said, had he been around. He would have censured Shanks for shirking his duty as a son. He would've spoken out about the need for grandchildren, the need for continuing the family name. The emotional blackmail was beginning to get to Shanks, and he could foresee a bleak summer ahead, when his mother came down for her annual six-month visit.

Like Shanks, Neel was also considered a pretty hot matrimonial prospect, up there in the hallowed echelons of prospective husband-dom. His parents presumed, and rightly so, that their son was quite capable of finding a girl for himself. After retirement from the army, Neel's father had chosen to spend a quiet life in the old family home in Defence Colony. They had many friends and relatives seeking them out, to hook

Neel up with their daughters, granddaughters, nieces, sisters, and so on. But his parents would politely turn down the proposals, saying that Neel was not ready yet.

Neel Sawhney was twenty-eight, and through the years, his steady string of girlfriends had not led to a single lasting relationship. This was beginning to seriously worry him. In his more introspective moments, he reflected that either he was too picky or emotionally challenged or just commitment phobic. Sometimes he wondered if—heaven help him—he was all of the above. Under the circumstances, the really smart thing to do would be to give the whole romance thing a miss and marry money instead.

And then there was Shri. He had pretty much grown up with Neel around and never considered himself competition. That very first time, when he'd chosen to introduce Shefali into the circle, it was with the full understanding that Neel was the uncontested ladies' man within the group. All other men like him lagged far behind. But the circumstance didn't bother him at all.

At twenty-seven years of age, Shri had never dated a girl. Inwardly, he baulked at the idea of settling down, but the family pressure was already on. So far, he had resisted matrimony, citing financial limitations for not taking the plunge. It had worked up to a point. Increasingly, over-zealous aunts and unconnected relatives had chastised him about his delaying tactics. If he did not move fast enough, they admonished, he faced the prospect of a lonely, loveless life of bachelordom forever.

But Shri had a huge personal dilemma that wasn't settled by a simple yes or a no. He had a secret, a deep and dark secret, buried inside him. A secret he'd kept hidden for twenty long years. And every single day he lived in fear of his secret exploding, like a time bomb, into the public domain. The fact was Shri didn't like girls. He liked guys.

He was homosexual, and had been one ever since he could remember. There was no overnight revelation, no single incident, that made Shri realise he was gay. It would have been considered highly unnatural to exhibit any such deviant behaviour, so every feeling, if it ever did surface, was firmly quashed.

Growing up in an Indian boarding school had often tested his sanity. When he'd discovered, with a sense of shock, that he was different from the other guys, it was like being born handicapped, with an arm or leg missing. Once, at school, he had been in a situation that could have led to physical intimacy with another student. But Shri had been too petrified to respond to the boy's advances. What if friends like Neel found out? What if the school rusticated him, for his wicked, wanton behaviour?

Shri had continued to conform to the middle-class stereotype of the boy who made his parents proud. There never was any question of revealing his true sexual orientation. Apart from being a model son, and a much-feted member of the family, he kept up the façade in his working life too. His career graph as a banker showed an equally blemish-free upward trajectory, with nary a blot in his copybook.

Then came the turning point. His parents migrated to the US. And, for the first time in his life, Shri saw that homosexuality was not a crime. Gay rights, gay television channels, gay parades, even gay marriages didn't raise any eyebrows. Being gay was accepted, even celebrated. In New York City, particularly around Chelsea, where he lived, he sometimes thought half the population was gay.

But sadly, that didn't change anything for him. *He* couldn't come out in the open and start participating in gay parades or seek out guys in gay bars—he was Indian! *His* job was to marry an eligible Indian girl and settle down.

"Shri, how much longer you want us to wait?" his mother would plaintively enquire.

"*Aai*, don't rush me," he'd say. "After all, it's a decision of a lifetime, I have to be sure about it."

He couldn't bear to hurt her, so there was no question of actually telling her the truth. It would have shattered his parents to know their only child was "a gay homosexual," as they called it. Even more unacceptable, they would become pariahs within their own circle. There would be finger-pointing and pity, but no sympathy. He, too, would become a social outcast overnight. Not that it mattered. The people who rejected him were probably not worth knowing anyway.

And yet, Shri was insecure about confiding to friends, even his closest friends. It was ironic, he reflected, he had always been the confidante, the guy who listened well, and offered sage advice to the lovelorn. But no one had thought to probe deep enough into *his* love life. In their college days, Neel and Shanks had often tried to pair him up in group situations, buy they'd always assumed he was super shy, or just hadn't found the right kind of girl. Over time, they'd simply given up.

So, as things stood, the Gang was still clueless about Shri's sexual leanings. He couldn't even begin to imagine how they would react if they knew. Even the thought that they might stumble onto his secret made him break out into a cold sweat. Lately, he'd been having nightmares about being discovered. He'd wake up breathless, covered in perspiration, his temples throbbing in pain.

And the reason was, Shri had recently acquired a boyfriend. Paolo. A couple of months back, Shri had attended a Citibank seminar at the Hilton, where he'd spotted Paolo among the other delegates. There was much to admire in Paolo's tall physique and bronzed good looks, and Shri had been all admiration, coveting Paolo from afar. He knew that Paolo worked for the credit cards division, servicing Latin America. Shri himself was on the trading side, so they'd never had an opportunity for any interaction in the workplace, not even a nodding acquaintance. In the circumstances, it seemed too forward to actually go strike up a conversation with a guy he wasn't even supposed to know.

Shri was therefore taken aback to find Paolo approaching him. Paolo came right up, his tanned face breaking out into a broad smile. "Hey, Shrikant, right? I've heard so much about you . . . I . . . oops, I got that wrong, didn't I?" Paolo had pronounced his name as "Shrik-a-n-t," American style, and was looking to Shri for a clarification.

Shri, overwhelmed by the attention, tried to laugh off the mispronunciation. "Hey, no worries, Shri works just fine for me. And I guess it's easier for you too." When Paolo had come by to say hello, it was almost like he'd sensed, with a built-in radar, that he, Shri, was available. What shocked Shri was not Paolo's overtures but how readily he had responded to them.

Within a week, they had become a couple. At twenty-seven years of age, Shri's love life had finally taken off! For the first time, he understood what had been missing all those years. For him, it was a huge deal, and he really wanted to share his newfound happiness with the Gang. He pictured the scene, probably at their Thursday night *adda*. He saw himself escorting Paolo in and making an announcement, something like, "Hey guys, meet Paolo, my date for the night."

The scene was so far removed from reality that Shri, who was sitting on a high stool in Neel's kitchen, inhaled sharply, and shuddered.

"'There is nothing either good or bad, but thinking makes it so.' Shakespeare." It was Neel, standing before him, and staring.

"You sure look like a man with something on your mind. What's up, bro?"

Unfortunately for Shri, Neel had walked in from his grocery shopping that very second, and witnessed his private little panic attack, up close.

"Umm, oh, nothing!" Shri responded. But Neel, who had offloaded his groceries onto the kitchen counter, continued to stare, with his hands on his hips. It was one of those bro-to-bro moments that demanded answers.

Shri shifted his attention to the grocery bags and, suddenly, got very interested in Neel's purchases. As he fished out a pack of kettle chips, Shri marvelled how the Shakespeare quote had hit closer home than Neel realised. Hoping to distract Neel, he tore open the pack and offered him first dibs. Nothing right or wrong about being gay, the quote had implied. Interesting, Shri mused. They often played the guess-whose-quote game, a school habit, which they had kept going through the years.

Shri happened to be at Neel's because his gym was in the next building. He had just finished a pilates workout, showered, changed, and let himself in with a spare key. This was their usual Sunday routine. After hanging together for a bit, they'd head out to meet Shanks, if he was free.

Shri helped himself to some more chips—they were amazing—and turned to Neel. "Okay, I love this one. 'Any man who reads too much and uses his own brain too little falls into lazy habits of thinking.'"

Neel scrunched his face. "Churchill? Gandhi? No, Einstein! When in doubt, always say Einstein."

Shri had to laugh. "Now *that* sounds like a quote by itself! But yeah, you're right, Einstein it is."

As Shri had intended, Neel had about forgotten all about his line of questioning, and gotten busy unloading his groceries.

"This stuff needs to be cleared away before the new maid gets here," he said, putting away the fresh coriander into a sandwich bag.

Shri was amused. "Isn't that *why* you have the cleaning lady? To clear things up?"

"Don't smirk, loser. Keeping the help happy is an important life skill. Otherwise you—"

Shri's cell rang at that moment. "Oh, my Sunday morning special," Shri announced, glancing at the caller ID. It was from his parents, in Atlanta. They called every Sunday morning and Shri listened with his usual patience, every Sunday morning. But this Sunday, as the conversation got going, Neel realised something was different. He had seldom heard Shri yelling at anyone, yet here he was, getting positively snarky with his parents. Something was terribly wrong.

When Shri finally completed the conversation, Neel was by his side. "Problem?"

"They want me to meet a girl. Tomorrow." Shri was more shaken than he was prepared to show.

Neel stared at him in momentary disbelief, then burst out laughing. "No! Seriously! Dude, you got to be kidding me! Look, if you're not interested, just pass her my way!"

"*So* not funny." Shri turned away before Neel could see his face.

Neel came round the kitchen counter and placed himself in front of Shri, suddenly dead serious. "Hey!" He caught Shri by the shoulders, looked him in the eye, and gave him a brisk shake. "Godbole!" A term of endearment from their school days. "Wake up and smell the coffee! They want you married, and if you think they're going to listen to any more of your bullshit, no, they're not! And boss, you better believe it!" He let go of Shri's shoulders. "Give it a try, man. I mean, just look at Shanks. Did you ever think Shanks would hook up with someone like Vivian? He just got lucky, right? I mean, it's basically a crapshoot, so the point is, you'll never know unless you actually go out there and—"

Neel shrugged. He was almost done stocking up the refrigerator, but he wasn't done with Shri yet. "So my advice? Just go meet this girl." He waved a spinach bunch at Shri. "Worst case scenario? You don't like her. You call your parents, say, no, not interested, thank you very much." To emphasise his point, Neel shut the fridge sharply. "Tell me, how hard is that?"

Shri didn't argue, merely did some sibilant sighing at regular intervals to make his point. The air-blowing, by way of a response, cut no ice with Neel. He picked up Shri's spring windcheater and tossed it in his direction. "Okay, bro, let's move dat sorry ass in da direction of duh doah. Can't keep mah Bloody Mary waitin', can we!"

Shri rolled his eyes at Neel's bad imitation of the inner city accent, plucked at his jacket in a half-hearted manner, and reluctantly hauled himself off the sofa. They had planned brunch and bowling with Shanks. And now, of course, there was Vivian. And Shefali too. Maybe Neel was right, he figured, he was getting too wound up about this encounter. He needed to chill with the Gang. Maybe the brunch would take his mind off things a bit.

But by the time they reached the bowling alley, Shri was more keyed up than ever. Meeting that girl was the very last thing he wanted to do, and for a wild moment, he even considered taking up Neel's offer and allowing him to go in his place.

So far he had managed to keep his parents off his back, by telling them he was active on Shaadi.com. His story was that he was actively trying to connect with a suitable life partner, but that nothing had actually worked out. The truth was he'd never visited the site in his life. Now, they were obviously getting impatient. They wanted to push him into making a decision.

The *mulgi*, apparently, lived in Atlanta and was visiting New York for a couple of days, because her best friend was getting married in New Jersey. This was an elegant way of getting them together, without her having to make a special trip just to meet the "boy." "Very suitable match," his mother had said. "She's a PhD, teaches at Georgia Tech, doing extremely well. We know the family, you know, very dear friends."

That was all he needed! The close connection made it impossible for him to back out. If he found an excuse, they'd simply set up another date and expect him to fly to Atlanta to meet her. The one thing going for him right now was that the rendezvous was happening on his turf, in New York City. So despite the anxiety attacks, he told himself it was best to get it over with, like he would an urgent dental appointment.

Soon after the call with his mom, he had called the girl, and got a tinkly, musical voice at the other end. "Sorry, I'm unable to answer your call right now, but if you leave a message . . ."

He left her a message, suggesting a time and place to meet, if she was free to make it. She texted him within half an hour, saying she'd be there. The "date" was officially on, at a small nondescript Indian restaurant he'd chosen, on the Lower East Side. Nobody he knew ever went there.

If Shri expected some R&R at the bowling alley, he was mistaken. He wished he'd had the foresight to tell Neel to shut up about the whole thing. But he had been too stressed to think about it, and now Neel had shared the news about his upcoming assignation with everyone. Cursing inwardly, Shri braced himself for the questions. Did he know her name? What about her photograph? Was she on FB? Where was he meeting her?

"Wear your grey linen jacket," Shefali advised. "It's really smart. Wear it with the tan shoes."

"Bro, you're taking her to a kebab joint. What if she's veg?" Neel said. He had a point, of course.

Everyone was only trying to be helpful, but the unsolicited attention was pushing Shri to a near meltdown. His friends, however, attributed his furtive and fidgety behaviour to nervousness and went out of their way to offer even more unsolicited advice. By the end of it, Shri had collected innumerable tips on how to ace the "interview."

The next day, Shri was practically a basket case. He was so rattled, that an hour before the meeting, he picked up his cell phone to call Neel, to ask him to stand in for him. But then, with a sinking feeling, he realised that that wasn't a solution. The girl had probably seen his photograph. Besides, he noted, all he was doing was postponing the inevitable. When his parents discovered he'd deputed a substitute groom, Shri reflected gloomily, he might as well enlist for the war zone in some *stan* or the other!

Finally, by the time he arrived at the restaurant, at the designated hour, his tension had escalated to a fever pitch. He was hyperventilating, his breath was constricted, his throat was dry, his ears were ringing, and a loud pounding sound was coming from his heart region. Even as his eyes scanned the restaurant, he wondered if girls experienced similar symptoms. However, the girl in jeans and a tee, seated alone at a table, was looking remarkably composed. She also looked like she was waiting for someone. That had to be her!

Shri hurried forward.

"Hi. Shrikant?" He noticed, once again, that her voice was like the tinkle of bells, and it wasn't only because of the ringing sound in his ears.

"Hi, Bhairavi Kalyanpur," she said, and held out a hand.

He cleared his throat and shook her hand. "Shri," he said. "I'm so sorry, I'm a bit late. Traffic was crazy. Really sorry."

"Oh, don't apologise. I'm early actually. New York traffic wasn't as bad as I expected," she smiled.

Shri liked what he saw. She had a pleasant, open face and a ready smile. Considering how casually dressed she was, he was glad he hadn't followed Shefali's linen jacket dress code advice. He'd have looked like a complete idiot. But that did not stop him from feeling like a fool. Here he was, on a date with this attractive girl, with no idea what to do next. The only gentlemanly thing to do was to disclose his sexual orientation. And yet, that was the only option not open to him. The deception made him hate himself. What was worse, this girl, Bhairavi, seemed really nice. Just the kind of person he would have loved to know under normal circumstances.

"D'you take the subway to work?" Bhairavi was asking.

He found it was easy to talk to her. They discovered that they shared a common love for Hindustani classical music. "Bhairavi, my favourite *raaga*," was Shri's opening line.

"As you can guess, my parents thought so too, though personally, I hate the *sound* of the name. But yeah, Bhairavi . . . and Yaman . . . Pilu. Those are some of are my favourites."

"You know, I have this hobby," Shri said, "connecting old Bollywood songs with *raagas*, like Yaman, Khamaj, Darbari, etcetera etcetera. That's where all the Bollywood classics originate, right!"

She was laughing. "Yes, we do that too. By we, I mean my music group. Back in Atlanta, we meet twice a week, and rehearse something new each time. In fact, in a couple of weeks, we are performing at a function in D.C. It's a Maharashtra Mandal function. You should come!"

"What will you be singing?"

She looked a bit embarrassed. *"Khamaj, tere mere milan ki ye raina."*

A couple singing a song about their wedding night. Shri swiftly changed the subject. When the discussion came to music, he realised that he tended to get a bit carried away. He must curb his natural enthusiasm, Shri reminded himself. There was no point giving the impression that he was interested. So, for the rest of the evening, he made a conscious effort to be boorish and bad-mannered and generally behave like a jerk.

If Bhairavi noticed the change, she didn't refer to it, in so many words. But he was aware that she was watching him in a puzzled way, as if she was trying to size him up, and was unable to find a fit.

Later, when Shri dropped her off at the nearest subway station, her smile had lost some of its sheen. Now, Bhairavi was smiling out of politeness, not because she wanted to. "Thanks for the dinner," she said. "I just want you to know, if you choose not to call, it's no problem, okay? I'll understand." Then, she inclined her head in farewell and made her way down the stairs and into the darkness of the station.

Shri turned away, full of self-loathing. True, it had not been his intention, but he had hurt this girl with his irrational and idiotic behavior. He wished, more than ever, that he could be like the rest of humankind and be a normal, happy guy, leading a normal happy life. Keeping up the charade, and the duplicity of leading two lives, was becoming more and more untenable. And he wasn't sure how much longer he could hold it all together, before he cracked under the pressure!

His ordeal, however, was far from over. Shortly afterwards, his parents phoned to ask what happened at the meeting and why he did not like the girl. Was she not smart enough? Was it the way she spoke? Or what she said? His answers appeared unconvincing, even to himself. Then there was the Gang. They were not about to let him off the hook. They demanded a blow-by-blow account of the encounter.

"She sounds very nice, Shri, and if she invited you to her concert, she likes you!" Vivian said.

"Did you guys hold hands?" Shanks, the budding expert on romance, felt he had to guide Shri through the paces. "Boss, come on, don't tell me you didn't even—"

"Shanks, cut it out, leave him alone!" Shefali, who had been sitting silently all along, could stand it no more. They all turned to stare at her, Shri included. They had never seen her so mad, not even on that fateful evening at Neel's. The peremptory command, however, had its desired effect. There was no more discussion on Shri's love life, the subject was closed.

They were all a bit bewildered by the strange outburst, but then that was Shefali, always high on drama! Neel saw it a little differently though. He felt it could have something to do with her fondness for Shri. He'd noticed that she'd been getting quite friendly with Shri, and was spending more and more time with him. Could it be possible that their easy friendship had morphed into a more meaningful relationship? But surely not?

Surely, she couldn't actually be in love with *Shri*?

5

Neel had a lot on his mind. To start with, work was a bitch. Office politics was progressively getting uglier, and lay-offs had become a way of life. He wouldn't be too surprised to walk in one day and find a pink slip sitting on his desk. While he was in the queue for his green card, it was going to be a long wait. Till then, he had to bide his time and stick with the job—if they kept him on, that was. In the ruthless hedge fund business, he knew his rivals would be only too happy to see his back, for good.

As an outsider, Neel was easy prey. Grimly, he reflected that his immediate work environment probably had more man-eaters than all the tiger territories of West Bengal. He was the guy who had to work doubly hard to stay in the same job, deliver to higher standards than his American peers, and, through it all, keep his smile intact.

Even more challenging than the iffy job situation was his iffy personal life. After Shefali's big revelation, Neel sensed something had changed between them. He understood her need to keep her Ms. Moneybags status under wraps, but now that it was out in the open, he had his own dilemma to deal with. It was a moral one. All along, he'd told himself he was looking to marry money—it seemed like the smart thing to do. But now that he had a golden opportunity to do so, clearly, it wasn't what he wanted!

Since they'd first met, Shefali had become more than just a friend. From the Broadway shows to art shows, from fusion cuisine to fusion music, they had enjoyed many shared interests in the city that never sleeps. Although they were not officially dating, at least not yet, the vibes were pretty hot. And the goodnight kisses promised an action-packed sex life ahead.

But here, Neel had to stop and ask himself, what did he *really* want? He'd already concluded that Shefali's fortune couldn't be an influencing factor in his decision-making process. However, there was another, much more fundamental question to ponder. And that was, if love was what he wanted, true love, then was Shefali *The One*? He thought not.

Neel was arrogant enough to assume that if he really wanted, he could get her to sign up for a committed relationship in a heartbeat. But in his present situation, he realised he was in a no-man's-land, *na ghar ka na ghat ka*. A single false move could send her the wrong signal, and then, where would he be? He knew he couldn't sit on the fence forever, but he needed more time to decide, one way or the other.

Little did he know that the following Sunday morning was to be his wake-up call, in quite the literal sense. He'd been sleeping in after a late Saturday night, when he was roused from his slumber at 8 a.m. His cell phone was ringing and, when he answered, it was a girl's voice on the line. She introduced herself as his cleaning lady Lida's daughter, Layla. "I'm calling to let you know my mom can't make today," she informed Neel. "She's in hospital, for a burst appendix. But if you need a replacement, I could come by around noon if that's okay?"

Neel was barely awake, but his first thought was that it was more than okay. The apartment desperately needed a clean-up. "Sure, yeah, you can come by. Let yourself in with the keys in case I'm out. Thanks," he mumbled. Then, he turned on his tummy and went right back to sleep.

Later that afternoon, as he entered the apartment after his usual Sunday grocery shopping, Neel saw that the living room had been dusted and tidied up. There was a lingering pine fragrance in the air. But Lida's daughter was nowhere to be seen. Neel offloaded his groceries in the kitchen and made his way to the bedroom. If she was still around, maybe she'd like some coffee. That way, he could brew two cups straight off. He stepped into his bedroom to find the bathroom door slightly ajar and the water running inside the loo. He knocked smartly on the door and opened it wider.

Whatever Neel was expecting to see, it wasn't this. He found Monica Bellucci on her knees, her long chestnut hair tucked in a barrette, busy scrubbing his bathtub. This could well have been every man's ultimate fantasy, and for a brief moment, Neel thought it was just that—his fantasy!

But the Bellucci was real all right. She turned off the bath water and stood up, revealing herself to be almost his height. Shaking hands was not an option: her rubber-gloved hands were dripping soapy water onto the tiled bathroom floor.

"Hi, I'm Layla. Lida's daughter?"

Neel swallowed. "Neel." He could not take his eyes off her.

She smiled and was down on her knees again. "Just finishing up . . . 'nother few minutes and I'm outta here."

That was when Neel noticed his pile of dirty laundry. His wash clothes were still lying on the bathroom floor, all heaped up right behind her.

"Oops," he said, flustered, and leaned in towards her.

"X'cuse me, how about I take those clothes off for you? Umm, off the floor, I mean!"

Layla stopped her scrubbing and viewed him through narrowed eyes. Her critical scrutiny, in response to his unintentionally lewd remark, made him want to duck behind the shower curtain. But of course, that wasn't even a last refuge. He'd just have to stop blathering on like the village idiot, like, now!

"You can get them later," she instructed, and resumed her scrubbing.

"And your mom? How's your mom doing?"

"Good, she's doing good," Layla said. She turned her attention to the wash basin, while Neel shuffled his feet.

"Some coffee for you? I'm . . . I'm making some." He knew he was sounding like an infatuated teenager making his first move.

"Great." She looked up, and saw him reflected in the wash-basin mirror, still shuffling about right behind her. "Yeah, that would be great, thanks," she said.

At that point, Neel had no choice but to tear himself away from the water nymph splashing about in the Kingdom of Neptune, and go attend to the coffee. He quickly put away the groceries and took a hasty peek in the hallway mirror. Hair, check, shirt, check, teeth, check. If only he could freshen up on the cologne, but that was in the bathroom.

Soon, two steaming mugs of coffee were ready and waiting on the kitchen counter. It was not an eat-in kitchen, but it had a pair of high stools that made for comfortable seating. When Layla came in, Neel was busy arranging biscotti on a plate. She looked even more alluring without the cleaning gloves and with her hair let loose. As she perched on the high stool, Neel pushed the biscotti plate towards her. "I have to thank you for rescuing me."

He had meant the cleaning up, of course, but after he said it, Neel caught his breath. Rescuing him from Shefali! Rescuing him from himself, actually. He had always been of the opinion that love at first sight was for pre-teen girls, or rich old men who fell for nubile young things. While he believed in love at some level, he hadn't thought of himself as a love-at-first-sight kind of guy. Yet, here he was, sitting next to a very beautiful young girl, inexplicably, inexorably, insanely besotted.

"I had a selfish reason for coming," she was saying. "You see, if my mom took a week's sick leave, the agency would simply lay her off. I'm filling in so she can keep her job. And I have to tell you that they don't even know she's sick and that I'm substituting, so I hope you won't . . ." She looked at him uncertainly and batted her lashes.

"Oh, mum's the word!" he replied wittily. "But hey, jokes apart, what about her medical bills? Doesn't the agency . . . pay?"

Layla lowered her eyes. "The agency gives her basic medical insurance, but she's part-time, like a temp, not on their regular payroll, you see, so they're not obliged to . . ."

Neel nodded. "I see."

When he heard she was a freshman studying architecture, he received the information with mixed feelings. That she would not be spending the rest of her life like her mother, cleaning up after other people, was certainly something to cheer. But she was in college, so much younger than him. Probably around ten years younger, he mentally calculated. Ten years, especially nowadays, was a lifetime.

After experiencing the Layla Effect, Neel understood the ennui he'd felt in his half-hearted moves with Shefali. True, Layla's sex appeal was off the charts, so maybe it wasn't fair to compare. But that was probably why he'd held out and not committed to a relationship with Shefali. She simply didn't wow him the way Layla did. She'd merely been a void to fill, until his *real* dream woman came along.

With Layla, it was different. Despite the fact that she'd shown no interest in him, he was shocked to discover her mere presence got his pulse rate skyrocketing. He could actually feel the serotonin surging through his system. He knew psychologists had demonstrated, in lab conditions, that you could fall in love in sixty seconds flat. Well, even if it was a completely one-sided attraction on his part, he was living proof of the practical side of the theory!

He wanted to enquire further, about her family, about why her father didn't help out with the finances. She had already mentioned that her Russian mother had met her Bangladeshi father in Lumumba University, in Moscow, and they'd married as students. But the marriage hadn't worked out. Just as Neel was starting out on a more probing line of questioning, they heard the latch key turn.

Neel went cold. He had completely forgotten about Shri, who usually made his Sunday appearance around this time. It *was* Shri, after his rejuvenating pilates workout, letting himself in with his spare key. He'd got one foot through the door, when suddenly, he stopped in his tracks. It took him less than a second to decode the tableau before his eyes. Two beautiful young people, two coffee cups, two high stools—all in a nice little confined kitchen space.

Neel hoped and prayed Shri would not use his favourite opening line, "I'm sorry guys, hope I'm not interrupting—"

"I'm sorry guys, hope I'm not—" Shri began.

Neel cut in smoothly. "No, no, Shri, not intruding, no. So, what brings you here today?"

Neel's frosty welcome caught Shri off guard, but he didn't miss a beat. "Knew you'd ask me that! Yeah, I figured, you know, it's been a while, so I told myself, I gotta see my buddy Neel today, it's been too long. So! Here I am!" Shri extended his hands in an open, I-love-the-world gesture.

Shri knew that, at that moment, Neel would have given anything to have his head on the chopping block. In fact, if looks could kill, he'd be dead meat by now. But he'd be damned if he was leaving without getting the details on the young Bellucci. If Neel could give him free advice on his love life, then he, Shri, was equally entitled to investigate the new developments in Neel's kitchen. Especially when things appeared to be unfolding thick and fast, right under his nose. It was payback time!

Neel smiled at Layla. "My friend, Shri. Shri, this is Layla."

Shri smiled too and gave her an extended handshake. "Neel's a *dear* dear friend," he told Layla. "We go back, like, *centuries!* I wish we could meet more often, but hey, this is New York, right! I mean, I *love* this guy!" He gave Neel a friendly punch. "Right, Neel?"

Only the strictest self-discipline stopped Neel from clobbering Shri then and there. "Yeah, right."

Layla eased herself off the high stool and turned to Shri. "Some coffee for you?"

Shri nodded enthusiastically. He wouldn't actually be drinking it—he detested the stuff—but it would give him a chance to start up a conversation. Usually Neel was pretty open about introducing a new date. With Layla, however, he was behaving oddly reticent, and Shri wanted to know why.

But Shri never did get that conversation going, because Layla seemed to be in a big hurry to leave. As soon as she'd rustled up his coffee and handed it over to him, she turned to Neel. "The laundry's in the dryer. It's going to be another," she consulted her watch, "twenty minutes. I'm sorry, I really can't wait. I have to—"

Neel interrupted, "You should be with your mom. Go."

She nodded and scooped up her bag. Then, she turned to Shri, who was dutifully holding onto his coffee mug. "Enjoy," she told him with a parting smile. And, within the next couple of seconds, she was gone.

Her departure left a loaded silence. Shri had a sixth sense about certain things, and right now his sixth sense was telling him to keep his mouth shut. If this girl, Layla, was helping out with Neel's laundry, it meant she'd almost certainly moved in. Or, at least, spent the night with him. And yet, something was amiss. Something wasn't right, and Shri couldn't quite put his finger on it.

Neel had had liaisons with married women before, but Layla looked a bit too young to be married. Not that you could tell. These days anything was possible. Maybe she had some other issues, like doing recreational drugs, or a foot fetish, or an eating disorder. Shri figured that he could speculate till the cows came home, and he still wouldn't know what Neel was trying to hide.

Neel unclenched his jaw. "I know, you're wondering where she sprang from."

"No, no, not wondering," Shri was careful with his words, "but I have to say . . . she's really gorgeous. She's—"

"She's the maid."

Shri thought he hadn't heard right. But, obviously, it was inappropriate under the circumstances to challenge Neel's statement. Shri did know that Neel had a new maid, but her appearance had not been discussed. Generally speaking, it could hardly be considered a topic for discussion. Of course, if the maid looked like the girl who had just left, it changed things a bit. Shri was aware that Neel always got lucky with women, but this was ridiculous.

"She's filling in for her mother." Neel ran his fingers through his hair in an overwrought manner. Then he turned to Shri and smiled dryly. "She was here to clean the place, just in case your active imagination is working over-time."

Shri nodded and remained silent. This was a different Neel, not the hard-headed Neel he was used to. This Neel was reacting spontaneously, from the heart, and Shri could see he was completely blown away by Layla's beauty—it was the Layla Effect! In rare moments like these, he seemed almost vulnerable. If Neel ever let the veneer slip, it was only with people he knew really well, in conditions that were extraordinary.

Well, the present situation certainly qualified.

6

The Layla Effect was not immediately apparent to the outside world. Neel chose to stay tight-lipped about the maid who was not really a maid. Shri had decided, early on, to mind his own business. So he zipped his mouth and looked the other way, thus ensuring Neel's latest passion remained below the radar, at least for now.

Shefali, therefore, had no idea that Neel was lusting after a new woman. She assumed all was well in their little paradise, and that their twosome evenings—you couldn't really call them dates— were moving along as they should. One such appointment, a dinner at a fancy new Michelin-starred restaurant, was something she'd been looking forward to. They'd booked for a Friday evening, and Neel was to meet her there directly from work. Shefali had lined up her manicurist that morning, the one who offered in-home services, for a price. She'd also decided that her sartorial theme for the evening would be d2k, as in, dressed to kill!

The effort, however, was quite misplaced. In Neel's scheme of things, Shefali was BL, Before Layla. Even as she was busy getting her manicure, he was at his desk, brooding about how to get out of the dinner date. The restaurant reservation had been made almost two weeks ahead, and at the time, he'd exulted in securing a corner table. But in his current state of mind, the last thing he wanted was to be cornered in an exclusive, candle-lit environment with Shefali.

By early evening, Neel was desperately working on his exit strategy. The crying off had to sound convincing, so he mentally rehearsed all possible scenarios. Something like, "Oh sorry, work's gotten really crazy!" seemed a little too unbelievable. Feigning sudden ill-health was an option, but the trouble was, he had only recently told her that his sick leave had piled up because he never got sick. What he needed, reflected Neel, was a how-to handbook on ditching your date. It would be one of his more worthwhile investments.

As he ran his hands through his hair, indicating his highly distraught state of mind, his cell phone rang. He glanced at the caller ID. It was Shefali. He *had* to respond. "Hey, 'sup?"

"Hi, listen, I'm so sorry, I know it's short notice, but we'll have to cancel tonight."

Neel inhaled sharply. "Oh? Everything all right?"

There was a pause at her end. "I-I'm not sure. My dad's flying in from London in an hour or so. I have to meet him. He has something important to tell me, he says."

The catch in her voice towards the end made him somewhat conscience-stricken. "Hey, it's okay, relax, I'm sure it's no big deal," he said, pausing delicately. "So anyways then, I'm cancelling the reservation for tonight. Call me later if you need anything, okay?"

He heard her whisper a word of thanks before she disconnected. After the call, he was almost ashamed about the surge of relief he felt. He liked Shefali and enjoyed being out with her—only, not enough. And especially not after he'd met Layla.

In normal circumstances, Shefali would have been pretty astute about sensing shifting loyalties, particularly if a rival was involved. But where Neel was concerned, the warning signs escaped her completely. At that point, she was more absorbed in worrying about her father's visit and wondering what could be so urgent.

She somehow knew that the trip meant bad news and couldn't help playing out all kinds of grim possibilities in her mind. Her grandfather had died of cancer at a young age, and a few years back, an uncle had lost his fortune on the stock exchange. Hopefully it was nothing as drastic as that. She'd know soon enough, she figured, and, to distract herself, called Rachna Ben to wipe the coffee table, yet again. Champakbhai Bhansali liked to see a spotlessly clean home.

Her father usually travelled within Europe and rarely ever visited the US. Regardless of destination, however, he always flew first class, with a cabin all to himself. His large retinue—his cook the *maharaj*, his personal secretary, and a majordomo—accompanied him in the economy section. But what Shefali didn't know was that on this particular trip, he was minus the entourage. He was flying solo. It was a strictly private trip, a dash across the Atlantic and back. In fact, it was so clandestine that even his wife did not know about it. He had told her he was stuck in London, on business, and would return home to Antwerp the following day.

His visit to New York was long overdue. He had to meet Shefali on an urgent personal matter. He had put it off till the last minute, but now, he could no longer postpone the inevitable. As his limo purred into her circular driveway, he braced himself for the encounter.

Thirty-two floors above, Shefali had been anxiously biting her freshly manicured nails. When she heard the building

71

security buzzer, she took a deep breath. Her father had arrived. Their reunion would be semi-formal, just like their relationship. Over the years, she had made an effort to infuse more warmth into their sporadic interactions, but it wasn't easy. Theirs was a complicated father-daughter equation, because there was always a third dimension to it. Money. Throughout her life, Shefali had had to come to terms with one simple maxim—she was compensated in cash for what her father couldn't supply in kind.

When Champakbhai emerged from the elevator, his daughter's door was already open. "Pappa!"

He came forward and patted her on the cheek.

"How was the flight?" she asked, leading him into the living room.

"Not bad, not bad." He sat down on her designer sofa and fidgeted about uncomfortably, not quite sure where to start. After hesitating a bit, he began with, "Shef, your *maasi* does not know I'm here, okay, and you must never tell her that I came." He referred to her step-mother as *maasi*. Shefali found it impossible to call her *ma*, considering she was barely a year older than Shefali herself. Calling Meena by her first name was also unacceptable. It would be disrespectful as a form of address for a stepmother. So *maasi* was a happy compromise.

"I wanted to speak to you alone, you see," Champakbhai continued, "and tell you myself. Shef, *beta*, the thing is, Meena is due next week."

"Oh?" Shefali raised her eyebrows. "She's coming here?"

Her father had turned all shifty-eyed. "Due in the family way. Having a baby."

Shefali went ice cold. Her head swam, and the blood seemed to drain right out of her body. Her father had just announced he was having another child. When he'd got married, she knew it would happen. He had never pretended otherwise. Why was

72

she suddenly feeling so very betrayed? "Next week, you said?" she whispered.

He nodded miserably, squirming under her steady gaze.

"What else, Pappa? I know there is something more." Her expressive almond eyes locked into his, demanding an answer. "You can tell me, Pappa, I can take it."

"Shef *beta*, she made me do it. She set all kinds of conditions before having the baby. If it was a boy, she said, I would have to transfer the inheritance in his name. Of course, when I signed the papers, I had no way to know it would be a . . ." he trailed off and covered his face, trying to control his emotions.

Shefali tilted her head up. "And happily for you . . . it *is* going to be a boy. Finally, your dream of having a son comes true. Congratulations, Pappa."

"I want you to know, nothing changes for you. The allowance continues, as always. You will be as precious to me, you know that." He looked at her imploringly. "See, *beta*, when your *maasi* gave me such an ultimatum, what choice did I have, tell me? I decided to wait to tell you, till we knew whether it was going to be a boy or girl. Then when I found out . . ."

He was too choked up to continue. Shefali wanted to get up and comfort him, but she just couldn't get herself to make sympathetic noises when the reality was, she wanted to scream out loud. *What about me*? she wanted to shout. *Why should I be squeezed out because your gold-digging wife wants her son, not even born yet, to grab what's rightfully mine?*

Champakbhai gazed up at his daughter with watery eyes. "I want to see you happy, Shef, whatever happens. Married, with children of your own. Is there nobody . . ."

"Nobody, Pappa," she said.

"You are now twenty-four, *beta*, the right age for marriage. If your mother had been alive, she would have seen to all that. Me,

I don't know how to handle these things. If you like I can—"

"No! No need, Pappa. If it has to happen . . . anyway, let's forget about all that. Tell me, when is the due date? What names are you thinking of?"

He brightened. "Ah, I was going to ask. What do you think of Sudhanshu?"

Shefali did not know how she got through the next couple of hours. By the time her father got up, to head back to the airport, her self-control was at breaking point. As they said their goodbyes, she sensed that their father-daughter relationship, as she knew it, was over. It would soon be replaced by a father-son bond, which, by tradition, was pivotal and all-powerful. In the Indian family, the "sun syndrome" was the established norm, where the world revolved around the male child, eclipsing all other family ties. From now on, she, Shefali, was on her own.

Neel was just getting out of the shower when his cell rang. All he heard was a series of sobbing sounds at the other end. "Shefali? Hello? Shefali!"

The sobbing got more intense. Neel was in the middle of towel-drying his hair, and the interruption was most unwelcome. After his shower, he'd planned to catch up on some urgent emails, but now it appeared that he had an even more urgent matter to attend to. "Shefali, I'm coming over, okay? Just try to stay calm. I'll be there as soon as I can."

Within twenty minutes Neel was outside her door. He gave her an appraising look as he stepped in. Before he'd showed up, she had scrubbed her face and tied her hair back. It made her look like a school girl, he thought. "Hey, you don't look so bad . . . you had me worried, you know!" Then he became serious. "You okay?"

She tried to smile. "It's weird, my getting so upset, but when he said they were having a baby . . ." She started sobbing again, her whole body shaking in spasms.

Neel got up and held her close till the outburst subsided. After she'd calmed down a bit, he drew away. "Come, let's get you something to drink." He moved towards the bar and poured out two extremely generous cognacs. Then, he got her to semi-recline on the chaise lounge, handed her her drink, and settled down opposite her to listen.

Shefali, as always, believed in playing to the gallery. She reached for a tissue, and sniffled. She was just warming up. "That creature must have been at least four months gone when I last saw her . . . in Antwerp. I just assumed she was getting fat on all the sugar she consumes. I mean, she's eating desserts, *mithai*, *all* the time." Shefali paused to blow her nose, and continued. "Then he springs this on me . . . like literally at the very last minute. *We're having this baby next week.* Next week! Couldn't you have mentioned it earlier! Hello! It's like, I'm going out shopping. Or, I'm seeing this movie."

Neel watched her warily, hoping she wasn't going to dissolve into tears again. She didn't. Instead, she took refuge in another handful of tissues and resumed her tirade. "Then, he happens to mention that he's cutting off my inheritance. Poof! Just like that. 'I will still love you and look after you,' he says. Like he's doing me one big favour! Does he think I don't know what's going on? I mean, what stops him from axing my allowance? One minute I'm like this . . . this heiress with my own apartment and everything, then, out of the blue, I'm on the streets, with God knows where my next meal is coming from! You know, even when he got married, I didn't feel so cheated. Now I'm just so mad that . . . that . . ." She shook her head violently. Then the tears started coming down again, fast and furious.

Neel was okay to let her just spew it out and get it out of her system. He noticed that she was becoming more vitriolic by the minute, but that was probably just the brandy talking, he figured. Not that he had any intention of giving her more alcohol. So he said, "Okay, I'm going to fix you some warm milk. Great way to relax. Then you should go get some sleep."

He got busy in the kitchen, and by the time he placed the mug of milk into the micro, he had decided it was time to exit gracefully. "I should be getting along," he told Shefali, "I've got an early start tomorrow."

She threw him a don't-desert-me look. It came quite naturally to her. "You can't leave me. I feel very fragile right now."

Neel, who had been hunting about for his windcheater, was in a bind. It was precisely her volatile state of mind that made him super-reluctant to hang about. He didn't want any crossed signals between them, and if she started becoming emotionally demanding, things could get messy. Moreover, he didn't want to lead her on. That would be an emotion-charged minefield he could never extricate himself from, alive!

So when Shefali came forward and clutched his windcheater, saying, "Don't go! Please! Please!" Neel chose to remain unmoved. He delicately prised the windcheater out of her grasp and shrugged it on. With a show of reluctance, he said, "I'd like to stay, really . . . but as things stand, I gotta go. There's some urgent mail to catch up on." At least that part was true. "Why don't I call you first thing in the morning? Okay?"

So saying, he placed her mug of hot milk on a tray and carried it out to the chaise lounge. Shefali reluctantly followed him into the living room and settled down once again. After he'd placed the tray beside her and plumped up the cushions for her, Neel considered his duty done.

Earlier, when she'd clung on to him, he'd been sorely tempted to change his mind and stay on. But once again, he reminded himself that spending the night in her apartment was going to put him in a very awkward position indeed. He didn't want that under any circumstances, not even in a seemingly benign situation like this one. So, as soon as she started sipping the milk, he muted the lights, dropped a chaste goodnight kiss on top of her head, and let himself out.

Not a moment too soon, Neel reflected, as he stepped into the elevator going down.

7

A couple of months into his relationship with Vivian, Shanks was still walking on air. During this period, he had freely and frequently shared his deliriousness with his two best buddies. He went so far as to describe Vivian as his soul mate, his heart's desire, his goddess on God's earth. Fortunately for him, Vivian adored him too, with equal fervour. The Gang watched the lovebirds with amusement, acknowledging that love did, indeed, make the world go round.

In a recent development, Shanks and Vivian had started living together, at his apartment. Like everything else in their relationship, it had happened quite seamlessly. One night, when Vivian was at his place for dinner, she had simply stayed over and not gone home. The very next day, she'd packed a suitcase and moved in with him. The new arrangement was perfect, because now, they could commute to work together, share the groceries, and consult one another on work-related issues. And, the nicest part was that they could spend the night on one bed!

But their new-found bliss had an expiry date. Shanks knew he had to come down to earth because his mother was coming. "I have to say this right now, my mother comes mid May," Shanks had told Vivian soon after she'd moved in, "and she stays till the middle of November. Once she's here, no way we can live together!"

Vivian understood perfectly. Her own mother wouldn't have approved of their live-in arrangement either. So the plan was that she'd continue paying the rent for her old apartment, which she shared with a girlfriend, and shift back there before Mrs. Revathi Subramanian arrived.

At that point, however, they were not aware that it wouldn't be just one but *two* Mrs. Subramanians flying in. Shanks' grandmother, his Tathi Ma, had decided to make the trip too. Her six-month visa had unexpectedly come through, and the seventy-four-year-old lady was pining to see her grandson. But Shanks was not the only attraction. Several decades ago, as a young married woman, she had visited New York City with her engineer husband, Mr. Subramanian. He had led an Indian delegation to attend a UN seminar on *Rural Infrastructure Development in India*, and she had accompanied him.

That was back in the Kennedy era, when America was an international superpower, at the peak of its glory. She had been dazzled by Manhattan and marvelled at the gravity-defying Empire State Building and the psychedelic Times Square. Now, the prospect of seeing her grandson making his mark in this capital of the world was like a dream come true. It was something she wanted to witness first hand, while she could.

The arrival of the two ladies necessitated some modifications to the living arrangements. However, Shanks and Vivian had been too caught up at work to make the necessary adjustments. All they'd managed was a quick, last-minute trip to Ikea for a sofa-cum-bed, and some extra sheets and towels.

The last-minute preparations had been challenging enough. But the last-minute packing had turned into a full-blown crisis!

An hour before the flight was due to land, Vivian was still in Shanks' apartment, frantically filling up her bags. "Honey, pass my belts, second drawer left. No, no, not armoire drawer, *dresser* drawer. Hurr-eee!"

She ran into the bathroom. "Mascara, lip liner, foundation," he heard her say. She emerged with an armload of assorted make-up and hair products and threw all the stuff into a suitcase. "You know, I came with one bag, now I've got three. Don't ask me how! And none of them will close. Hon, find me one more bag! Please!"

Shanks was time-crunched too: he needed to get to the airport for the pick-up and was already running behind schedule. As he hurried off to find her a bag, Vivian sat on top of a particularly bloated suitcase, and tried to zip it up. Once matters were somewhat under control, Shanks turned to Vivian. "I've got to run, okay? Shri's picking you up in ten-fifteen minutes. Think you'll be done by then? If not . . ." He rolled his eyes theatrically and dropped his head sideways.

Vivian smiled at the high drama. "Relax, Mr. SS," her new acronym for Slavedriver Subramanian, "by the time you're back, the crime scene will be all cleaned up. Vivian Hsein will have vanished, without a trace."

"No, don't say that . . . don't ever say that." He wrapped his arms around her and held her tight. "I don't want you vanishing anywhere, okay?"

She dimpled and pulled away. "Umm, let me think about it. Now's my big chance to negotiate more loo time, before I sign up again!" Then she gave him a push. "Go, go, go! You don't want to keep them waiting."

Shanks had hired an SUV for the pick up, knowing full well that his mother and Tathi Ma would come armed with kitchen supplies. Fortunately, the economy baggage allowance was a deterrent, and excess baggage meant heavy penalties. He was hoping they'd have considered that before loading up on all manner of non-essential items, and lugging them half way across the world.

Shanks finally made it to Newark Airport well after the Air India flight had landed. Within minutes of reaching Arrivals, he spied the first baggy-eyed Chennai passengers emerging. In New York, Shanks always recognised Indians from a mile away, simply by the way they dressed. They were more colourful than the general population, and were usually over-clad, regardless of season.

But even by Indian standards, his mom stood out. She was among the older sari-wearing generation of women and determinedly clung to her six yards of silk like it was going out of style (which, in a sense, it was!). After she was widowed, she'd conformed to tradition and worn white for a year. Then, she'd reverted to her multi-hued collection of South Indian silks.

Shanks, therefore, had no trouble spotting his mom in the crowd. She was in a chrome-orange Kanjivaram silk and sneakers. A porter was trudging along wearily by her side, wheeling what looked like half a dozen bags. His grandmother was close behind, being assisted in a wheelchair.

Shanks hurried forward to waylay the little procession. And a classic, Indian-style reunion ensued, with lots of hugging, laughing, crying, and more hugging. When Shanks bent down to touch his grandmother's feet, his gesture of respect had the old lady in tears. "Sankar, I never thought in my life this day would come! I am so blessed, so blessed! Oh my dear God, look at you, even taller than I remember! And so exactly like your father! Handsome *kanna!* Revathi, remind me to ward off the evil eye as soon as we get home. I am talking too much!"

The porter, standing by for his payment, was also of the

opinion that she was talking too much. He cleared his throat. An apologetic Shanks quickly offered him a generous tip and then turned to the wheelchair assistant to make a similar pay-off. That accomplished, he led the way towards the parking area. They crawled along, with his mom wheeling her mother-in-law, and Shanks pushing their luggage trolley, impeded by the column of suitcases stacked so high that even a tall guy like him could barely see two feet ahead.

Later, as Shanks navigated the SUV towards Holland Tunnel, he turned to his mother. "That's two extra suitcases, *Amma*, and all so heavy. How much did they make you pay?"

Mrs. Revathi smirked. "Nothing." She preened a bit before elaborating, "You know, your father's old school friend, Srinivasan? He's become director of Air India, so I just gave him a call . . ."

Shanks couldn't help smiling. Nothing had changed, he reflected.

When they got to his apartment, and started unpacking their suitcases, Shanks saw that his fears had not been unfounded. The 450-square foot apartment had no space to stand! All kinds of pickles and *pappadums* were strewn over the floor, making their pungent presence felt. Shanks picked up a large bottle containing a spicy pickled mango in chilli-red oil.

"*Avakkai?*" He stared at his mother. "What, they let this through customs?"

His mother raised her eyebrows. "I use techniques to distract them. We women have to learn these things, otherwise how do you think we survive? How do you think I have managed, now that your father is no more?"

Shanks could see her chest was heaving, a sure sign that the tears were about to flow. Ever since his father had passed away, these attacks of self-pity, where she went into dry, hacking sobs, had punctuated every conversation he'd had with her. He quickly mumbled something about sleeping arrangements, and pretended to get busy with the sheets and pillows. He'd planned for Tathi Ma to be sleeping on his bed, while his mother would be assigned the new Ikea sofa-bed. He'd have to settle for the air mattress, which still had to be pumped up.

That night, as Shanks fidgeted about on his air mattress, he felt like a man doing time in a penitentiary. He was cool with any degree of physical discomfort. Nor did he mind being bossed around or even emotionally blackmailed by his mom. But the separation from Vivian was unendurable.

Earlier that day, when he'd walked into the apartment along with his mother and grandmother, his eyes had scanned the place, almost hoping for some trace of Vivian. There was none. And yet, had it been his imagination, or was there a faint whiff of her signature perfume, Tresor, still hanging in the air? But minutes later, as soon as the suitcases were opened, every other olfactory nuance had been overwhelmed by the invading aroma of spices. Vivian's lingering presence had been very effectively obliterated, in no time at all!

Shanks sighed inwardly and continued to fidget on his mattress. Dealing with his mom was tough enough, but with Vivian banished from his life, his morale had sunk to an all-time low.

Shanks was not the only one with Mom-related issues to battle. Shri had his own Armageddon looming up. One fine day, just as life seemed to be on cruise control, his mother called and commanded his presence in Atlanta. Apparently, another matrimonial prospect had popped up. The candidate looked like Madhuri Dixit and came with a Mensa-level IQ, his mom informed him. "Shri, we are expecting you home this weekend. Girls like this don't last forever." Whatever that meant. *No*, Aai, he wanted to say, *she might get spoiled, like leftover pizza that someone forgot to put in the fridge.*

"Trouble at home?" It was Paolo, coming up from behind and wrapping his arms around Shri's yoga-sculpted torso.

Shri did the famous Indian head bobble, conveying a yes and no at the same time. "Yeah, the usual," he said, "they want me to visit them, in Atlanta—"

Paolo raised an eyebrow. "You should go, man, if only to keep the peace!"

Shri was thinking the same thing. Not making an appearance was non-negotiable, he had accepted that. But going through the whole charade of seeing another girl?

He sighed. He really hated the idea of meeting a girl and rejecting her outright, for no valid reason. It was all so unnecessary! He mulled over the possibility of feigning insanity during the introductory meeting, a theme he remembered from an old Bollywood movie. Or he could tell the girl he had AIDS or something!

Just then, his cell rang. It was Shefali. She informed him that she was in the process of scheduling an informal lunch with a fashion consultant, potentially for freelance writing work, and was keen to have him in at the meeting. She considered Shri's input valuable and wanted him there to help her negotiate the opportunity. Would the coming Saturday work?

Shri froze. The very thing! He interrupted, "Shefali?"

There was a pause at her end. "Shrikant Godbole, you haven't heard a word I've said!"

"No," he admitted. "Listen, I need you to do me a favour. Okay, not just *any* favour, a huge *big* favour actually."

"What."

"Come with me to Atlanta this weekend . . . be my new girlfriend."

There was a protracted silence at her end.

"Please? That's the only way they'll get off my back. I'll owe you for the rest of my life, till my dying day, God promise!"

Again, no response. Why wouldn't she say something? Was his cell connection acting up again? "Shefali? You there?"

"Yes, I'm here." She hesitated. "Hey," she seemed to make up her mind, "we need to talk. Urgently. You need to come over."

Half an hour later, Shri was at Shefali's door. The very second he saw her face, he knew that she knew. Her eyes were saying it all, and her eloquent silence was only confirming it. He wasn't sure when or how she had guessed, but guessed she had.

Shri felt like he was going to pass out. That there was another human being in the known world privy to his dark and deadly secret was almost too much to bear. He'd have blacked out, then and there, if Shefali hadn't dragged him in, and made him sit down.

For Shri, it was like being pulled out of an abyss and rescued by a guardian angel, an angel with strong arms and a firm grip. This do-gooder angel had led him straight to the safety and salvation of her designer sofa, and offered him some water to drink. (After her dad's recent visit, her sofa seemed to have become the designated hotspot for all kinds of soul-baring sessions!)

However, unlike her dad, who had revealed all right away, Shri took his time opening up. After chewing his lip in deep thought for a length of time, he looked up, trepidatious. "How did you guess? Who else knows?"

"No one knows. And I guessed because . . ." Because he was very much like her gay friends in London. He had a highly developed EQ, always second-guessed what she was thinking, and even chastised her on her fashion faux pas. Of course, it was entirely possible for a straight guy to possess all these amazingly useful qualities, but the truth was, she didn't know any! What had really clinched it for her was how disturbed he became whenever he was paired up with a girl—Bhairavi being a case in point. However, this wasn't the time to tell him all that. It would only upset him further.

"Because?" He was waiting.

"Because women have a better 'gaydar' than men, that's all!"

"You know, I've grown up with Neel . . . maybe he knows, maybe he—"

"No," Shefali interrupted firmly, "he doesn't know. Neel's so self-absorbed he can't see beyond the end of his nose. And as for Shanks, he is such a sweetheart he wouldn't remotely suspect anything like this." She hesitated. "Hey? You tell them when you're ready to tell them, okay?"

"You think I should tell them?" The mere thought was making him quake.

She rubbed his arm reassuringly. "That's up to you . . . but I wouldn't worry about it. They're your friends, right? They're going to accept you for who you are . . ."

Finally, Shri was beginning to relax. He had unburdened his soul to a fellow human being and had not just survived the ordeal, but come out of it in one whole piece. His surge of relief was like a meditative, out-of-body experience, where a heavy, brooding presence seemed to have physically lifted itself out and drifted away.

Shefali rang a discreet bell for Rachna Ben. What Shri needed was a nice hot cup of chocolate. So, very soon, Shri was curled up on the sofa, sipping steaming hot cocoa. Along with the cocoa, he could feel contentment seeping in. Shefali had not judged him. She had not crossed him off her friends' list. In fact, she'd sounded pretty matter-of-fact about the whole thing. It felt awesome to be able to finally share his secret and open up to a sympathetic listener. Of course, he still had to tell her about

Paolo, but after this watershed moment, he felt he could do it.

"So now, what happens to Madhuri Dixit?" Shefali cut into his thoughts.

Shri started. He had completely forgotten about the Dixit gal. (Funny how they'd started calling her that!) "What about my plan?" he asked. "If I take you along . . . as my bride prospect . . . then obviously, they won't be showing me the other girl. Worth it just for that, isn't it?"

She was forced to acknowledge that he had a point there. So they decided he'd tell his parents he couldn't meet the girl they'd shortlisted, because he was going to be accompanied by his new girlfriend, Shefali. Of course, what they were doing was unethical, it was morally wrong, but, as Shefali saw it, the subterfuge was only a stop-gap arrangement. Eventually, Shri would have to come clean. How he chose to do it, and when, was up to him.

However, till Shri got his timing right, Shefali figured she had to do her bit, for her friend in need. Her mandate was to play decoy girlfriend and she busied herself doing just that. For starters, she needed to pick an appropriate wardrobe. She directed Rachna Ben to lay out some conservative outfits, those that projected a suitably coy image.

It was ironic, Shefali reflected, as she chose her accessories, being Shri's pretend girlfriend was easy-peasy, but becoming Neel's real-life girlfriend remained as elusive as ever! She'd finally woken up to the fact that Neel was distancing himself from her. He avoided being alone with her, and was always finding excuses to have the Gang around. Surely she didn't need chaperoning! The only explanation was that there was someone else in his life, but if there was, surely the Gang would know? Even Neel couldn't hide a grown woman under the carpet, could he?

And then, there was her friendship with Shri. Could Neel be bowing out because he was heroically allowing Shri first rights?

But here, Shefali had to admit to herself that that was probably just wishful thinking. When Neel had heard about their trip to Atlanta, he'd appeared to be quite blasé about it. Not really caring that she was flying off with Shri, into the sunset.

Although that was quite a dispiriting thought, Shefali decided to play it safe. She resolved to let Neel know, as soon as she was back, that her trip to Atlanta had been purely altruistic. She had done it for Shri out of the goodness of her heart, and that was all there was to it. On the plus side, all this might get Neel feeling a little jealous. At least, she hoped it would.

When they landed at the Hartfield-Jackson airport in Atlanta, Shri's parents were waiting to receive them. As they approached the old couple, Shefali felt like a criminal. It was so unfair to do this to them, even as a short-term measure. She glanced at Shri, and saw that he was not looking very happy either. But keeping up the charade was all-important, so, as designated drama queen, she braced herself for an accolade-worthy performance.

When Shri ushered her forward, saying, "*Aai*? *Baba*? This is Shefali," she folded her hands in a namaste.

"Shri has spoken so much about you! I'm so happy to be here. And thanks so much for having me!"

Mr. and Mrs. Godbole were dazzled. What a charming girl, so refined, and respectful! Shri's new girlfriend had exceeded their wildest expectations. Mrs. Godbole cast surreptitious glances at her as they made their way to the car, quite certain that Shefali's ensemble must have cost a fortune. And as for the jewellery, she wasn't much of a judge, but surely stones that size had to be fake! Where on earth could Shri have met a girl like this one?

Shri sat in front, next to his father, and the ladies got comfortable at the back. As the car headed out towards the idyllic Atlanta suburb of Acworth, Shefali steeled herself for the inevitable line of questioning that must follow. And her answers came so pat that even when they reached their destination, Shri's mom was none the wiser about what she did, where she stayed, or who her parents were.

Once they got to the picket-fenced home and deposited their bags inside, Mr. Godbole insisted on taking Shefali for a conducted tour around the property. They started on the front lawn. "The garden is my domain," Mr. Godbole informed Shefali, as they walked along the grassy periphery. "See? I replanted the tulip bulbs here. Should be out in a week or two."

Shefali smiled. "And who does Shri get his cooking skills from?"

He laughed. "Ah, his mother, she's the expert cook!" He guided her towards the backyard. "In fact, she's in the kitchen right now, finishing up a traditional Maharashtrian-style dinner, especially for you!"

Shefali was overwhelmed with their warmth and affection, and the trouble they were taking to make her feel at home. It made her want to cry. This was really very difficult to do! She guiltily told herself that for every minute she stayed in this house, she was giving them false hopes and abusing their trust. But the problem was that there was no viable option.What would their reaction be if they were told their only son was gay? Would that be any less cruel than what she was doing now?

They had taken care to install her suitcase in a pretty guest bedroom that was as far away from Shri's bedroom as possible. In fact, the length of an entire passageway separated the two bedrooms! Indian parents really had some sweet, old-fashioned ideas about non-married couples sharing a bed under their roof, Shefali noted, with a touch of amusement. And that didn't look like it was going to change anytime soon. True, she did know of a few Westernised *desi* families who chose to wink and look the other way, but if they did, it was a huge break from tradition.

Mrs. Godbole had half-expected Shri to protest against the sleeping arrangements, and was pleasantly surprised when he didn't. He was being a respectful son, she thought gratefully. And his Shefali too appeared ready to accept the rules of the house.

After a sumptuous meal of *wantania chi ussal, subudaniache wade,* and *amti bhaat,* Shri's parents were very keen to get down to business. But they needed to catch him alone. The opportunity arose shortly after dinner, when Shefali excused herself to go upstairs to freshen up.

Shri had been sitting at the dining table, savouring his second helping of *shrikhand* when his mother and father hemmed him in from both sides, effectively cutting off all escape routes. "Shri! Have you proposed yet?" His mother did not believe in meaningless chatter. The road to grandchildren was a slippery one, and when negotiating its twists and turns, speed was of the essence.

Shri looked around surreptitiously, like he expected Shefali to be lurking about in the doorway. "No, no, of course not!" He swallowed. "I—we are taking things gradually. If we find we're compatible, then we'll—"

"So how much longer to find out? I decided on your mother in ten minutes flat."

His father made it sound as if the clock was ticking, and his time was starting—*now!*

With great dignity, Shri squared his shoulders and cleared his throat. He wasn't going to be heckled. "Aai? Baba? I love you both very much, you know that, but please understand and bear with me. These things take time, I can't give you a wedding date just yet."

They stared at him with puzzled frowns. What was the hitch when the girl seemed perfectly ready to say yes? Why was Shri unnecessarily delaying such a momentous, life-defining decision?

"Something wrong, Shri, some problem? Her family?" his

mother asked.

"We can speak to her father if you want," his father added.

Shri quickly shook his head. "No, no, please. Things haven't reached that stage yet." He paused, deliberating on what to say next. "See, back in your days, things were different . . . but now life is more complicated. There's so much to think about before actually deciding . . . my career, her career, where we'll stay, how we'll—"

"So you stay together now?" his mother interrupted.

"No, not exactly." Shri squirmed, hoping Shefali would hurry up and come back.

The questions were becoming increasingly tricky. While he and Shefali had gone over the broad details of their supposed liaison, they had not discussed specifics. If his parents were to quiz her separately, discrepancies were bound to crop up. He needed to tread carefully, his parents could be pretty sharp. He was well aware that his mother, particularly, was equipped with an in-built lie-detector. Being on her radar had frequently tested him through his childhood.

Just when he thought it was all over, his parents nudged in a little closer. They were still awaiting an answer. Shri could have sworn he was in the interrogation cell on an episode of *Law & Order: Criminal Intent*. "Okay, it's like this," he said finally, "we sometimes stay at each other's apartments, but no, not actually living in, no."

By then, his nerves were seriously beginning to fray. So, when Shefali walked back in, at that very moment, Shri heaved a sigh of relief. He was off the hook, thank goodness, at least for now! The idea was to keep the hope alive, without making any concrete commitment. He was aware that most Indian parents thought of romance as a sort of dress rehearsal, a necessary evil, before their commitment-phobic offspring could be persuaded to tie the knot. In his case, the courtship would have to be carefully calibrated over an extended period of time, and aborted just before reaching the altar.

After getting the initial status report, his parents decided to leave him be. The important thing was, their son had brought a girl to meet them, thereby demonstrating that he was serious about settling down. Relieved to find that Shefali was just the kind of girl they'd have picked for him if they'd done the choosing, they knew that was reason enough to be content. At this point, pushing for a wedding date would be pushing their luck. All they could do was hope and pray that the grandchildren would be on their way in the not-too-distant future.

So, the status quo was maintained, and the rest of the visit turned out to be surprisingly tension-free. Then came the time to say farewell. By this point, the play-acting had taken its toll on Shefali. She had to concede that being a pretend girlfriend, studied and scrutinised 24/7, was exhausting work. Moreover, she had become increasingly attached to his warm and wonderful parents. His mother, particularly, had embraced her like a daughter, and Shefali knew she was going to miss her.

His parents were keen to see them off at the airport and despite Shri's protests, they had insisted on the send-off. *The curtain call*, thought Shefali, with a sense of closure.

"Keep in touch, *beta*," Mrs. Godbole said, wiping her tears.

Shefali gave Shri's mom a big hug and turned away, trying to keep her own tears in check. When Shri glanced at Shefali, he was surprised to see her crumpled face. If she was acting, it certainly was the performance of a lifetime. Once his parents had disappeared from view, Shri turned to Shefali, concerned. "Hey, you okay?" he asked.

She shook her head in an overwrought manner and, unable to contain herself any longer, burst out sobbing on his shoulder.

8

After the Atlanta trip, Shefali got down to some serious introspection. She couldn't help feeling that her emotional rollercoaster at the Godbole residence had gotten way more intense than the situation had called for. Her seesawing sentiments, therefore, had to be symptomatic of a larger problem—her vulnerability.

She'd been devastated after her father's announcement, and was still trying to work out her new equation with him. Denting her self-confidence further was her uncertain scene with Neel. Their twosome outings might be a thing of the past, but they hadn't made a clean break either. So she was at the crossroads, unwilling to cut loose, and unable to move on.

Of course, Shefali was well aware that all the self psychoanalysis in the world couldn't offer a solution for her Neel-mania. She needed to share her pain with a sympathetic soul. But unfortunately, Shri couldn't be that soul. He was too close to Neel. Just as she was wondering which of her girlfriends she could confide in, Vivian called.

Vivian was at a loose end. Shanks, apparently, was preoccupied with his mother and grandmother, so was Shefali free to meet up? Shefali, as always, had time on her hands, so they decided to catch brunch at the neighbourhood bistro. It was a beautiful Saturday morning, perfect for relaxing in the outdoor patio and enjoying the sunshine.

Once they'd placed their orders, Vivian filled Shefali in on the latest in her life. Or rather, *Shanks'* life. "Shanks is out again, today," Vivian began. "He's taking them to see a movie in Secaucus. They're also doing some Indian groceries. His mom wants to make some, umm, some sweet snacks? Something with *j?*"

Shefali frowned. "*J?* Oh, I don't know. I know, in the South, they make some kind of *jalebi*, starting with *j.* Something that sounds like Jehangir . . . I don't remember now…" She was referring to *jhangiri*, the bright orange sweet that resembled the *jalebi*, its Northern counterpart. She gave Vivian an appraising look. "You haven't met her yet, have you?"

Vivian shook her head. "Oh my God, no. No way. Truth be told, I hardly meet Shanks either, outside of work."

Shefali clucked sympathetically. "Must be hard."

Vivian sighed. It *was* hard. Summer was round the corner, and they'd be missing out on park outings, and cycling along the riverfront, and simply being a part of the night-time buzz in the city. She had to make an effort to shake herself out of her despondency. "At least we work in the same place . . . we see each other every day but—" Her voice cracked into a sob.

"Hey, hey, it's okay." Shefali squeezed Vivian's hand. "He loves you very much, and that's all that matters."

Vivian nodded in agreement. "Yes, yes, he does. That's what makes this almost bearable."

For the next few minutes, they sipped their cosmopolitans in companionable silence. By this time, Shefali had decided that she wasn't in the mood to confide in anyone. She preferred to keep her Neel-mania private. So, when Vivian looked up and said, "You know, I've been going on and on about me and my problems. What I've been meaning to ask is, how are things between you and Neel?"

Shefali raised a haughty eyebrow. "What things?"

Shefali's act didn't fool Vivian for a second. She simply smiled and said, "Oh, I'm sorry, I didn't mean to upset you or anything. If you don't want to talk, it's fine, I—"

"I want to talk." Shefali knew she had been rude and now, suddenly, she actually wanted to share her anguish with Vivian.

"But, Viv, I'm not sure what to say! I mean, I thought we had something going, and then, I find, maybe not. Maybe there's someone else. Maybe he just isn't a one-woman guy."

Vivian could see that Shefali was deeply affected by Neel's indifference, if it was that. It was difficult to tell what Neel was thinking. His intense, inscrutable dark eyes gave nothing away. Vivian herself wasn't immune to his charm, and his unattainability only added to his other attractions. Neel was always going to be a player, she reflected, and any woman who fell for him needed to keep that in mind.

They had no idea that, at that very moment, Neel happened to be on the line with his latest love interest, Layla Quereshi. The call, however, was strictly business. Layla had phoned to say she wouldn't be able to make it for her usual Sunday slot. She wasn't free.

"Oh? Not free Sunday?" He'd waited all week for her to show up! Now, she was calling one day before and cancelling what should have been the highlight of his weekend. "So, umm, how about re-scheduling then, for later today?"

"Yeah, today works," Layla replied. "I can make four-ish today." She was already out and about on the Manhattan sidewalks, striding along in her stiletto boots with practised ease.

Her fuchsia cape flapped about her, making her look like an exotic tropical bird among the raven-black New Yorkers around. After she'd signed off with Neel, her attention was caught by a store display showcasing the season's latest swimwear. She decided to step in.

When Neel got off the phone, he realised that he'd just messed up his entire day. To accommodate Layla, he'd be ditching a colleague's wedding lunch that very afternoon. But he didn't care. His priority was to be at home—and available—when Layla arrived. Aware that he was behaving like a love-struck teenager, Neel found that he just couldn't help himself. In fact, he'd sunk to the depths of stalking Layla on Facebook. Although her status didn't specifically mention it, he suspected that she had a boyfriend. When she came in that afternoon, he was determined to find out!

By the time she rang the bell, at 4.15 p.m., Neel already had the coffee going. He welcomed her with a nonchalant air. "I figured you might want some coffee before you get started."

She smiled. "Sure."

"Your mom's home now?" He handed her a mug of the aromatic brew. "She's recovering well?"

"Umm, not so great. She's home, but she reacted to some medication, so the recovery's taking a bit longer." She sat on the high stool and crossed her legs. Neel tried not to stare as he sat opposite her, sipping his coffee.

"And how's college? You're closed for summer?"

"Yes and no. I'm doing a couple of catch-up courses through summer, so it's gonna be busy." She surveyed him through her lashes. "Your friend, he's not visiting today?"

"Oh, no, no, he's pretty sporadic, you know. Drops by on Sundays, occasionally, but—" Neel brushed off the casual friend with a casual wave of his hand. "But as it happens, I-I'm free this evening." He took another sip of his coffee. "So, if you're up for it, once you're through with the cleaning stuff . . . we could go check out this amazing Irish pub in the neighbourhood."

She looked at him, hesitated. "Umm, I'd love to, but . . ."

Neel waited.

"I'll need to make a couple of calls. If I can wiggle out of my commitment . . ."

Neel shrugged his "whatever" shrug. It usually worked with women. The more he appeared not to care, the more clingy they became. But the tried and tested may not work with Layla, he reasoned. She probably *did* have another guy lined up for Saturday evening.

She did. Layla had first met Jonathan almost a year back, when she had served him warm goat cheese and carpaccio as hors d'oeuvres at the restaurant where she'd worked as a part-time waitress. She still remembered, the blonde girl with him had ordered French fries. The very next evening, Jonathan had walked into the upscale Italian bistro again, without the girl. He had sat at the same table, so she had been forced to serve him again.

He told Layla that the girl was just a casual acquaintance, but Layla hadn't believed him. To prove his point, he'd turned up at the restaurant night after night, every single night, alone. Each time, he'd reserved the same table, and each time, he'd asked Layla out. He tipped her very generously, indicating that he could be well off. Either that or he was just trying to impress her.

On the sixth night, Layla *had* been impressed—by his perseverance. He was an older guy, probably in his early forties, extremely suave, and sure of himself. He looked like a man who gave orders and expected acquiescence. She'd wondered why he was pursuing her so relentlessly, when he could have easily moved on to a more willing woman.

Her reluctance to go out, even on a casual date, was because she was emerging from a messy relationship and wanted to remain man-free for a while. But that was not happening. Men like Jonathan Goldstein made sure that women like Layla Quereshi did not stay single for long. She had read *Fifty Shades of Grey* and couldn't help comparing him, in some ways, to the protagonist in that novel.

"I don't want you serving me, I want you sitting next to me," he'd said. "So, how about we step out for a drink?"

Finally, she had agreed. He'd escorted her to a fancy hotel, where they'd sat at the bar and ordered daiquiris. He told her he was visiting from Miami and that his family was into real estate there. He also mentioned that he owned a gym franchise, with multiple centres across Florida.

So her first impression had been right. This guy was loaded. But Layla was pragmatic and was pretty sure he was married too.

"What would your wife have to say about us being out together?"

"I didn't say I was married," he responded.

"But you wear a wedding ring. I can see the white strip on your ring finger, the part that isn't tanned."

His eyebrows rose, partly in amusement. "Right. So you're a fan of all those crazy detective shows!" He saw she was waiting for an answer. "Okay, yeah, I admit, I *used* to wear a ring. I'm married, but hey, not for long. I'm in the middle of a divorce, as we speak."

"Really?"

"Really!"

She didn't know why, but she'd chosen to believe him. Maybe because she wanted to. She felt flattered to be sought after by such a wealthy guy. Whenever Jonathan had come into town after that, he'd called her up to arrange a rendezvous at some exclusive club or bar in the city. It was Layla's first exposure to the rich-and-famous lifestyle, and she'd loved every minute of it. From there on, the progression to his penthouse suite at the Hilton was just another hop up the lifestyle ladder. Soon, she and Jonathan Goldstein became part-time lovers.

Jonathan, or John, as she now referred to him, had been due to fly in that Saturday evening. But a short while earlier, he'd called to say he might have to postpone the Saturday to Sunday. That had forced her to change her Sunday schedule at Neel's, and even now, on Saturday evening, she *still* didn't know his plans.

She'd been kept dangling till the last minute, and she was fuming. He was really taking her for granted. As she took her cleaning stuff into the washroom, she tried John's cell once again. "John."

"Hi, beautiful. I was just gonna call you," he said smoothly. "Looks like I'm gonna be stuck here in Miami tonight . . . I'm sorry." He paused, sensing that she was mad about being stood up. "But hey, catch you tomorrow? Usual place, around noon?"

She'd have to wait another day. But what was another day, another week, or even another month, Layla asked herself. She had waited almost a year for him to be a free man. And every time they met, he'd sweet-talk her into waiting just a little longer. The settlement was just around the corner, he'd assure her. His lawyers had come close to finishing up the paperwork, now it was a matter of days, he'd insist. The divorce was *almost* through, *almost*. Layla told herself that she shouldn't be taken in with any more talk. She had too much at stake. And sticking around as temporary mistress was not an option. *Her* target was trophy wife!

However, now that her "commitment" was postponed, she

could do as she pleased. She had her Saturday evening free, and Neel was a pretty hot John substitute. So hot, really, that maybe it was just as well John had chosen to stay away. She found Neel in the living room, reclining on his leather armchair, looking busy on his laptop.

"Umm, sorry to disturb you," Layla said, "but I'm okay for the evening, that is, if you still want to—"

"I still want to." He tried to keep the elation out of his voice. "So we leave in, like what? An hour?"

She sashayed up to him and inclined her head slightly. "Why leave at all . . ." she whispered and drew closer.

Neel didn't waste another second. He quickly cast his laptop aside and transferred her onto his lap instead. Almost instantly, their lips met, in scorchingly hot kisses. Then, he scooped her up in his arms and carried her into the bedroom.

"I wanted you the moment I saw you," he breathed into her ear.

"Me too," she murmured.

The passion was already escalating beyond control. As she submitted to his expert love-making, it was raw, sexually charged, heat-of-the-moment action. The best sex she'd ever had. He was aggressive, and he was insatiable, and yet, it was more than just a tumble between the sheets. Neel made her feel special. She guessed he'd had a lot of practice satisfying many different partners, in different positions!

The bed looked like a war zone by the time they came up for air. "Wow, that was some workout!" Layla panted and laid her cheek against his chest. "Oh my God, that was fantastic!"

The next morning, as she got ready to leave, Neel watched her dress. She wore the same outfit she'd come in, but her hair was freshly washed. She was in front of the mirror, busy blow-drying her chestnut tresses.

"You headed back home?"

"Umm, not right away," she responded, using his hairbrush to slick back her unmanageable mane. "I have a couple of detours."

"Errands? I'm out for my usual groceries, so if you want to pick up stuff, we could—"

"Oh no, no, thanks. I'm meeting a friend, actually, for coffee."

"Aha. Rendezvous with the secret boyfriend!" Neel smiled.

She was still in front of the mirror, applying her lipstick. So he hadn't observed the way her hand froze, smudging the bright carmine colour right out of her lip line. Irritably, she picked up a tissue. "That's not funny, Neel."

"I agree, and I apologise."

He was surprised when she turned around and bent over the bed to kiss him impulsively. "I'm sorry, I'm being bad-tempered." She glanced at the time on her cell. "Oh my God, I have to run." She held out her hand to stop him from getting out of bed. "No, don't, I'll see myself out." Another quick kiss and she was gone, leaving him with a bright carmine moustache.

Neel sighed and flopped back into bed. He wasn't sure where he was headed with this particular one-night stand. What he did know was that it had been one of the most amazing nights of his life. He smiled to himself as he re-lived some of the highlights. He shut his eyes and decided to laze about till Shri made his appearance. The groceries could wait.

A short while later, Layla's taxi was pulling up in front of the Hilton, on Avenue of the Americas and 54th. She made her way up to Jonathan Goldstein's penthouse suite. In the elevator, she quickly appraised herself in the full-length mirror. She looked just as she should—perfect. Then, as the elevator door opened, she put on her most provocative pout, and stepped straight into Jonathan Goldstein's palatial abode.

"Hey, beautiful." The standard greeting, at the standard Hilton suite, to be followed by standard sex, within minutes of seeing each other. She tried to step past him into the plush interior, but before that, he caught her by the waist. "I missed you." He pressed his mouth to hers. But he was surprised to find that his absence hadn't made her heart grow any fonder! She wasn't being the sultry seductress he'd come to expect. "Hey, you okay?" He pulled away, looking slightly hurt.

"I'm fine." She tilted her chin up and went over to the window. The penthouse commanded magnificent vistas of the Manhattan skyline in all its glory. The bird's eye view gave her a sense of power, and privilege. She turned away from the window, and faced her part-time lover. "So what's the story, John? What d'you have to say to me *this* time?"

"Layla, look, I've told you, time and again, negotiations are in the final stage. Be patient, okay? It's gonna be just a little longer, but it's happening." Then he paused, like he'd remembered something. "Oh yeah, before I forget . . ."

She saw him unzipping a suitcase. "It's somewhere here, I know it is . . ." He poked around and produced an oblong box. He handed it to Layla. "Open it."

She knew, even before she saw it, that it would be another expensive piece of jewellery. Another sop to keep the hope alive. The necklace—a diamond and ruby choker with a pearl clasp at the back—was certainly spectacular. He reached out to help her with the clasp. "Let's see how it looks."

It looked stunning. As she studied herself in the mirror, she knew she was a little too young to be wearing such a heavy, ostentatious piece of jewellery. But she wasn't complaining. At least she was getting *something* out of this relationship!

"It's beautiful," she said, smiling at John. "You really didn't have to do this." Her voluptuous red lips pouted into a kiss, and she led him to the kingsize bed. Just as the steam was beginning to build up, her cell phone rang. The phone was on the bedside table and she glanced at the caller ID. Neel!

"Who the *hell* is that? Put that phone on silent, for chrissakes!" Wedged under her, John sounded muffled, but miffed. So Layla put Neel on silent and gave John her complete, undivided attention. She had her priorities totally figured out. As long as John was in town, she couldn't afford to give Neel a voice.

Neel would have to be on mute till John was safely back on the flight to Miami.

9

Summer officially arrived on the 21st of June, bringing with it so many secrets that soon, something had to give. Neel still hadn't told a soul about his red-hot affair with Layla (except Shri, of course, who had stumbled upon it quite by accident). Shri was keeping his sexuality, and Paolo, under wraps. And Shanks was hiding Vivian from his immediate family, at least for now. The subterfuge was hardest for Shanks, because it went against his grain. His basic instinct, to be upfront and open, was being compromised, and the sneakiness was beginning to get to him. So despite his mom's fabulous cooking, Shanks was losing weight.

The Gang had gathered for their Thursday evening get-together, only this time, the girls were not present. Shefali had flown to Antwerp for her baby brother's naming ceremony, and Vivian had a birthday party she couldn't miss.

So it was the usual suspects, sitting around, and sharing their woes. "My parents are in touch with Shefali, they're like, totally in love with her, and they want me to 'approve' her, asap!" Here, Shri used his fingers to indicate quote, unquote. "Man! I'm so stressed, don't know what to do, I—"

"Shefali's a very special girl," Shanks interrutped, pointedly. "So what's the problem, bro, I don't understand why you won't—"

"Stop! Stop right there. This is so not happening!" Shri was sounding so agitated that Neel stared at him in surprise.

Neel knew Shri was very close to Shefali, so much so that on a couple of occasions, they'd gone out together and excluded him. But what he couldn't understand was Shri getting all hyper about it. Maybe it was time to speak to Shri, man-to-man. "Dude just so you know, if you think *I* was dating her at some point, I wasn't, you know, so—"

"I *know* you weren't." Shri eyed Neel contemptuously. "*You* were just giving her a hard time."

"What's that supposed to mean!" Neel was four drinks down and not cool about having aspersions cast his way. "Surely I'm within my rights to choose my own dates, without you telling me who—"

"Oh really? Then why not go official with Layla? Why not include her in our—" Shri stopped abruptly, but it was too late.

"Who's Layla?" Shanks the Inquisitor was on high alert.

"Oh, she's nobody, nothing!" Shri waved a dismissive hand.

Neel turned to Shanks. "Okay, she's not nobody. She comes over to clean my apartment, and I'm seeing her, as in we're, umm . . ." Neel averted his eyes. "I'm not sure how serious it is."

Shanks and Shri looked at each other. They could see right away that he was sleeping with her. There were some things Neel couldn't hide.

"Aren't you going to introduce me?" Shanks wanted to know.

Neel promised he would, if only to change the topic, and veered the conversation to Shanks' situation. "What about your scene? When does Vivian meet your mother?"

This had been troubling Shanks for a while. He was

wondering how to orchestrate a casual meeting, because, unlike Neel, he was sure that he was very, very serious.

"Do a dosa do!" Shri said, inspired. "Vivian loves dosas!"

"She does? You know, I'm not sure, when we went to Saravana Bhavan, she—"

"Shanks, chill, that isn't the point! *You* tell your mom your co-worker Vivian loves eating dosas. So you're inviting her home."

Shanks brightened. "Now that's an idea. And hey, you guys better show up too."

So it was all settled. Vivian was to be introduced to Mrs. Revathi in the guise of a dosa-lover. When Shanks cornered his mother and announced that he wanted to have Vivian over, his mom was sceptical. A dosa-eating Chinese girl? "Are you sure she will enjoy? Or we can order some samosas specially for her. Just like their fried wontons it'll be, no?"

Shanks assured her that Vivian wanted to come expressly for the dosa, and not to check out samosas-posing-as-wontons. Mrs. Revathi was not convinced, but promised to do her best. "Soup, I can make very good sweet corn soup. Without egg, of course. She knows, I hope, we are strict vegetarian?"

Shanks was curling up inside. He was already on tenterhooks about the initial meeting, and this kind of talk was not helping. He had better prepare Vivian for sweet corn soup without egg. Definitely a first for her.

Whatever his misgivings, Shanks hoped that the dosa do would serve as Vivian's backdoor entry into the Subramanian household. The whole idea was that his mother and grandmother would be so charmed in her presence that they would scarcely notice she was not Indian. In his heart of hearts, Shanks knew this was the height of wishful thinking.

The reality was that even in the age of the internet, time had stood still for Mrs. Revathi Subramanian. Browsing the net for new ideas, or any kind of mind-expanding activity, was not for her. But when it came to hunting down prospective daughters-in-law on Shaadi.com, her computer screen came alive with the possibilities. The only slight deterrent was that her conservative and closed-minded views restricted the search within her own community and, therefore, limited the choices.

Nevertheless, her requirements were quite clear. She sought a daughter-in-law who conformed to the stereotype of a Tam Brahm wife. If Shanks also found the girl suitable, so much the better, she wasn't complaining. Otherwise, no doubt, he'd learn to appreciate the girl's sterling qualities over the many decades of married life.

Given his mom's views, Shanks was perfectly aware that he and Vivian were eventually going to face some stiff resistance. It was particularly comforting that, at least for the initial meeting, Vivian would have the full support of the Gang behind her. Apart from Neel and Shri, known to his mom from their Mumbai days, Shefali would be coming too. She was back from her Antwerp trip and delighted to be part of the clandestine "girl showing" operation.

On the morning of the dosa party, Mrs. Revathi was at the door with a smile on her face. When Neel and Shri arrived, she greeted them warmly, proclaiming how wonderful it was to see them, and praising their enduring ties of friendship with Shanks. But when Shefali walked in a few minutes later, she blinked. As always, Shefali had tailored herself for the occasion, socially and sartorially. She was attired in a kurta with flared pants, and her demure, docile manner was pitch-perfect. The whole package was quite riveting, and Shanks' mom, definitely, was riveted.

Vivian was the last guest to show up. Mrs. Revathi was so eager to make the Chinese girl feel at home that she paid extra attention to her. "Vivian, what a pretty name!" She ushered her towards a chair. "Come, dear, come, sit down."

Vivian smiled self-consciously, and sat on the edge of the sofa. When she looked up, she saw an old lady observing her closely. "I'm Sankar's grandmother, his Tathi Ma," she told Vivian. "You know, I first came to America when I was a young girl, like you."

Vivian was genuinely interested. "That's amazing. Did you like it then?"

"Oh yes, very much, *kanna*," Tathi Ma used the Tamil word of endearment to address Vivian. Then, she regaled them all with stories of her visit to America, a journey she'd made almost half a century ago. The notorious Times Square of the sixties was a highlight of her account. "Walking walking here and there, I was, and I got lost, so by mistake, I came towards Times Square. *Ayyo*, my God, such strange kinds of people I saw! One man came to me, man with orange hair, and said he'll pay me to just stand on a stage and pose, because I was wearing a sari and a small blouse!" She touched Vivian's cheek and cackled happily. "I was quite pretty then, *ma*, just like you! I ran so fast from there, my sari was slipping off, so I had to hold it and run!"

The scene must have been funny, reflected Vivian. This pint-sized Indian lady, running about Times Square, hanging on to the folds of her sari! She shared her own grandmother's experiences when she had first visited the US. She had come to San Francisco, Vivian told Tathi Ma. Shanks observed their conversation from afar and smiled. Given his limited social skills, he didn't want to interrupt, and upset the good work. Wisely, he decided to keep his distance.

Mrs. Revathi, meanwhile, was concentrating on Shefali. From her vantage point in the open kitchen, she had a full view of all her guests. She saw Shefali helping Shanks lay out the chutneys and pickles, and immediately her antenna went up. Oho! Nice girl, with good manners. Pretty too. Her Sankar seemed to like her. He was laughing at something she had said. She spooned the dosa batter onto a sizzling hot pan and continued to watch the action.

As she expertly flipped the dosa over, Vivian appeared by her side. "Oh, Mrs. Subramanian, I have to see this!" She turned to Mrs. Revathi. "You don't mind if I watch?"

"No no, you can watch, no problem." Mrs. Revathi had two dosa pans going simultaneously, but she still found time to chat. "So you work with Sankar, I hear. Same office, ah?"

"Yes, we do some projects together. He's very good."

"He was always very clever, you know, always first in class!"

"Wow!" The exclamation wasn't for Shanks' academic prowess, but for the dosa his mother had turned over. "It's so perfect! Golden brown, and so crisp!"

"You start taking them out while they're hot. And you eat hot also, no fun eating a cold dosa!"

Vivian followed her advice, and emerged from the kitchen with two plates of freshly-made dosas. Before she could even pass the plates around, Shanks was at her elbow. "So how was it?"

"How was what?"

"Talking to my mom!"

"She seems nice." Vivian drew away slightly. "Don't stick so close to me, she'll suspect something! You better go help her in the kitchen."

Reluctantly, Shanks retreated. This was crazy! These days he got so little time with Vivian, and now, even in his own home, he had to treat her like a stranger!

He got busy refreshing the soft drinks. There was no scope for consuming alcoholic beverages in his mother's presence, so even Neel had to make do with lime juice.

"More *nimbupani*, boss?" Shanks was at Neel's elbow, solicitous.

Neel smiled at him nastily. "What d'you think? No, thanks!" He gave Shanks a mock punch on his shoulder. "Hey, you look like you could use a drink even more than me, and I'm pretty desperate myself! Say we head out after we're done here?"

Shanks nodded in a careworn manner. "You're on, man," he said and moved away to refresh Shri's empty glass.

Neel had been wondering how soon he'd be able to exit. He was craving for a vodka on the rocks. But even more than that, he was craving Layla's company. He'd made it to the dosa do only because she had cancelled her Sunday cleaning appointment. Sure, she was not obliged to come by and work for him—by filling in for her mother, she was actually doing him a favour. He only hoped that after their recent encounter in the bedroom, she wasn't avoiding him altogether.

When Shefali spied Neel sitting all by himself, and looking a bit preoccupied, she came up with a loaded plate. "Food?"

He accepted the plate with a smile. "Where's yours? Why don't you come and join me?"

So she got her own plate and sat down next to him. "Umm, brilliant dosa . . . wish I could cook like this!"

He had to smile. "Yeah, right. That'll be the day—you slaving away in the kitchen, churning out dosas!" Then he got serious. "So how was Antwerp?"

"Not too bad. My baby brother's pretty cute actually."

Neel looked for signs of bitterness, but she seemed to have made her peace. She was taking it well, he thought, and was about to congratulate her on her new equanimity when they were interrupted by Shanks' mom. "*Kanna*, what a pretty salwar suit you are wearing! I wanted to ask you, bought from India, ah?"

What followed was a series of probing questions about her family, her job situation, her accommodation, her financial status. For Shanks' sake, Shefali tried to keep her temper in check. But when Mrs. Revathi wanted to know how much she paid her household help, she almost asked her if she was looking for the job.

Sensing Shefali's growing irritation, Neel turned to Mrs. Revathi. "Aunty, superb dosa, superb! This is the dosa I remember from my college days, best dosa on the planet!" He turned to Shefali. "And did you know she also makes the best *payasam* in the world?"

Shefali saw that Mrs. Revathi was actually blushing with all the attention. Sixteen or sixty, she reflected, Neel really knew how to charm them! Quite flustered with all the flattery, Mrs. Revathi rose and hurried off to procure some *payasam* for him.

Shefali exhaled slowly, letting out the pent-up steam. "Thanks for coming to my rescue. God, she makes Shanks' inquisitions look positively benign!"

"I guess she's just trying to be friendly," Neel said, not sounding very convinced himself.

"I hate it! Hate when they behave so *Indian*, if you know what I mean."

"Yeah, I know what you mean."

Neel had often felt like distancing himself from the "Indianness" too. Being Indian was a way of life. It meant having tons of relatives, friends, and neighbours, all landing up home at odd hours and often staying on for meals. The open house concept entailed having neighbours' friends and relatives coming over as well, as part of a larger contingent. Equally welcome were relatives with their friends, and their friends' friends, an extension of the happy Indian family. The extra guests were almost always not invited, but always accommodated.

On the plus side, it meant you were never without company. You also saved money on a shrink, because you could carp on without a care in the world, and there was always someone to listen. The downside was, you needed to be prepared for a constant stream of unannounced visitors, who had to be given endless cups of tea and snacks (preferably home-made).

In a city like New York, the *desi* get-togethers were much tamer affairs. Guests got formally invited, and if they were coming, they formally accepted. Some even showed up on time. But regardless of which part of the world the get-togethers were hosted in, predictably, some things didn't change. Between the food and the drink, the conversation always became deeply, deeply personal. The talk usually revolved around matrimonial prospects, latest updates on paychecks, and private family matters. Far from being considered intrusive, this was seen as taking a healthy interest in your fellow brethren. In fact, not making inquiries in sufficient detail was misconstrued as being too standoffish. "No time for your own family" was the verdict.

But the highly Westernised younger generation wanted to have its cake and eat it too. While they desired the close intimacy of their family circle, when it came to their own personal lives, they demanded a hands-off approach.

After lunch, the Gang helped with the clean-up. Then, in true Indian style, they all departed, en masse. Shanks, who was supposed to have stepped out with Neel for a drink, had declined the invitation. He'd stayed back to get his mom's report card on Vivian. He needed to know! So, after Tathi Ma disappeared into the bedroom for a late afternoon siesta, Shanks hung about in the living room, looking for the right moment to broach the subject.

"Sankar, come, *kanna*, come sit here, I want to talk to you." His mother patted the sofa encouragingly.

Shanks did a double take. His mom was inviting *him* for a discussion, even before he'd had a chance to sound her out! What could that possibly mean! With a deep sense of foreboding, he placed himself by her side, his fingers and toes firmly crossed.

His apprehension seemed unfounded. Mrs. Revathi smiled tremulously and went all misty-eyed. "You think you can hide anything from your mother, hah? A mother's heart always senses, always, always knows what her child wants!"

For an awful moment, Shanks assumed Vivian had revealed all. But no, it couldn't be! He knew Vivian better than that. He squirmed. "What, Ma? Honestly, I don't know what you are talking about!"

His mom smacked him smartly on the cheek. "Ah ha ha, don't know what we are talking about? How long has this been going on, I'd like to know?" she said. Then she leaned closer and whispered, "But I must tell you, I like her, very much!"

If it were possible for a strapping young man to swoon, Shanks would have swooned. "Oh," was all he could manage.

"See, I will not lie to you, Sankar, I would have preferred an Iyer girl. But for the sake of your happiness, I am prepared to . . . to . . ." Her bosom heaved, she was too overwrought to continue.

"But, Ma, you always said, you preferred—"

"You don't have to tell me what I said!" She looked at him keenly. "She is not of our caste, I know, but . . ."

"Ma! I don't believe this! I don't know what to say." Shanks shook his head, uncomprehending.

"You do not know your mother, *kanna*, I can make any sacrifice for my children! Even your father does not know what all I have had to give up for you two! But no point discussing all that. I am just happy that she is from a similar family background. Just like us, they are. Good, decent, God-fearing vegetarian family."

Shanks felt his stomach churn, as if he'd eaten too much chutney. She was talking, of course, not about Vivian, but about Shefali. And that was why she was suddenly so amenable to the whole proposition. It wasn't about the family being vegetarian, but about them being wealthy. He heard her say, ". . . she mentioned they are jewellers, from Amsterdam. Must be very, very rich, *iliya!* Her own apartment, in New York, just imagine! Even gold is nothing for them, *pa*, these people, they live like the film stars, dripping in diamonds!"

Shanks was feeling quite dizzy. "Antwerp, Ma, not Amsterdam." Later, he would wonder why he wanted to get that inconsequential detail right.

When Shanks told the Gang about what had happened, Shefali didn't know whether to laugh or cry.

"Okay, this is crazy! At least with Shri's mum it was intentional, but Shanks, your mum? *Why* would your mum think I'm a prospect? I never gave her any indication that I'm . . ." Shefali shook her head in disbelief.

She told herself that given her high popularity with mothers, she should probably meet Neel's mother right away! *That* certificate of approval would be worth having! But frustratingly, that wouldn't be happening anytime soon.

10

"I'm so done with all this double-dealing," Shri announced to Paolo. He'd lied to the Gang about not being free that evening, because he was out with Paolo, checking out a happening new gay bar in Chelsea. He looked into Paolo's eyes. "You know, I think I'm ready to take up that offer, if it's still open."

Paolo couldn't believe that Shri was finally coming around. "You mean you'll move in? With me?"

"Yes." Shri had decided he wanted to share his life with Paolo, and moving in with him was the first step in that direction.

He also wanted to share his happiness with the Gang. So far, of course, the only Gang member who knew about Paolo was Shefali. But they hadn't met yet. Shri was therefore very keen to get them together, and, after consulting with his partner, he decided to invite Shefali for a cosy little dinner at Paolo's place.

For the momentous occasion, Shri planned to cook up a storm. He was doing a full-on Mediterranean spread, with antipasti appetisers, blackened sea bass, salads, and baba ghanoush.

Paolo was hosting the wines and the most amazing cheesecake from a local deli.

The get-together turned out to be quite a riot. Paolo had a wicked sense of humour, and he kept Shefali in splits all through the evening. The high spirits continued over Shri's outstanding dinner and, after they'd gorged themselves silly, the three of them settled down in Paolo's living room, with coffee. Then, quite out of the blue, Shefali had a sudden impulse to rock the status quo.

"Guys, guys, guys. Listen up." She waited till she had their undivided attention. "So what I'm saying is . . . let's go for it."

She didn't need to elaborate. Both of them knew exactly what she was talking about. They stared at her, trying to absorb the implication of her words. She was talking, of course, about Shri going public.

"How about the coming Thursday?" Once Shefali decided something, she was not one to allow the grass to grow under her feet.

"*This* Thursday?" Shri was scarcely breathing.

"Yes." Shefali was firm. "This Thursday. Shri, once everyone's there, you make the announcement, and after that, Paolo, *you* show up. And . . ." And let's hope for the best, she wanted to add.

So the eventful Thursday evening kicked off with Shri and Shefali arriving together, hand in hand. Shanks and Neel exchanged speaking glances. Aha, so they were finally going to go public. About time too!

However, Shri's two best buddies had no idea that how it looked was not how it was. Shefali was holding onto Shri, not because love was in the air, but because she was trying to stop him from bolting. The problem was, Shri was having cold feet and wanted to make a run for it. But Shefali had him on a tight leash. And, until Paolo made his appearance, she had no intention of letting go.

Even as the main players rolled out their agenda, the rest of the Gang looked on, viewing the developing situation as a Shri-Shefali romance that was about to go official. Neel told himself he didn't feel the slightest trace of jealously. He was just so happy for them both. "Guys," he told them, "I'm over the moon. I knew you'd make this happen!"

Shanks echoed the sentiment. "Congrats, people! This is so amazing, I'm so happy for—"

"Shanks! Stop!" Shefali was stamping her foot.

Everyone froze. They didn't know what was happening, but this sure as hell didn't look like a regular boy-loves-girl announcement. Maybe they'd had a tiff or something? Maybe the timing was off?

"Why don't *you* tell them?" Shri begged her.

"No, you tell them. They have to hear it from you," Shefali replied.

"I can't, I *cannot* do it!" Shri backed away, like trapped wildlife seeking an escape route. His hunted expression told her he was going to flee any second now. "Shri! Stop!" Shefali commanded. "You can't run away. I won't let you! I—" Suddenly, she broke off, and stared ahead. "Oh my God!"

Following her line of vision, the Gang swivelled their heads in unison. They saw a handsome and well-dressed young man headed their way. "Oh my God, no! No! No!" Shri had seen the guy too, and was almost epileptic.

The hot guy came right up to them and stopped in front of Shri, smiling mysteriously. And then came the moment of truth. They saw Shri shake off his slouch and square his shoulders. Right before their disbelieving eyes, he reached out, and threw his arms around the stranger, in what was an unmistakably intimate clasp.

The Gang collectively dropped their jaws and went into a synchronised stupor. Shri—their Shri—was in another man's arms, in a lover-like clinch, in full public view! In the blink of an eye, he had turned into a stranger, a person they didn't know, and had probably never known at all!

The moment seemed to hang in the air, like time standing still, until they heard Shefali's voice, an echo from the distance. "Guys, he needs us right now."

When Shri drew away from Paolo, he found that he could finally breathe again. At last, it was all out in the open. But when he turned to his friends, expecting some sort of reaction, all he got was frozen stares. It was like walking into Madame Tussaud's waxworks, where you enter and discover all your best friends have been waxed.

"Guys? Say something!" Shri pleaded. "Yell, shout, curse, just say *something, anything,* please!"

Paolo touched his arm gently and shook his head. "Let's get outta here."

That was when Neel suddenly came to life. "No! No, wait!" He walked towards Shri in a zombie-like state of disbelief. "Why didn't I see it! Why, why, why didn't I see it!"

Shri stared, not sure if Neel was ranting at him, or talking about his own shortcomings.

Neel's voice shook. "All these years, these stupid, wasted, pointless years, I should have been there for you, *yaar.*"

Shri let out something between a sob and a hiccup. The next second, they were hanging onto one another and bawling like schoolgirls.

Shanks turned to Vivian. "You know, I was so busy pairing him with Shefali . . . I just didn't see this coming! Didn't see it, at all!" He was shaking his head, vexed about how dense he'd been.

But it wasn't too late to make amends. He stepped over to Paolo. "Hey, man, umm, we just want you to know we all love Shri very much . . . and always will. So now, that includes you too."

Vivian gazed at him proudly. He had truly spoken for them all.

A short while later, Shri pinched himself, just to be sure. Here he was, actually sitting with his partner at a bar in Hell's Kitchen, Manhattan, in the company of the Gang. The whole thing was so unreal! They had embraced him, literally and figuratively, with open arms. He was fortunate to have friends like these, friends who accepted him for who he was. He was just so madly, deliriously, ecstatically happy!

Shefali, meanwhile, couldn't wait to have it out with Neel. She caught him at an opportune moment. "So. This sets the record straight, I hope."

He bowed his head, acknowledging her right to be resentful. "What can I say! I'm sorry! All I can say is, obviously, I don't know my friends as well as I thought!" He paused. "When did he tell you?"

"He didn't."

"You mean you guessed? Impressive!"

She gazed at him thoughtfully. She wanted to say, "You would have seen it too if you hadn't been so self-centred." But Neel was on the backfoot, so there was no point rubbing it in. Now that Shri was officially out, she wondered if Neel would see her in a new light. At least, he'd no longer be speculating about her and Shri being an item. But for her, the guesswork continued. Was he or wasn't he interested? Was he or wasn't he seeing someone else? Shefali sternly told herself to stop. She was getting a little too obsessed with this supposed other woman in Neel's life.

Little did she know that there *was* another woman, and Neel, for his part, was already obsessed. The fact was that his feelings for Layla were escalating to an out-of-control kind of craziness that was scaring him. That was one of the reasons why he was being so secretive about her. Unlike his previous liaisons, in this particular link-up, *he* wasn't calling the shots. For once, *he* was at the receiving end, waiting for his phone to ring!

A couple of nights after Shri's big announcement, Paolo happened to be travelling, so Shri was hanging out at Neel's. And that was when Shri really understood the full impact of the Layla Effect. He'd been ordering dinner for both of them online when Neel's cell rang. He saw Neel immediately disappear into his bedroom, cell phone in hand. It didn't require extra sensory perception to guess who the caller was, so as soon as Neel emerged from his room a short while later, Shri fixed his eyes on him. "Layla?"

"Yeah."

"I'm your friend. You can tell me, you know," Shri said, in his best mother-hen tone.

Neel sighed. "Nothing to tell. We're doing a casual dinner on Saturday evening. Before that, she'll be cleaning the house. "

"Oh. Her mother's still recuperating?"

"I think she's had some post-surgery complications . . . after she got home. But she's on the mend now, should be back on duty by next weekend," Neel said. Then he looked up at Shri, and hesitated. "Look, not sure I should be telling you this, but it's getting kind of weird with Layla."

"Weird how?"

"Like, she won't return my calls. She's secretive, you know . . . blocks her mail access, hides her cell phone, things like that. All of last week, she—"

"Dude, she just called you, didn't she? Okay, maybe she's not falling all over you, like they usually do, but that's no big deal.

Why would you let that bother you?" Shri couldn't help feeling that Neel was getting unusually clingy about this Layla of his.

By way of reply, Neel raised his glass for a refill. That was the other problem. Earlier, even when he consumed large volumes of alcohol, Neel knew his limits. He had seldom lost control. His hard-drinking finance colleagues often admired his ability to hold his liquor. And stop when he needed to stop. But now, he was letting the alcohol rule. His speech was slurring, and his hands were shaking.

Just as Shri was wondering how to pull the booze away from Neel, and make him eat something, the bell rang. It was Shanks. He'd left the stifling confines of his apartment and, aware that Shri was with Neel, had decided to stop by to enjoy some face time with his friends. But his chill-out night was clearly not happening, not tonight. Neel was boozing non-stop and brooding sulkily into his single malt. Shri was playing the self-appointed shrink, and Neel, totally wired with the alcohol, was ready to bite Shri's head off.

"I just don't get it, bro, why does this Layla get you so worked up? I mean, why won't you chill and—"

"Why? Okay, I'll tell you why. Because she's seeing someone, that's why." With his sixth scotch down, Neel was finally loosening up.

This was news. Shri and Shanks had not expected it. But before Shri could open his mouth, Shanks spoke in a hushed tone. "You *saw* her with someone?"

Neel turned to him, impatient. "No, of course not, but one knows these things."

"How, precisely?" Shanks was not going to give up.

"FB."

"FB!" Shri and Shanks chorused in tandem.

Neel ignored their incredulous faces and looked away. Don't

say anything, and they're all offended. Tell the truth, and they don't believe a word of it. Really, what was a guy supposed to do? "Will you guys stop shrieking like a couple of teenage girls!"

Coming from Neel, at this juncture, it was a bit too much. Here he was, deriding all female teendom, as if he was a model of adult decorum. This Neel was stalking a girl on the internet, and if that wasn't juvenile enough, the girl in question was, in all probability, barely out of her teens herself. Whoa, whoa, whoa! Shri had seen Neel in love several times before, but this was insane!

"Okay, okay, I know, it's crazy," Neel admitted. "I don't know what got into me. I checked out her status. It said 'it's complicated.' And we all know what that means! But I don't know who the guy is. She doesn't mention a name."

Neel stared fixedly into his single malt, hoping for his answer there.

11

It was almost July. The blazing New York summer was reaching its peak, and tourist traffic was at an all-time high. Out-of-towners pretty much had the run of the city and its sidewalks, prompting many New Yorkers to seek refuge in their air-conditioned apartments. The Gang hated being caught on the sidewalks between the photographers and the photographed. Being background fodder for "Our Family Trip To New York City" was not their idea of fun.

Vivian shared her experience of how she'd once been actually *physically* knocked over by a photographer who chose to reverse, camera in hand. He hadn't even turned back to look! Shri related his own horror story about a girl who asked for directions, then talked him into wheeling one of her bags to her destination, which turned out to be a good many blocks away. There were advantages too, as Neel had discovered, but he wasn't talking. You could meet some really attractive women, on vacation from different parts of the world, happy to spend an evening with a local New Yorker!

However, they all agreed that, with their city under siege all through summer, retreat was the best form of defence. The Fourth of July weekend was coming at a time when everyone was really looking for a break. Shanks and Vivian, in particular, wanted to get away and spend some quality time together. They were all sitting around at Neel's, downing strawberry margaritas, when Vivian decided to take up the cause in right earnest. "Guys, this shouldn't be one more of those armchair discussions. This time, let's actually *go* somewhere. Please!" So, in the best tradition of the Gang, they decided to put the options to vote.

When it came to choices, everyone was, quite literally, all over the place. Paolo proposed a drive to Atlantic City, for the casinos. Vivian wanted a three-day cruise to Florida. And Shri mooted the idea of going abroad, to Canada! "My vote goes for Montreal. All those who say aye, hands up," said Shri, raising his own hand. Not a single hand went up. He looked around, crestfallen.

"Montreal? Duh, it's a wannabe Paris. I'd rather do the real thing." said Shefali. "Even the French they speak there is different, I don't think—" Suddenly, she sat up, her eyes shining. "Hey! Vegas! How about Vegas, guys? Now that's the real McCoy! Vote for Vegas!" She raised her hand. Then, seeing no other hands were going up, she raised her other hand too. There were still no takers. Shefali pouted and dropped both her hands. "God, what a bunch of wusses! Haters!"

The remark got her just the reaction she'd anticipated. Everyone heckled her to shut up and stop being such a drama queen. Once the light-hearted banter had subsided, Neel cleared his throat. "Okay, here's a thought. Does the Hamptons sound interesting?"

He was greeted with an awed silence. Then Shri spoke, tentative. "You mean, like, the *Hamptons* Hamptons?"

"Oh? I didn't know it was a repeat, like Baden Baden or Bora

Bora or whatever!" Neel laughed.

Shri laughed too, but he secretly wondered whether Neel had used favours to get access there. Shefali was thinking exactly the same thing. She had stayed at the Hamptons a couple of times, with family friends. It was the preferred summer destination for loaded Wall Street movers and shakers. Neel was doing well financially, but a Hamptons holiday? Was he actually renting the place himself?

Neel appeared to read their minds. "Yeah, I know, playground of the rich and famous and all that, but my boss actually offered me his villa, because, oh well, because I got this deal through, you know how it is. So in case anyone's wondering, it's all quite kosher." He looked around speculatively. "People? What's the verdict?"

"What I don't understand is, why the big secret? Why are you telling us just two days before? I needed to work on my beach body, you know…" Shanks joked.

"It was a surprise for me too. I got the confirmation only last night, so good timing, I guess." He didn't add that the confirmation he'd been waiting for was from Layla. She had agreed to come, at least for now. Her erratic responses were driving him insane. He seriously wondered if she was bipolar, or just plain hard to get.

The verdict for the Hamptons was a resounding, unanimous "Yes!" But there were questions.

"Can I invite Paolo?" Shri wanted to know.

"Oh, yeah, partners are welcome. Any plus ones are fine, it's a huge place." Neel braced himself for the questions. "I'm getting a plus one myself." But no one wanted to ask who the lady might be. To avoid Shefali's searching eyes, he quickly filled in the silence. "We'll hire two cars, it makes for a comfortable ride, and—"

"Oh! I forgot, I have a plus one too!" Vivian interrupted suddenly. They all turned to her in horror. What! Was she proposing a threesome or something! Shanks looked ready to faint. But Vivian seemed to be enjoying herself. "Hey, why is everyone looking so shocked? I just heard Neel say we could—" Looking at their faces, she couldn't contain her mirth any longer, and burst out laughing. Then, she turned to Shanks. "Sorry, honey, I just couldn't resist it. I'm dog-sitting for a friend, over the Fourth of July break, so I'll be bringing Dumbo along. He's adorable."

A dog! While they all sank back in relief, Shanks was not amused. Vivian shouldn't be giving him heart attacks like this, it simply wasn't done. Not even in jest! Now, the million-dollar question was, who Neel's plus one was going to be. While the guys were pretty sure it had to be Layla, with Neel, you never could tell. He always played his cards close to his chest, depending on how the hand was dealt.

All in all, Shefali couldn't help feeling that *she'd* gotten the raw end of the deal. To her, the message was loud and clear. Neel wasn't interested, and she could look out for her own plus one, if she so desired. She was upset enough to want to give the entire thing a miss. She'd simply say she was unwell, or offer some other creative excuse, and drop out. She pulled Vivian aside and spoke to her privately. "Viv, listen, I've decided I'm not going. I can't even *think* of hanging about and watching him with—"

"Honey, you have to come!" Vivian broke in. "We can't go without you!"

"Can't go where?" Shri had overheard Vivian's remark.

"People!" Shefali didn't want Neel to hear. "Why is everyone yelling!" She turned to Shri firmly. "I've decided I'm dropping out."

"You can't." Shri took her hand in his. "If you don't go, *I* don't go."

"Rubbish!" Shefali sounded convincing, but secretly, she was quite pleased with the fan following she was acquiring.

"It's like this," Vivian told her, "we—Shanks and I—we were so looking forward to this trip, the time together. But if you insist on not going, then . . . " She dropped her head, and let out a deliberately long, wistful sigh.

The emotional blackmail was getting to Shefali. Both Shri and Vivian were laying it on thick, and she was beginning to feel guilty. So, when Shanks too went down on his knees and clasped his hands in supplication, she hastily changed her mind about ditching the trip. She would come, she told them, if they could please cut out the histrionics, like, now! She glanced towards Neel, to see if he had caught the little drama that was being played out. But fortunately, he appeared to be quite engrossed in an intense discussion with Paolo, on the topic of derivatives.

So, with matters smoothened out, at least temporarily, the Gang were all set for some much-needed R&R. A sprawling estate in the Hamptons, a part-time housekeeper, no airfare costs—it seemed almost too good to be true. Neel described the property as a five-bedroom mansion, located on the beachfront. He had been there once before, for a Christmas party.

But the usual last-minute hitch, a pre-requisite for any trip, had to happen. The entire party—Shri, Paolo, Shanks, Vivian, Shefali, and Dumbo—had congregated in Neel's car park, but there was no sign of Neel. When an exasperated Shri texted him, he got a cryptic reply that said, "coming coming coming!"

After waiting another ten minutes, Shri figured that Neel's grace period was up. "I'll bet he slept in, lazy dog," he said to Shanks. "I'm going up *right* now, to haul him out of—"

He broke off abruptly. In fact everyone stopped whatever it

was they were doing, and stared ahead. Walking towards them, hand in hand, were Neel and Layla. In her microscopic denim skirt and bustier, she looked straight out of a couture ad. Shefali and Vivian exchanged glances. She was GQ cover material, and she knew it.

Neel was clearing his throat self-consciously. "Really sorry, guys. We had a slight delay getting started this morning, but hey… let's get everyone introduced!"

After the introductions, there was an uncomfortable pause. No one seemed to know what to say next. So Neel took it upon himself to be the life and soul of the party. He smiled all around, slapped Shri genially on the back, and said, "So, guys, this is it! Woo-hoo! Off we go! Who's in which car?"

Shefali wanted to be in the car that didn't have Neel in it. So she quickly made her way towards the four-wheeler that Shanks and Vivian were designated and hopped into the back seat behind them. Dumbo, she observed, was already an occupant there, and seemed only too happy to have her sit beside him.

The second car had Paolo driving, with Shri next to him. That left Neel and Layla to occupy the back seat, which they did, almost immediately. And, even before the two SUVs had hit the road, Neel and his new girl got all cuddly and cosy, like they hadn't seen each other for eons. Shefali looked away, disgusted. All that PDA, when this Layla creature had barely been introduced!

Soon, the two cars were cruising along the Brooklyn Bridge, towards the Long Island Expressway. Given the number of bags and food cartons they'd packed, the party looked like it was setting out on a long journey to a remote destination in the developing world. No one would have believed they were merely undertaking a one-and-half hour drive to the Hamptons. Shefali's beach wardrobe alone could have stocked a small boutique in Chelsea, and Vivian had carried vast quantities of supplies for Dumbo, including his special cushion, special ball, and even a special sweater, just in case it got cold, in the middle of summer.

As they made their way out of the congested city limits, it was refreshing to get New York out of their lungs! Breathing fresh air was a whole new experience. Given their pressure-cooker lifestyles, to suddenly be breezing past bucolic fields, with grazing horses and butterflies—real, live butterflies—was completely liberating.

Funny, reflected Shri, you realised how much you missed nature only when you were in the midst of it. Otherwise, living within slabs of concrete, your deadened senses got used to never seeing the earth, or the sky. You quickly forgot how living things survived and thrived in their natural habitat. An ardent bird lover, he had carried along his high-end camera and binoculars to catch nesting habits of the local winged populations.

Exactly an hour and a half after they'd set out, the two SUVs were pulling into the circular front driveway of the Hamptons mansion. Calling it a mere villa would have been an understatement, because it *was* a mansion, in the classic Cape Cod style. In fact, Neel's description had not adequately prepared them for the beauty of the place.

"Oh my God, this is straight out of Architectural Digest!" Vivian exclaimed.

She was right. The front lawn sprawled across several acres, with silver birch and poplars lining the property. They spied a tennis court on one side of the estate, and a pool on the other. The water-touching property backed onto a small private jetty, where a couple of boats were anchored. Beyond the jetty lay the beach. Although it wasn't a sandy beach, the pebbly coastline was picturesque indeed.

Even before they'd unloaded their bags, the hostility between

Layla and Shefali was out in the open. Neel had picked up Layla's fancy Louis Vuitton overnighter for her, and ignored Shefali, who was struggling with her own suitcase. Although Shanks came to her help immediately, it was enough to get Shefali gnashing her teeth!

Observing the unpleasant vibes, Vivian couldn't help feeling somewhat anxious. She hoped tensions wouldn't escalate to a point where they spoiled the trip for everyone. So far, she hadn't found the opportunity to speak with Layla. Maybe if she unstuck herself from Neel, they could actually have a conversation.

But that didn't look like it was happening anytime soon. As soon as everyone had settled in, Neel and Layla vanished from sight. First, they stepped out for a twosome walk together, and then, right after coming back, they disappeared into their room again. It was nauseating, Shefali told herself, simply nauseating! She was in the kitchen with Shri, helping out with lunch. Vivian was busy sorting out their supplies, and loading up the fridge.

"Shef, careful with that knife!" Shri's terse warning brought her back to reality. She'd been chopping carrots for the salad, and he was right, she had almost cut her finger off! That was when Shri decided he wanted her out of the kitchen, asap. "Okay, girls," he said, "I'm done here, no more help needed. Why don't you take that mutt out for a walk before he pees on the hardwood!"

Vivian frowned. "He's *not* going to pee."

"Look at his expression, *so* going to pee. You better hurry."

Both the girls gave him exasperated looks, but decided to follow his advice. In any event, he certainly had lunch under control. The housekeeper was also due to come in shortly. She would help with the cleaning up.

So Shefali and Vivian picked up their beach totes, got Dumbo leashed, and made their way towards the sparkling blue ocean. They meandered along the curved, pebbly stretch of beach, dotted with many spectacular waterfront mansions very similar to theirs. The area was quite densely populated, and local residents were out in full force to enjoy the sailing and snorkeling along the shore. It was a beautiful walk, and they strolled barefoot along the water's edge, allowing the waves to lap around their ankles. Just as they reached a cluster of rocks, Dumbo began barking his head off, at nobody in particular.

But Dumbo had his reasons, because seconds later, the girls saw Shanks and Paolo over the top of the same rocky outcrop. The guys waved and headed down towards them. Earlier, they'd both stepped out to check on bikes for hire. The boats on the property were not for their use, so they had also made some enquiries about getting a boat large enough to accommodate them all.

"You go ahead and join them," Shefali told Vivian. "I think I'll carry on further, till that little cliff out there. The view from that point would be amazing. And, oh, why don't I take your plus one with me?" She took over Dumbo's leash and smiled at Vivian. "*My* plus one actually, *I'm* the partnerless one, right?"

So saying, Shefali continued ahead, while Vivian backtracked to meet up with the guys. Shefali walked at an easy pace, enjoying the sunshine, the seagulls, and the briny ocean spray on her face. She reached the sloping cliff and climbed all the way up, with Dumbo following close behind. Once they were on top, she let him free and settled down on a rocky ledge to enjoy the view.

Meanwhile, Dumbo went about chasing crabs in the rock crevices, but he couldn't seem to catch any. Then, all of a sudden, Shefali saw that he'd disappeared from sight.

"Dumbo!" Shefali called after him. "Dumbo, come here!"

She didn't want Dumbo running loose all over the beach—it wasn't allowed. So she quickly rose, and peered down on the other side of the cliff. Sure enough, he was at the bottom of the rocks, still sniffing around. "Stupid mutt," mumbled Shefali to herself, as she started making her way down. But halfway down, her feet began to slide over the slimy-wet rocks, and, within seconds, her momentum accelerated, like a downhill skier descending to the finishing line. Braking was not an option, and when a swimmer suddenly appeared from behind the rocks, she cannon-balled straight into his wet arms!

"Oh my God," Shefali gasped breathlessly. "Oh, I'm so sorry!"

He helped her steady her feet before he let go. "Hey. You okay?"

She glanced up at the guy. He was against the sun, in silhouette, so Shefali had to squint through her Dior sunglasses to see him properly. Very promising, she noted with appreciation. He was super toned, with a great tan, and the bluest eyes she'd ever seen. He introduced himself as Ryan Giffords.

"Hi, Ryan. Shefali." She extended her hand.

By then, Dumbo had ditched his crab hunt. He was apparently more interested in meeting Ryan. Shefali laughed. "Oh dear, he's feeling left out. This is Dumbo!"

Ryan looked at Dumbo. "Great meeting you both."

Shefali thanked him once again, and was about to turn away, when he spoke to her, tentative. "Mind if I walk with you? If I'm not intruding?"

"Not at all."

"You're British."

"Indian." Shefali hated to be boxed in. When Ryan assumed she was British, she was determined to contradict him, and be Indian. Just as she had corrected Shri, telling him she was British, when he'd said she was Indian.

"Indian." Ryan smiled. "I love chicken *tikka!*"

Shefali smiled too. She had been scrutinising him closely, and she liked what she saw. "You live here?"

"I live and work here." He paused. "I do odd jobs."

"Odd jobs?" She gazed at him earnestly. An idea was suddenly floating about in her head. "*Any* odd jobs?"

"X'cuse me?"

"Would you do an odd job for me? I'll pay well."

He raised his eyebrows in amusement. "Really? And how well would that be?"

"Five grand."

"Whoa, lady, you gotta be kidding me!" He came to a standstill and crossed his arms, watchful and attentive. The easy, laid-back beach boy had morphed into a businessman. "Anything for five grand! What did you have in mind?"

Shefali had to smile. "Nothing very exciting. No jewel heist, nothing like that. You'd simply have to pose as my friend, umm, my boyfriend. Okay, no, my *ex*-boyfriend, who comes back."

His grin was widening by the second. "Okay, let's get this straight. You want me to be your *ex*-boyfriend, who has reappeared, magically, in your life because you have to make your *present* or *potential* boyfriend jealous. Right?"

"How do you know that?" Shefali demanded.

"Why else would you be paying me a big fat sum like that!"

"So? Will you do it?"

He was looking at her thoughtfully. "It's a lot of money. I'd do it for less. I'd do it for free, actually."

"No!" Shefali reacted so sharply she surprised herself. She wanted this weekend relationship to be transactional. There should be nothing personal about it. She didn't need any favours from anyone.

"Okay," he said. "You're on."

"Two thousand advance, balance on completion of job."

He smirked. "'On completion of job.' I like that."

She gave him a quick lowdown on what to say and when to keep his mouth shut. She told him he'd get his first instalment when he showed up at their villa later that day. Then, along with Dumbo, she made her way back to their property. Ryan headed off in the opposite direction, to get some clothes on.

Shefali made her little announcement as soon as she got back. "Hey guys, guess what? I just bumped into my ex-boyfriend, ex *ex* actually! And believe it or not, he stays a few minutes down the road!"

"Get out! You can't be serious!" That was Vivian, sitting up in disbelief.

"Absolutely serious! Crazy, isn't it?" She looked around. "I invited him to come by a little later. Hope it's okay?"

More than okay, everyone assured her. But Shanks had a question. "Wasn't he the guy you ran off to meet, in that limo?"

Shefali froze.

"Yeah, that's right. I remember, you mentioned his name . . . Karan!" Shanks had an amazing memory—she knew that from when they'd first faced off on cricket trivia.

She decided to laugh it off. "Oh no, no, this guy was *between* Karan and my ex, Mansoor! He's been, sort of, in between. A half ex?"

Everyone looked thoroughly confused, which was the whole idea. But be that as it may, they were all quite impatient to see this "half ex" for themselves. When he finally arrived, a couple of hours later, they'd dozed off on the lawn after a big lunch. Neel and Layla had retired to their bedroom once more, and the rest of them were sprawled on the grass, dead to the world. Only Shefali was awake, keeping vigil.

So Ryan's appearance was like an early evening alarm going off. The entire group was startled into wakefulness, when suddenly, Shefali said, "Ryan! There you are!"

Ryan was impressive indeed. He towered over Shefali and made her look even more petite. They made a very striking couple.

Neel, who was at his bedroom window, was thinking the same thing. This ex, whatever his name was, looked quite besotted by Shefali. Maybe not so ex after all.

"Oh, is that him?" Layla was curious about the old flame, or the new guy, whichever way you wanted to look at it.

Meanwhile, Shefali was wondering how to play it. At Shri's place in Atlanta, she'd had two unsuspecting old people to satisfy. But right now, with the entire party watching, and every eye upon her, she'd have to be super careful about her next move.

As she introduced Ryan around, he appeared to be very much at home. He smiled, and shook hands. Neel was still at his window, screwing up his eyes to see better. "Why does this guy look familiar?" He racked his brains, but it eluded him.

"You mean you've met the boyfriend before?" Layla was amazed. "Now that makes it a double coincidence. Is there any word for it?"

"Don't think so!" Neel smiled. "Hey, how about a dip, while the sun's still up?"

"Skinny?"

"Umm." Neel got closer.

Shefali glanced up to see them in a passionate clinch. Damn Neel and damn his sleazy girlfriend!

A short while later, when Neel and Layla came downstairs, Ryan leaned towards Shefali. "I'll bet he's the one."

She smiled. "Yeah, that's the target. Do what you can."

To her utter amazement, he swept her off her feet, quite literally, and, with a lover-like intensity, locked lips with her. Instinctively, she tried to fend him off, but then she realised, just in time, that Ryan was doing a really great job. She must relax and learn to enjoy the perks, just as he was.

The Gang was finding it hard to keep up with the fast-unfolding developments. Shefali's unexpected plus one certainly had them riveted. It had been all very sudden, for sure, but she looked very happy with all the attention he was showering on her.

By then, Neel had decided he didn't need to go dipping, skinny or otherwise. He turned to Layla. "You know what, I'm up for a drink. How about you?"

So Neel became the official bartender once again. Shri couldn't help noting that for the first time since they'd arrived at the Hamptons, he was actually spending time with the rest of them. He suspected that they had Shefali's plus one to thank for that.

Fortunately, the undercurrents didn't come in the way of a perfect evening. After the sunset, they sat around a little bonfire with their drinks, and asked Shri to sing. Paolo had carried his guitar, so he tried to accompany Shri, who was singing classical ragas. Much to the delight of the assembled party, they hummed and strummed together, in an informal jam session. And, going by the frequent applause, their impromptu duets were turning out to be quite a hit.

Shanks and Vivian leaned against each other and held hands. "It's so beautiful," she whispered in his ear.

"I know. Let's make the most of it," he replied. The weekend was their little interlude, their precious time together, before they got back to the harsh realities of the real world. Shanks knew he'd have to figure a way out of their problem soon, while his mom was still in the US. Because if he didn't introduce Vivian to his mother this time, they'd have to wait till the next summer. Obviously, he didn't want that.

All through the evening, Neel had been drinking steadily. He was on his third drink when Layla's cell rang. *Urgent call*, she told Neel, and excused herself. By the time she joined him again, he was five malts down, and in a foul mood.

"It's been over an hour! Where on earth did you disappear?" he lambasted her, as soon as she returned.

"Oh, baby, it turned out to be one of those longish call." She caressed his chest and leaned forward to kiss him. "I'm sorry."

Neel was somewhat mollified, but he was getting increasingly irritated about her constant absences. Even when she stayed over at his place, she'd excuse herself for chunks of time, and be on her cell. She never had a conversation when he was around, and if he happened to come by, she quickly signed off.

Their second day at the Hamptons was pretty much a repeat of the first. They swam, they boated, they ate, then swam, boated, and ate again. It was an idyllic existence. But the Gang could see that Neel was not a happy camper. He'd been drinking all day, and was getting more angsty with every passing hour.

Nothing, however, could prepare them for what was to come. At around seven that evening, Layla came up to Neel, and whispered something to him, something that made him go completely ballistic.

"What is *with* you!" he ranted. Then he turned to them. "Okay, peeps, announcement." His speech was slurred. "Layla's leaving, to go someplace else." He turned to her. "Bye, sweetie, nice knowing you." He waved to her.

Layla looked at the rest of them, embarrassed. "I'm so sorry. Something came up, and I have to rush off, I . . ." She shook her head helplessly.

"Not bad news, I hope? Everything okay?" Vivian tried to be polite.

"Sure, everything's very okay. Her boyfriend's in town, so—"

"Neel!" Layla was furious.

"You didn't know, did you? I saw his message on your cell last night."

"You went through my *messages*? How dare you!"

Neel shrugged and turned to his friends. "I need a drink."

Shri went up to Layla. "I think you better go, before things get any worse."

She nodded and, after a brief glance around, disappeared upstairs to pack her things.

Neel was still holding up his glass. "Will someone around here get me that drink? Hello?"

Shri took his glass, hoping Layla would leave quickly, so that he could get Neel up to bed. Neel saw him procrastinating. "Shri . . . I want my drink, and I want it now. If you won't get it I'll . . ." He got up unsteadily and took a step towards the bar. Shanks came forward and tried to get him to sit down, but Neel was beyond reason.

"Out of my way!"

Shanks would have resorted to force if necessary, but it wasn't required, because, at that moment, there was a diversion. A mad-as-hell stranger had appeared out of nowhere, shouting, "Where is she!"

The "she" he was referring to was obviously Layla. This was a whole new twist to the tale. Ryan, who was standing beside Shefali, was incredulous. "Whoa, you guys sure get a lot of action around here! Is all this normal, everyday kind of stuff for you?"

She glared at him, and just as she was about to come up with a curt reply, Layla breezed down the stairs, Louis Vuitton case in hand. Then suddenly, she spied the stranger and stopped in her tracks. Her free hand flew to her face.

"John!"

"Hey beautiful, you look surprised," John said, smiling nastily.

She continued to stare at him, shaking her head, speechless.

"It's called GPS," he told her. "That Vuitton I gave you? You'll find a little GPS device inside the lining. I've been tracking you beautiful, and here I am!"

Layla put her suitcase down and curled her fingers into little fists. "Stalker! Pervert! Psycho!"

John took a few quick strides up the stairs and caught her roughly by her shoulders. "My instincts were right, weren't they? So which one of them is it?" His eyes swept to Neel, and then to Ryan. He was obviously checking out possible candidates.

Layla contemptuously brushed him aside and picked up her bag again. She continued down the stairs with a new determination. "I'm so outta here." She turned to Neel. "Don't bother to contact me again, ever." And, still hanging onto her GPS-enabled Louis Vuitton bag, she made her exit.

The guy called John hurried out after her.

Neel's head was reeling. The whole incident was not just shocking, it was deeply, deeply embarrassing. In full view of the Gang, Shefali included, he'd just been passed over for some random older guy called John. His ego had suffered a huge blow. He wanted to crawl into the polished maple woodwork of his bedroom and die a slow, painful death.

To think that she'd been a traitorous, two-timing bitch the whole time, and he had allowed her to lead him on! *He* should have been the one to dump *her!* From what he'd seen, John obviously had first rights to Layla, and, as far as he was concerned, the guy was welcome to keep her. John could continue to be her sugar daddy and shower her with gifts and Vuitton bags and whatever else. Meanwhile, he, Neel, needed a drink.

"Hello again. Shri? Shanks?" He held up his empty glass.

Shri knew they'd have to fix him a small one, if only to persuade him to go upstairs and sleep it off. So he poured Neel a diluted single malt, with lots of rocks. Then, with some help from Shanks, he escorted him to his bedroom.

But what Shri didn't know was that Neel had his own stash of alcohol under the bed. Soon after they'd left him to sleep off the effects, Neel simply got himself a refill. And another. And another. His plus one that night was his single malt. Like a drowning man clutching onto his floatie, Neel embraced his bottle of scotch, until he'd downed every last drop.

Then, he fell to the floor, and passed out.

12

The next morning—their last day in the Hamptons—there was no sign of Neel at breakfast. They'd all planned to grab a quick bite and head out as early as possible for a sailing expedition. A boat had already been hired, and Ryan, who was expected shortly, was accompanying them as their local guide. The idea was to explore the beautiful coastline and try some fly-fishing under Ryan's expert guidance. "Great season for blues and stripers," Ryan said. (Stripers, he told them, were striped bass.)

But when Shri got to Neel's room to rouse him, he got the shock of his life. Neel was lying spread-eagled on the floor like a dead man. Shri quickly bent over, and tried to shake him awake. He couldn't. His head spinning, Shri sprang up and scrambled out, yelling for help.

The panic in his voice got them all racing up the stairs. The sight of Neel's prone body, lying with his head twisted at a funny angle, hit them right between the eyes. Shefali cupped her hands to her mouth, and let out a silent scream. Paolo, with great presence of mind, was already dialling 911, and Shanks was on the phone with Ryan, checking out how far the local hospital was. Meanwhile,

Vivian, who had been gazing at Neel in horror, looked up at the assembled party. "Is he . . . is he . . ." She couldn't get herself to actually ask the question. And even if she had, they wouldn't have had an answer to give.

Within minutes, an ambulance was shrieking into the driveway. The paramedics rushed upstairs, and got Neel hooked on an IV drip right away. Then, they transferred him onto a stretcher and spirited him into the waiting ambulance. Turning down their collective plea to jump in, they allowed only one person to accompany Neel. There would be papers to fill out, and they needed to know exactly how much alcohol had been consumed.

After checking with Shanks, and getting the nod, Shri stepped into the ambulance. The door banged shut, the sirens screamed, and the vehicle disappeared down the driveway. It all happened so fast, it was almost as if they had imagined the whole thing.

Literally, within ten minutes of his being discovered comatose on the floor, Neel had been whisked off to the ER. They hadn't been able to talk to him or even touch him. In that short span of time, it was as if he had moved into another world, a world they were not permitted to enter. Unsure about what to do next, they turned to each other to review their options. But before they could decide, another vehicle drove up.

It was Ryan Giffords, in his hybrid Bimmer. When Shanks had called him, he'd already been in the car, on his way to join them for the fishing trip. So he was dressed in casuals, for a day out at sea. However, had they paid attention, and looked beyond his appearance, they'd have noticed that this was a very different Ryan from the drifter kind of guy they were familiar with. They'd have seen a guy who was used to taking charge, especially in crisis situations such as this one.

After Shanks' call, Ryan was ready to volunteer his services in any way he could. As soon as he arrived, he offered to drive them to the hospital, in the shortest time possible. His own car was too small to accommodate everyone, so the depleted bunch—consisting of Vivian, Shanks, Paolo, and Shefali—piled into the SUV, with Ryan at the wheel.

The Southampton Hospital was the only medical facility in the area. When they got there, the staff informed them that they couldn't see Neel just yet. He had been rushed into the ER and was being examined by doctors. They had to wait.

Even when Shri showed up in the waiting lounge, a short while later, there was no fresh news. Shanks turned to him fearfully. "Shouldn't we call his mom?"

Shri was hesitant. "Let's wait till we have something to tell them." Two old people, in faraway New Delhi, didn't need to hear over the phone that their son was in hospital, hovering between life and death. If they could have physically been with him, then, sure, it made sense to call. But as things stood, a few minutes here or there weren't going to change anything.

It was a good half hour before a doctor finally came to see them. By that time, Shri and Shanks were close to needing medical attention themselves. The doc introduced herself as Dr. Natasha Singh—she was Indian. She informed them that Neel was stable, but not out of danger yet. "Everything that can be done is being done for him," she assured them.

If Shri hadn't been so stressed, he'd have observed, once again, that Neel's luck with women was really holding out! Even his *doctor* was exceptionally good-looking. She was tall and lissome, with liquid brown eyes and long brown hair. She didn't actually look like a doc, except the kind that showed up in Bollywood movies.

After she left, Vivian and Shefali googled "alcohol poisoning" on their iPhones. It was so scary that they didn't want to share the results with the guys. "It says, even when someone's unconscious and has stopped drinking, the alcohol continues to be released into the bloodstream." Vivian turned to Shefali. "That means the level of body alcohol continues to rise. The person does not sleep off the alcohol poisoning! Oh my God! That sounds so—!" Vivian wanted to cry.

Shefali was reading something even worse. If the alcohol poisoning was extreme, the patient could go into a coma, and eventually die. Neel was already in that coma! Obviously, the doc wasn't telling them the bad news. "Not out of danger yet" didn't mean anything. All they could do, at that point, was wait and watch. Paolo and Ryan offered to get some food from the hospital cafeteria, but there were no takers.

After another excruciating couple of hours, one of the hospital staff came up to them. She directed two of them— any two—to follow her. With sinking hearts, Shri and Shanks hurried behind her. She led them straight to Neel's ward. When they saw him lying corpse-like on the hospital bed, hooked up to all kinds of tubes and needles, they almost gave him up for dead.

What on earth were they going to tell his parents?

But when they saw the nurse smiling encouragingly, they slowly stepped forward. Shri reached out and touched Neel's hand, holding it in a tight clasp. To his utter amazement, he detected a feeble pressure, an answering touch from Neel. He turned to Shanks, jubilant. Neel was responding! He was alive! Shanks, who had almost passed out upon seeing Neel's condition, broke down. He couldn't seem to stop the tears, and finally the nurse had to offer him tissues and ask him, kindly, to cut out the sniffling, because Neel could hear him.

In the visitors' area outside, Vivian had been praying. She was a firm believer in meditation and the power of positive energy, which she believed could heal the world. Her thoughts went to Neel. She saw him in a happy place, thriving, doing well. His mental anguish is what he needed to resolve, thought Vivian to herself.

Till early evening, the Gang continued to keep vigil outside Neel's ward, hoping that the worst was behind them. A round-the-clock nurse remained by Neel's side, monitoring his condition. When Dr. Natasha Singh made her next visit, around 6 p.m., she allowed Shri and Shanks to follow her into the ward.

As they entered, they saw Neel drifting in and out of an uneasy slumber, and mumbling something incoherent in his sleep.

"Is he okay? Why is he so restless?" Shanks asked the doc.

She motioned him to be silent because, by then, she was busy checking Neel's vital signs. After completing a full physical check-up, she turned her attention to his medical reports and consulted with the duty nurse on his current condition. Once she had all the details she wanted, Dr. Natasha Singh shifted her focus to Shri and Shanks.

She smiled at them, a full, all-is-well kind of smile. "He's responding well, better than I expected. The good news is, the alcohol's almost completely flushed out. It makes him a bit fidgety, you know, but that's to be expected, nothing to worry about. He's gonna be just fine." She didn't mention that once the alcohol was washed out of his system, he could well have some serious withdrawal symptoms. Instead, she waved her stethoscope at them. "You're his friends?"

Shri briefly explained that they were old friends, and that they were in the Hamptons for the long weekend. He added that they were extending their stay, until such time as Neel was ready to be discharged.

The doc nodded. "I'll be talking to him before he leaves, about—" she paused, frowning, "—about his condition. I can't say more. You know, how it is in the US, doctor patient confidentiality and all that."

"We understand," Shanks said. "We only want to hear from you that he's gonna be okay. Actually, I have to tell you, we almost called his parents—they're in India— you know, to inform them."

Her melting brown eyes swept over them, serious. "Since his parents aren't here, and he's not married—is he?" When they shook their heads, she continued. "So basically you guys, his friends, you'll have to be looking out for him. Oh, I don't mean physically, but there'll be psychological issues. You know, emotional upheavals, or undue mental stress . . . that sort of thing could trigger off another binge, so those are the things to watch for." She smiled. "But hey, you guys? I'm pretty sure you'll do a great job."

The following day, shortly before he was discharged, and just as she had promised, Dr. Natasha Singh did manage her little chat with Neel. When she walked into his ward, he was sitting up in bed, reading the previous day's copy of the *WSJ*.

"Hi, Neel. How are you at this time?" she asked, seating herself in front of him.

He looked at her. She was in her white doctor's overall, with her long hair tied back in a French braid. This was the first time he was really seeing her properly, and he couldn't help noticing that her melting caramel eyes were surveying him rather critically. "I'm good. Feeling a little weak, but otherwise—" he flashed a smile.

Natasha nodded. "Now that it's over, I can tell you I have seen two patients—*two*—die from alcohol poisoning, at levels lower than yours."

"Wow, that's a lot of drinking happening here in the Hamptons!"

"This is serious stuff, Neel."

"I know." He sighed. "I admit, I was way out of control."

Understatement of the year, she wanted to say. "Your friends got you to the hospital just in time. Believe me, it was a close call. Absolutely touch-and-go . . ." After waiting for the implication of her words to sink in, she became brisk and businesslike. "Now. For the next one week, I'd advise complete rest. I've prescribed some pills . . . multi-vit, iron, stuff like that. But you have to be careful." She stared at him. "Strictly no alcohol."

The message was abundantly clear. No messing around this time!

"Yes doc," Neel said meekly. "I'm many things, but I'm not stupid."

She relaxed a bit. "You'll have to see a guidance counsellor on a regular basis. And connect with AA. I've referred your case forward. It's all in the hospital pack you take away with you." She glanced at her watch. "Okay, so you're good to go. They'll be discharging you soon." She got up. "You take care, Neel. Any problems, call me immediately."

"Problems such as?"

"You're going to have withdrawal symptoms," she informed him bluntly. "Severe symptoms. As you must know, heavy drinkers experience it. You will too."

Neel lowered his eyes. He had gotten so used to reaching out for that single malt he wasn't sure how he was going to last out.

She reached out and clasped his hand. "Good luck." She smiled and turned to go.

He wanted to say "Don't leave me!" Her low, soothing voice and down-to-earth bedside manner was very comforting. She was gorgeous, too. Beneath the white overall, he'd caught glimpses of her ramp-model curves. The good doctor was pretty hot, no question about it!

The Gang was only too thankful that Neel's near-death experience hadn't ended in tragedy. They knew he was really blessed to be coming out of it alive and well. Happily, the ordeal was almost over. But it had completely killed the joy of the Hamptons holiday. They just couldn't wait to bundle Neel out of the hospital, and head back home to New York City.

Before leaving, Shefali had to say goodbye to Ryan. The rendezvous took place along the waterfront, where they'd first met. "So, Mr. Odd Jobs Man, who are you?" she asked him.

"I'm sorry, I should have told you, but," Ryan laughed, "when you offered me the money, I couldn't resist it!"

"Yeah, right!"

"Okay, I figured it would be fun, but as it turned out . . ." He shook his head, smiling.

Shefali had googled *Ryan Giffords* and had come up with *Ryan Giffords Jr.* He was a very wealthy guy from a very wealthy family. If they'd visited his home in the Hamptons, it would have been twice the size of theirs. He had given up Wall Street to run a not-for-profit centre, working in the field of renewable energy.

Shefali and Ryan paused by the same rocky outcrop where she'd bumped into him (quite literally!) just four days ago. As they faced each other, she felt an urge to burst into tears.

"Hey." He took her hand. "I'm sorry things didn't work out for you."

She shrugged, and found she could be philosophical. "Life happens." She tried to smile. "I met you, right here at this very spot . . . so it's not all bad!"

He said, "I'd like to keep in touch."

She nodded. "I'd like that too." Then suddenly, she reached for her bag. "Oh, and how could I forget?" She pulled out a cheque, with the details already filled in.

"You know I won't be taking that," Ryan said.

But Shefali pressed the cheque into his hand, saying, "A deal's a deal, that's what my dad always taught me. And hey, you earned it! You were very convincing, Mr. Odd Jobs Man!"

Although he took the cheque, and tucked it away into his pocket, they both knew it would never be cashed. Then, he leaned down and kissed her gently. As the passion began to escalate, Shefali withdrew. "Ryan, I can't." She was in tears. "I shouldn't!"

He didn't say anything, just pulled back and surveyed her thoughtfully. Then he stepped backwards, in reverse, with his eyes still on her. With a little nod of farewell, he turned on his heels and walked away. She saw him getting smaller and smaller, a solitary figure on the horizon. She turned back too, slowly, and made her way to the waiting cars.

Meanwhile, Dr. Natasha Singh had repeated her warning once again. Just before they departed, she'd taken Shri and Shanks aside, and told them that it was their responsibility to see him through this tough phase. It was absolutely imperative to keep Neel away from alcohol. He needed to be monitored, she exhorted, 24/7!

After seeing Neel lose control the way he had, and almost lose his life in the process, the Gang knew they had to take Dr. Natasha's advice very seriously. Although most of his Wall Street cohorts were diehard drinkers, and lived the work-hard-play-hard ethic, Neel would have to revise the rules and re-invent himself. All this while, booze had been his escape valve. But now, whether it was his pressure-cooker work environment or his steamy love life, Neel could no longer use alcohol as an excuse to "let off the steam."

The consensus, therefore, was that Neel be put on round-the-clock surveillance. But no one actually told him so. Instead, they talked him into staying with Shri, as a temporary measure, for a couple of weeks, till things settled down. Neel knew he had no choice. Much as he hated being nannied, he'd have to accept it as the new normal. After all, he'd been responsible for ruining their holiday, and the least he could do, under the circumstances, was remain trouble-free for a while!

Fortunately for him Shri hadn't shifted to Paolo's yet. Shri had planned to make the move after the Hamptons holiday, so now, he could simply postpone his plans, and have Neel come to stay over. He didn't mind, Shri told himself, he was happy to do it, for Neel. Not that there were any other options: Shanks' apartment was houseful and, of course, there was no question of Neel moving in with Shefali.

13

Upon their return to New York, Shanks regretfully bid Vivian goodbye and dragged his feet homewards. It had been really great to share a bedroom with Vivian again, and talk about their future, a future that seemed very far away. His present, he reflected ruefully, was the mattress, and the nagging Mom.

After the dosa do, his mother had kept pestering him, wanting to know why he wasn't getting Shefali home to visit her. She was keen to spend time with her future daughter-in-law, she had told Shanks. When he'd flat-out denied any link-up, she had only smiled, and shaken her head, like she was humouring a wayward child. Shanks had tried to remain unaffected by it all, but it was hard, very hard indeed.

Half an hour later, a really depressed Shanks let himself into the apartment, and called out to the residents-at-large. "Hello, I'm home!"

He was greeted by an ominous silence. "Hello? Amma? Tathi Ma?" He put his bag down. Where was everyone?

That was when Mrs. Revathi appeared at the bedroom door. "You're back."

Shanks was never terribly perceptive, but even he could see things were far from okay. His mother had her tragedy-queen look, and Shanks knew, from experience, that that particular look didn't bode well.

"So how are you, how's everything?" Shanks went forward to hug her, but she recoiled.

He stared at her, nonplussed. What was the matter with her? Why was she freaking out?

Then, to his horror, his mom held up a lacy red bra. Followed by matching red lacy panties. And a bunch of other assorted lingerie.

"She was living here! In this house!" Mrs. Revathi was breathing fire.

"The neighbour's laundry . . . I-I must have picked it up by mistake." Even as he said it, Shanks knew it sounded really lame.

"Neighbour-*ah!*"

At that moment, Tathi Ma appeared in the doorway. "Sankar! You're back!" The same greeting as his mother, but with so much more affection!

"That Shefali was *staying* here with you?" His mom was on the warpath.

"No!"

Mrs. Revathi frowned. If Shanks had been lying, she'd have known right away. She always did. But he wasn't lying. Her frown deepened.

Tathi Ma turned to Shanks, and gently stroked his shoulder. "Vivian, *illiya*? She is a very nice girl."

"Vivian? Vivian! What are you telling me? You are in love with that . . . that Vivian girl?" Mrs. Revathi was making scary choking sounds.

Shanks hadn't wanted the newsflash out through some recently discovered lingerie, but now that it *was* out in the open, he figured he might as well come clean. "Yes. She . . . I . . . w-we love each other very much."

Mrs. Revathi's bosom heaved menacingly, and her eyes went slitty. "That girl can never—*never*—become part of this family, remember that!"

"She's a nice, sensible girl, Revathi," Tathi Ma said placatingly. "She will make Sankar happy. What more do we want?"

"Amma, how can you say this!" her daughter-in-law fumed. Then she turned her attention back to Shanks. "And what do you think your poor father would say, tell me, hah?"

Shanks was of the honest opinion that his poor father would certainly have kept his mouth shut, but he could hardly say so. "Ma, listen. Take your time thinking about it. Meet Vivian, spend time with her—"

"No, no, no, no!" Mrs. Revathi shut her ears with both hands. Then she collapsed on the sofa, buried her face in her hands, and let out a hacking howl. Shanks might as well just have confessed to murder.

Shanks and Tathi Ma glanced at one another. They knew there was no point in reasoning with her at this moment. She'd only work herself up to an elevated state of hysteria.

Shanks bowed his head. "Okay, we'll talk tomorrow, Ma. I'm really tired, I—"

"Over my dead body you'll see that girl again!"

Shanks, who had been wheeling his little suitcase towards the bedroom, stopped in his tracks. When he heard the ultimatum, delivered so unequivocally by his mother, something inside him just snapped.

"Okay then." He looked at his mother, unflinching. "Till you don't accept her, till you don't welcome her to this house, I refuse to stay here!" He paused, making sure it was sinking in. "I'm not coming back home, you understand?"

With that, he turned on his heels and walked to the front door, wheeling his suitcase behind him. Before either his stunned mother or grandmother could react, he had shut the door behind him.

Never before had Shanks defied parental authority so flagrantly. As he hit the sidewalk, the enormity of what he had done struck him. His mother's emotional blackmail had led to the final rift. It was the reason he'd chosen to walk out of his own home. He was glad he had made it very clear that he was not going to take any nonsense where Vivian was concerned. *No regrets*, he told himself.

For a while, he wandered aimlessly on the streets of Manhattan, dragging the suitcase about like a dog being taken for a walk. Then, driven to the point of exhaustion, he found a bench and slumped on it. What was he going to do? He didn't want to call Vivian, because he knew she'd be very, very upset. All things considered, it was best not to speak to her, at least not that night. He'd talk to her in the office tomorrow and tell her everything face to face.

So he called Shri and told him he was coming over for the night. "I'll explain when I'm there," he informed him.

The conversation was so cryptic that it left Shri none the wiser about what was going on. He turned to Neel, who was lounging on the sofa with a ginger beer in hand. "That was Shanks. Looks like he's missing us already."

Neel didn't get it. "Missing us? How?"

"He's on his way here, to stay the night!"

"No!"

"Yup, so you'll stay on your couch, and he'll have to sleep on the air mattress." Shri sucked in his breath. "Shit! Forgot to ask him if he's had dinner!"

When Shanks arrived, a short while later, he looked like

something the cat had brought in.

"What happened to you?" Shri demanded.

"You look bad, man, really bad!" Neel added, not very helpfully.

Shanks gave a gusty sigh and sank back into Shri's leather armchair. A spent force, he mopped his brow feelingly. Although the suspense was killing them, his friends waited for him to find his groove. These were not things you could rush.

"I've left home," Shanks announced finally.

There was a pin-drop silence. Then, after a longish gap, Shri ventured to speak. "Boss? You can't 'leave home'! I mean, how can you, when it's *your* home?"

"I'm not going back. Till she accepts Vivian." Shanks' voice had taken on an obstinacy they'd seldom heard before.

So that was what all this was about! Neel glanced at Shri. They both tacitly agreed that the situation was a delicate one and would require careful handling. Shri said, "Shanks, bro, we are totally with you. You should stay here till things sort themselves out. Neel and I—"

"No, no, I'm staying here one night only. Then I'll move in with Vivian."

They left it at that. Shri made him a cheese and lettuce sandwich, and Neel insisted he have the couch. Shanks cheered up with all the fuss around him. After he'd eaten a hearty sandwich and banana dinner, he turned his attention to the practical side. "You know, I was just thinking, I'll have to find a way to give them cash to manage their groceries and all that. And I just realised, my work clothes are all still in the apartment! What am I going to wear tomorrow?" His suitcase had beach shirts and bermudas, and even those weren't clean!

"My stuff won't fit you," Shri said. "Neel's my size, but you're too tall for any of my—" Suddenly, he brightened. "Hey,

Paolo's left a couple of suits here. *Those* would definitely work!"

So it was the three of them together again, in Shri's tiny Manhattan studio apartment. It reminded them of their college days—the all-night cramming sessions on the eve of exams and survival on *anda pao*. Luckily, Shanks had learnt to eat eggs by then, because otherwise all he'd have got was bananas in the bread. Mostly, that was all they could afford, and sometimes, after the twenty-fifth of each month, not even that!

Suddenly, Neel got up from his couch, all senti. Shanks and Shri stepped forward, on cue, for the threesome hug and the theme song. The little ritual was their renewable energy source, to be used when they needed each other the most. It was an emotion-charged moment, sacred and sacrosanct.

Shanks could run away from home, Shri could spring a same-sex partner upon them, and Neel could scare them witless with his bingeing bouts. But none of it mattered—they were a team! Shri really wanted to open up his bar, in celebration of the team spirit, but of course, that was out of the question. As it was, Neel seemed to be trying very hard to maintain his sanity.

Over the course of the evening, Neel was feeling more and more nauseous. He also had a splitting head. The tranquillisers and anti-anxiety pills prescribed by Dr. Natasha had calmed him slightly, but the doc had instructed him not to exceed the dosage. So, despite the medication, he was still feeling pretty hyper and high strung. Later, as he lay down on his air mattress, he found he couldn't sleep a wink. His throat was parched and his headache was killing him.

Not sure how long he dozed off, Neel suddenly found himself jerked awake by a really scary dream. In the dream, a black coyote was chasing him over a barren desert landscape into a long, dark tunnel that didn't seem to end. The claustrophobia of being trapped underground had him in a panic.

It was only when he heard the gentle, reassuring snores of Shanks on the couch, did he relax a bit. Shanks was nearby, thank goodness! And Shri was only a little distance away, on his bed. As he lay awake, staring up at the reflected city lights on the ceiling, his alcohol craving was getting urgent, too urgent to ignore. One drink, Neel told himself, even one sip would do.

Stealthily, he crawled out of his air mattress, and crept past Shanks' couch, making his way towards the bar. (Though he needn't have worried about Shanks. Shanks was a sound sleeper. Even with his life in turmoil, Shanks, one of mankind's favoured mortals, slept the sleep of the just, with nothing on his conscience.)

As Neel got to the liquor cabinet, he had absolutely no idea that there was a duty night watchman tracking his every move! Unlike Shanks, Shri was not asleep. He'd been lying awake, waiting for something like this to happen. When Neel tugged at the cabinet handle, and discovered it locked, Shri heard him cursing under his breath.

Shri leapt out of bed. "Neel!"

Neel swung around guiltily. Shri was at his elbow, steering him back to the godforsaken air mattress.

"I can get you some coffee if you want," Shri urged, softly.

"I don't want coffee!"

"Tea then? Hot chocolate? Juice?"

"No, no, no!"

"Then you just have to go back to sleep." Shri was firm.

"One small shot, *yaar*, and I'll sleep, I promise you!" Neel was begging for his life.

Shri placed his hands on his hips and peered at Neel through the semi-darkness. "I'm calling that doc of yours, what's-her-name—"

"No!" It was bad enough being caught in the act by Shri,

but to have Dr. Natasha Singh woken up, with news of his misdemeanor, was unthinkable. Neel desperately summoned the teeny weeny bit of self-control he still had in reserve and crawled right back onto his mattress. The thought of Natasha—he thought of her as just Natasha now, no prefix-suffix required—was strangely soothing. He smiled, remembering her cool, soft fingers on his brow. Finally, at around five in the morning, he drifted off into a troubled sleep.

The next morning, Neel was a huge mess. He was shaking, and sweating, and looking so scary that he couldn't look at his own face in the mirror. Seeing his condition, Shri was rattled enough to immediately contact Dr. Natasha Singh, to ask her what to do.

"It's the aftershock, it's going to happen," she told Shri. "Someone has to keep an eye on him, round the clock, otherwise he might go hit a liquor store."

"Doc, I have to be at work today, I can't—"

"I understand. Is there any another friend? Or relative?"

Shri was at his wits' end. He knew Shanks wouldn't be able to spare another day either. They'd already stayed back an extra working day at the Hamptons. Asking Shefali to come by was an option, but that would be grossly unfair to her. He knew the humiliation she'd endured when Neel had flaunted Layla right under her nose. Now, to call upon her to pick up the pieces after Neel's excesses would be a serious violation of human rights! And besides, Neel himself wouldn't agree to have her around, playing nursemaid. His sky-sized ego would never permit it.

"Shri, I'm sorry, the recovery is a gradual process," Dr. Natasha was saying. "He'll have his good days and bad days. I suggest you call the helpline. The contact info is in the pack I gave him."

"Okay, I'll do what I can. Meanwhile—"

"Hey," she interrupted, "what I'm thinking is . . . I have the day off. I could make a trip into the city." She paused, then took the plunge. "I'll be there in a couple of hours. Text me the address."

Neel was getting a house call.

14

Neel would have been surprised to know that in his Manhattan neighbourhood, there was another insomniac who'd started having "withdrawal symptoms" at exactly the same time as he had. That fellow sufferer was Mrs. Revathi Subramanian. Like Neel, Mrs. Revathi too had had a sleepless night. After Shanks had "withdrawn" from her life, she'd tossed and turned about on her Ikea sofa-cum-bed, distraught. She'd agonised about her Sankar's cavalier behaviour, and his blatant disregard for his own mother! How could he be so heartless, she'd moaned. That too, all for the sake of that girl, that *Chinese* girl, Vivian.

To make matters worse, the very next morning, her mother-in-law cornered her after breakfast. "You want to lose that boy forever?" Tathi Ma asked bluntly.

Of course she didn't want to lose Sankar—he was all she had. Okay, she also had a married daughter, and two granddaughters, but a son was a son. And right now, her son was distancing himself from her. In fact, she had felt closer to him when she'd been in Chennai! All she could hope, right now, was he'd see reason, and come back to her.

The boy had gone a little crazy, she told herself, but surely, it had to be a temporary spell.

But Tathi Ma dispelled any such illusions. She sat her daughter-in-law down and told her she needed a reality check. "He will not return till you agree to meet Vivian." She paused delicately. "Should I call him back?"

Mrs. Revathi shook her head violently. No way she was going to concede. Next thing she knew, they'd be thrown out of the house to accommodate that harlot! Bright red underclothes, indeed, thought Mrs. Revathi—was that how decent, God-fearing girls dressed! She bristled at the thought of having such a creature ever gaining even a toehold in the family. If only it had been that nice girl, Shefali. So modest and cultured she was, and dressed so traditionally, in a proper salwar suit.

Meanwhile, Shanks wasn't worrying about his mother worrying. He was more concerned about how Vivian would take the news. As soon as he got to work, he sought her out, and gave her a gist of the developments. But he was surprised to find that not only was she not perturbed, she actually started giggling! "I *knew* I'd leave something behind. I barely had time to get *myself* out that day! Why it had to be the crimson lingerie, I don't know!"

Shanks figured he would never know what she was actually thinking, or why. He said, "Well, I suppose, the bright side is, now they know!"

"Now they know!" Vivian echoed, still smiling. "Now we give them a little time to get used to the idea. Meanwhile," she glanced at her computer, "I've got a deadline." Then she looked up. "How about lunch at Macy's? We'll get you a couple of suits, shirts, ties, whatever. I'll meet you downstairs, front entrance. One o'clock?"

Shanks nodded and slouched off, disconsolate. He had

better go focus on work too, he told himself. He had a lot on his plate. He'd have to take it one day at a time. In the afternoon, he was off to buy new officewear. That was a start.

Later that same morning, Natasha arrived at Shri's as scheduled. By the time she came, Shri was already dressed and ready, waiting to dash off to work. So like a relay runner passing on the baton—Neel, in this case—Shri was only too happy to hand the patient over to her, and run. On his way out, he gave Neel a speaking look. "Hmm, have a great day! And be *good!*" Then he went wink-wink and shut the door behind him.

Neel hoped Natasha hadn't seen the now-you-can-pounce-on-her suggestiveness. But of course she had. And she was smiling, looking like she wanted to laugh but was trying not to. Neel, however, was terribly embarrassed and tried to diffuse the awkward moment. "I could use some tea. Would you like some?"

"Umm, how about masala chai? I'll make!" She moved with her easy grace into the kitchen, and he followed her. Neel was struck anew by her statuesque beauty. In skinny jeans and an environment sloganed tee that said "Peace, Love, Recycle," and she didn't look old enough to be a doctor. Soon, she was busy boiling the milk and water along with the spices and sugar to produce the most amazing made-from-scratch masala chai he'd ever had.

She watched him sipping his tea. "How bad was last night?"

Neel wasn't going to divulge the details. "Bad."

After the chai, she gave him a quick check up and made sure he was up to date on all the medications. "It does get better, you know. And you're very lucky to have the friends you have."

"Lucky to have the doctor I have too," he smiled. With her encouragement, he spoke a little more about his friends and his foray into the fast-paced world of New York high finance. She listened intently, her eyes never leaving his face.

Throughout the conversation, Neel was a little disconcerted by her direct, analytical gaze. Sure, she was seeing him as a patient, but never in his life had a woman, a beautiful woman, eyed him with such clinical disinterest! After a moment of pique, he had to remind himself that she was not there with any amorous intent. She had come in her capacity as doctor, and he could hardly expect her to behave any other way.

In fact, she'd got her laptop along with her, and had mentioned at the outset that she would be busy studying for her next exam. She told him she was specialising in Trauma Surgery.

"Hmm, trauma surgery . . ." Neel frowned. "Must be pretty traumatic for the doctor too!"

"It's our job," she said matter-of-factly. Then, she picked up her laptop, and got busy. Neel, therefore, was obliged to open up *his* laptop, and pretend to be hard at work too. He even managed to respond to a few mails, and browse about a bit.

It was weird spending time in the same room with a very desirable woman, who, in normal circumstances, he'd have gone all out to woo. When he was distracted, which was pretty much once a minute, he would glance in her direction. He saw her referring to a couple of thickish hardcover books, checking her comp from time to time, and making some notes. And yet, she appeared to be keeping tabs on him as well.

"Trouble concentrating?"

"Umm, yeah. It's hard," Neel said, and quickly turned his attention back to his laptop. He'd been admiring the way her slender fingers fluttered over her keyboard, and the cute little crease that appeared between her eyes. She'd looked like she'd been deeply engrossed in her work, but obviously not. Or maybe she was just very good at multitasking. As Neel opened his inbox again, he tried to mentally shrug off any further thoughts about Dr. Natasha Singh. Enough was enough. It was time he got his shit together!

For lunch, they scanned Shri's takeout brochures. He discovered that Natasha shared his love for Far Eastern cuisine, so Korean food was the order of the day. By the time the takeout arrived, they were both quite famished. "Umm, miso's my all-time favourite," she said, sipping her soup appreciatively. Neel nodded. The simple pleasures of life.

"So tell me," he waved his chopsticks about, and got chatty, while he had a chance, "does your family live here too? I mean, your parents . . ." What he meant to ask was, did she have a boyfriend living with her?

"My parents are in Noida, you know, and my grandfather lives with them. I have an older sister, married. She's in Toronto."

"And you've been here, how long?" He hoped he didn't sound too inquisitive, like those Indians Shefali detested.

"Oh the usual story . . . came four years back to do my post grad, stayed back, etcetera, etcetera."

He still had no clue about her status. "So . . . you're not married?"

She looked like she wanted to laugh. "No. And I've no intention of getting married till I'm done with my fellowship . . . and *that* seems, like, light years away!"

"Wow, pretty work focused. That's great!"

"Is it?" She was laughing quite openly now. "Neel, if you are trying to get me into your bed—"

"No, of course not! I wouldn't *dream* of—"

"Oh, no, don't misunderstand. I mean, I'm all for an active sex life, it's healthy . . . *essential* even!" When she saw Neel staring at her, she clarified further. "Sex, with no strings attached!"

He couldn't believe it. Was she propositioning him? That would have to be a first—he'd never been seduced by a doctor before.

He said, "So you don't mind the, er, sex, but you won't get involved?

"Yeah, something like that," she admitted. "I'm quite clinical about it actually. I don't believe in chasing relationships, you know. Such a waste of time."

Considering those had always been his sentiments, exactly, Neel should have felt no astonishment. But this, coming from a woman, and that too a woman who was his *doctor*? Times were a-changin', that was for sure! She made it sound so matter-of-fact too, she could have been talking about a high school reunion, he thought, amused. Then, she calmly went back to her notes, as if nothing had happened.

Neel continued to brood over what she'd just said. He'd probably have to re-calibrate his views on the good doctor, and make his moves accordingly. But as he was working on possible options and opening lines, the effects of the drugs kicked in. And the previous night's insomnia caught up. His eyelids drooped, his limbs loosened, and before he knew it, he crashed out on the couch.

When she left, in the early evening, he was still sleeping. So she let herself out without waking him up. Shri was due within the half hour, and she had wanted to head back before the peak of the commuter crush.

When Shri got home, he found Neel fast asleep on the couch, and wonder of wonders, food on the table. There was a note. "Rajma is my specialty," the doc had written. "Eat with *chawal* from the rice cooker. Enjoy!"

Shri sampled the rajma. It was delicious. She had worked on the canned kidney beans in his kitchen to produce this quick-fix meal. It felt great to have dinner waiting, and Shri realised he was actually very hungry. All that remained was to rouse Neel to the dining table. He bent forward and shook Neel's shoulder. "Oye, wake up, *yaar!* Guess what you're getting for dinner!"

Neel's healing process continued to require hands-on care. They knew the first few days were crucial, and they all tried to help him through his rough patch, best as they could. All except Shefali. She had consciously chosen to keep her distance, because she didn't want to invite any more heartache than she could cope with. She'd been emotionally vested in the one-sided relationship with Neel, so switching off her feelings like a light bulb was hard to do.

But Shefali was no fool. She was well aware that she seriously needed to move on, and get a life. And, the sooner she initiated the process, the better. A full-on personal makeover was what she needed, Shefali told herself, a makeover from the inside. Maybe some hot yoga classes? Or a spa vacation? As she turned over the game-changing possibilities in her mind, her thoughts were interrupted by her ringing cell phone.

It was Shri, and he was sounding weird. "Hi . . . Shef?"

She knew immediately that something was hugely amiss. "Shri, what is it? Is it Neel?" She hoped Neel hadn't had to be rushed back to hospital.

"No." A longish pause. "Shef, I lost my job."

Shefali wanted to be absolutely certain she'd heard right. "You mean . . ."

"Pink slip." Shri paused. "Citi laid off over two thousand employees today, they sent us packing, no notice, nothing. So I'm home right now. Neel's here, with me."

"I'm coming right over," she said. She was already pulling on her sandals and grabbing her handbag. As she sat in the taxi, looking out at the vibrant streets of Manhattan, she wondered how people who got laid off survived. She recalled how *she'd* gone into a tailspin, when she'd assumed that her father might snip off her allowance. (Although, of course, he hadn't.) But having no income at all? Not knowing when—*if*—your next paycheck was coming? It had to be a soul-shattering experience.

When Shefali got to Shri's apartment, she found him sitting with his head in his hands. Paolo and Neel were trying, unsuccessfully, to console him. During her brief phone conversation with Shri, he had seemed to be holding up. But now, seeing him in person, it was clear that he was coming unglued. He barely acknowledged her presence and, instead, stared fixedly at the carpet and shivered. This, despite the blanket they'd wrapped around him. Being in denial wasn't going to help, thought Shefali worriedly, he needed to pick up the pieces and stay positive.

Paolo, who was with Citi too, had been spared. His department—credit cards—had had no casualties so far. But that didn't mean it couldn't happen. He'd been in a client meeting, with his cell phone on silent, when the news broke. When he emerged from the meeting, the whole office was abuzz about who was in and who was out. He'd tried to contact Shri, repeatedly, but hadn't been able to reach him. So finally, he'd landed up at the apartment, and found him there.

Meanwhile, Neel tried to reach Shanks. But both Shanks and Vivian were in a seminar, at work, and could not be contacted. Neel had left them a text message, giving them a brief status report, but no details. At that point, he himself had been unsure about the facts.

Earlier, as soon as Paolo had arrived, Neel had tried to grab a moment with him alone, for a first-hand account. When he finally managed to catch Paolo in a quiet corner Shefali had joined them too, to hear the full story, unabridged. "It was a bloodbath out there," Paolo told them, in a low voice. "I mean, literally, the number of people they've axed is unbelievable!"

He went on to describe how the lay-offs had been conducted in the utmost secrecy. Apparently, no one had had any inkling that the downsizing was going to be implemented on such a massive scale. When the announcement came, it had caught everyone by surprise. "It was done like precision surgery," Paolo continued. "The slips came in around four, I believe, and people were told to leave their computers, cell phones, and files exactly as they were. They were all told to take their personal belongings, and leave immediately."

A sombre tale. They brooded over what Paolo had just said. Neel was desperate for a drink, but he knew the last thing anyone needed was a repeat of the Hamptons weekend. He'd have to somehow get through the day—and night—if only for Shri's sake. He had hoped things would get easier, but so far, that hadn't happened. It had been sheer hell.

"Coffee, all round?" It was Paolo, playing host on Shri's behalf. Shri was still curled up in his corner, refusing to budge.

"Yeah, sure, I'll help," Shefali said, getting up.

"Oh no, sit, sit, sit. I'm the coffee expert around here, so—"

That was when Shri finally stirred. "I make good coffee too. Even if I don't drink it."

Paolo quickly took advantage of Shri's transition from still life object to a more animated life form. He persuaded him to change out of his suit and tie and freshen up. "A nice warm shower and you'll be good as new," Paolo instructed. Shri, still functioning on autopilot, followed his advice and meandered off into the loo.

With Paolo busy in the kitchen, Neel and Shefali were face to face, alone, for the first time since the Hamptons incident. "How's it going?" she asked, feeling she had to say something.

"Well, I haven't binged myself under the table yet, so I suppose that's a good sign." Neel was being quite brutal about his affliction, making her position only more awkward. A damned-if-you-ask, damned-if-you-don't kind of situation.

But Neel was being unnecessarily harsh on himself. The truth was, so far, he'd done a pretty good job of staying sober. Only now that the Layla Effect was wearing off, the cynical lines around his mouth had deepened. And the furrows between his brows appeared more etched. She'd been wondering how to take the conversation forward, diplomatically, when he caught her by surprise. "So how's Ryan?" he asked.

She quickly bent over a supposedly chipped fingernail. "Oh, he's good." When she looked up, she saw Neel observing her quite keenly. She'd have to watch what she said next.

"Does he come into town often?" he wanted to know.

Shefali could feel a dampness on her upper lip. "N-no, not that often." She rose. "I-I'll go help Paolo with the coffee."

Shefali didn't know that Neel had already done his homework on Ryan Giffords Jr. His house arrest at Shri's had afforded him ample time to google the guy, and get all the details, just as Shefali had done. And that was when the penny had dropped! He'd suddenly realised why Ryan had looked kind of familiar! The search had thrown up some interesting info on the Giffords' family fortune and the environment protection organisation that Ryan spearheaded.

Neel had speculated about why Shefali had never mentioned this trophy boyfriend of hers before. He'd have thought that dating Ryan Giffords Jr. would have been something to crow about—even if she risked being labelled a show-off! But here, Neel had to acknowledge to himself that although Shefali moved in exalted circles, she was not a name-dropper. That was simply not her style. So maybe, this once, he had to give her the benefit of the doubt.

When Shri emerged from the shower, in his pyjamas, he was still looking like the living dead. "Guys, just so you know," he announced, "I'm not going to be around much longer. The moment they lay their hands on me, they'll shunt me back to India," he sighed. "Y'know, I always thought there was a grace period, like a few months or something, to find another job? I never bothered to check, because I never thought I'd be the one to . . ." He flopped onto the nearest armchair, and turned to Paolo with a twisted smile. "But P, they tell me there is *no* grace period! My clock is ticking. I'm illegal, as we speak!"

"Hey, let's not get ahead of ourselves here . . . and remember, you're not alone in this, okay? I'm with you." Paolo sat down on the armrest of Shri's chair and held his hand. "And I'm gonna see you through this, whatever it takes. You'll move in with me, we'll be together, and we'll handle it together, right?"

Paolo's pep talk had its desired effect. Shri calmed down, just a little bit. He really *was* looking forward to moving in with Paolo. He told himself that, as soon as Neel could get back to his own apartment, and function independently, he'd be ready to move out too. It all depended on how soon Neel recovered.

But by then, Neel had had a little brainwave of his own. His immediate plan was to haul his ass out of Shri's, as speedily, adroitly, and unobtrusively as possible. He'd concluded that his presence was no longer required. Shri already had Paolo by his side, cossetting him and coddling him to death. So the time to skedaddle—*satko*—was *now!*

He turned to Shefali and spoke in a low voice. "Umm, you know what I'm thinking? Makes sense to leave them together tonight, give them their space, and so on. So I'm, like, headed out." He paused. "I can drop you back, if you like. It's on the way."

She avoided his eyes. "Fine."

For Neel, the prospect of being out and about again was very liberating. He couldn't wait to get the hell out of Shri's, head back home, and resume his normal routine. Privately, he told himself that if he took any more "sick leave," he might well be in the same boat as Shri—jobless! With a little bit of persuasion, he managed to cajole Shri into letting him go. So before Shri could change his mind and revert to nanny mode, Neel was stuffing his belongings into an overnighter and getting set to depart.

Soon, he was seated in a yellow cab going uptown, with Shefali by his side. The taxi ride turned out to be even more awkward than they'd anticipated—the conversation between them was stilted, and the space between them, on the back seat, could have accommodated another whole person!

As they reached her Upper West Side destination, Shefali turned to him. "Hey, keep up the good work. I know you can do it." She smiled. "Thanks for the ride. Take care."

Neel was touched by her concern. He reached out and tapped her arm. "Thanks . . . your support means a lot, you know. I really appreciate it."

Then, as the cab continued on its way, Neel's cell rang. It was Shanks, all agog to get to the bottom of Neel's bizarre text message.

15

Over the next couple of weeks, Neel settled into a fairly predictable routine at home, and at work. He was well aware that the Gang were monitoring his comings and goings closely. Short of setting him up with a tracking device, the vigilance committee was on to his every move! But he didn't mind too much. He was especially touched to discover that, in deference to his no-booze constraint, there would be no more boisterous bar nights at various watering holes around the city.

Instead, from now on, Thursday nights would be low-key affairs. They'd meet in each others' homes, and try to stay "dry." To support the cause, Neel volunteered to host their first alcohol-free Thursday night at his alcohol-free apartment. He'd made it his mission to donate his entire collection of extremely expensive malts to Shri. Now, all he stocked was organic juice, coconut water, and ginger beer. And if his guests really needed a quick fix, Red Bull was the go-to drink for the evening. (He himself chastely stuck to coconut water.)

As it happened, the first "sober night" had the original threesome again, with no add-ons. Paolo was away on a business trip, Shefali had pleaded a "headache," and Vivian had simply said she was "busy," whatever that meant. Shanks only hoped that she wasn't getting fed up with all the waiting, and lining up some other guy, a la Layla!

Where Shefali was concerned, they strongly suspected that the "half ex" was back in her life. Ryan had probably come into town, and she had a date lined up. She was bailing on them to spend more time with him, but hadn't wanted to say so.

However, the Gang was wrong, on both counts. Shefali *had* lied about the headache, but only because she was squeamish about seeing Neel again so soon. Their forced meeting at Shri's had convinced her she needed more time before she was ready to party. She couldn't pretend the Hamptons never happened. Neel's PDA with Layla, and the way he'd flaunted her about so brazenly, had left her emotionally scarred, perhaps for life!

Vivian, too, had her own reasons for ditching the Thursday special. And, like Shefali, it had nothing to do with another guy. She was meeting a girl friend, but she couldn't tell Shanks what it was all about. Had he known what she was up to, Vivian was pretty certain that he'd have put his foot down, quite unambiguously.

The sober night, meanwhile, was turning out to be very sober indeed. Despite the Red-Bull-gives-you-wings slogan— as advertised in the Red Bull campaigns—morale was not high. And it wasn't only because of the lack of booze.

Shanks was agonising over Vivian's mysterious disappearance and what it could all mean. Shri was pretty depressed too, about his alien status. And Neel wasn't so hot either. Battling a booze ban and betrayal, all at once, was enough to test anyone's limits. Observing them, an outsider would have concluded that someone near and dear had recently died!

Something needed to be done, Neel was thinking, they couldn't all just sit around, staring into their non-alcoholic drinks, and behaving as if—

His cell broke the brooding silence. Neel stared at the caller ID and then, very deliberately, disconnected the call. But both his friends had seen the look on his face.

"Layla." Shanks said before he could stop himself.

"Yes." Neel spoke carefully. "She's tried calling before. A few times."

Everyone went back to silent mode. Shanks and Shri were not prepared, not yet at least, to volunteer any advice. Secretly, they were very relieved that Neel was cutting off all contact. They had never seen his love life in such a mess. Never. He had always been the one to have the upper hand in a relationship, but this time, clearly, the shoe was on the other foot.

While they knew he would eventually get over his Layla, it was not happening just yet. To mourn his lost love, Neel had embraced the bottle, Devdas style. And the Devdas legacy, by its very nature, involved a painful, protracted, and pathos-filled grieving process. However, unlike the older version, Neel was fortunate enough to have access to AA—his modern-day Devdas came with the resources to script his own happy ending.

He seemed to be working very hard towards that end. He had his regular group therapy sessions, where he sat down with other recovering alcoholics and discussed common problems. They articulated their day-to-day difficulties and bonded over coffee, looking for solutions. When they found themselves in stressful situations, they called each other, seeking timely support. The goal was to contain their dependence on alcohol and hopefully, over time, conquer it completely.

At least Neel could seek help. Shri had no such recourse. If he appeared the glummest of the three, it was with good reason. He could do nothing but wait for the phone to ring. Or watch out for interview calls in his mailbox. A few days earlier, he had given up his apartment, and moved in with Paolo. But there too, he'd continued to exhibit an irrational moodiness. Often, he'd go into a huddled position and not respond to anything that Paolo said.

"Shri! Love," Paolo would plead, "don't sweat it, man. Something's gotta give . . . it's just a matter of time before—"

"—and time is what I don't have, remember?"

Shri's anxiety attacks had gotten so debilitating that he couldn't even work on his résumé without help. Often, when Paolo got back from work, or from an out-of-town trip, he'd have to patiently sit with Shri and take him through his job application process, with lots of coffee breaks in between. Every case was different, and it took them forever to finally send out the right CV to the right recipient.

Shri hadn't been cooking either, so Paolo would coax him to step out to eat. He'd noticed that wandering about the happening streets of Manhattan lifted Shri's spirits. "Okay, so today we're going to The Out," Paolo would say. "Great reviews on Yelp, let's check it out!" Yelp was the online site that offered star-rated user reviews for dining out, and the theatre.

Although Shri continued to remain depressed for the most part, he did have some happier moments. For the first time in his life, he was at leisure to participate wholeheartedly in his alternate lifestyle. He'd always known about the omnipresence of the gay universe, particularly in a city like New York. Now, free from time constraints of a job and unconcerned about how the world might view him, he enjoyed exploring the many facets of the gay sub-culture. In the process, he was beginning to understand himself a little better.

While the boys continued to wallow in varying levels of misery, Vivian was putting her absenteeism to good use. She was busy trolling the streets between 26th and 30th, on Lexington, in Manhattan's Little India. It was the hub where all the *desi* shops, restaurants, and grocery stores were clustered. Accompanying her was her Sri Lankan colleague, Latha Vellesamy, lieutenant and advisor, hand-picked for this particular covert operation!

"Curry powder is too general," Latha was saying. "There's *sambar* powder, *rasam* powder, *puliotharai* powder, gunpowder—"

"*Gunpowder!*" Vivian was horrified.

"That's the really spicy red one," Latha said, as if the rest was self-explanatory.

She educated Vivian on the different kinds of rice—regular white rice, idli rice, and red rice—used for different purposes in the Tamil kitchen. She also got Vivian to load up on coffee beans, dals, and other spices. The vegetable section was amazing too, with every shade of green and purple and red on display. Most of the veggies looked strange to Vivian, but some were familiar.

"Oh look, this is like our bitter melon!" she told Latha.

"That's bitter gourd, and I should warn you, it's really, really bitter." Latha reached out for a chunk of raw jackfruit.

"Boluomi!" Vivian exclaimed. "That's what we call it."

The trip was quite an eye-opener. Vivian hadn't ever seen so many varieties of pickles or sniffed such a mind-boggling array of spices. She treated Latha to a quick coffee and idlis that came accompanied with a delicious coconut-based dipping chutney. Then Vivian thanked her friend for all her help and, before saying goodbye, held on to her nervously. "So . . . wish me luck," she sighed. "I'm going behind enemy lines. They could shoot my face off!"

"That won't happen," Latha reassured her. "Good luck to you, and hey, call me. Let me know how it goes."

So, even as Shanks was fretting about his beloved Vivian's absence, his beloved Vivian was ringing the doorbell of his apartment. Mrs. Revathi had been watching a soppy Kalaignar soap, her daily dose of Tamil TV entertainment. She always wept during the high-decibel confrontations between the mother-in-

176

law and daughter-in-law and kept an emergency tissue box handy. This soap was turning out to be more heart-wrenching than most. She had come to the part where the son must bid farewell to his mother, because his nasty, conniving wife has driven a wedge between mother and son. She felt the entire scene could have been directly scripted from her own life. It was all too real!

The doorbell gave her quite a start. From the bedecked and brightly coloured living rooms of Chennai, she was transported back to her own immediate surroundings. Her hands flew to her face. "Sankar!"

Upon hearing the bell, Tathi Ma too had drawn the same conclusion. It had to be Sankar. So far, apart from a text message saying he was to be contacted only for emergencies, and a weekly cash envelope in the mail, they hadn't heard from Shanks at all. But obviously, he'd finally seen the folly of his actions, relented, and decided to return home.

Mrs. Revathi forgot all about her TV drama. *This* was a going to be a mother-son reunion that would make TV soaps look like nothing! Her happy ending was about to be played out in real time, here and now! She rushed forward to open the door for her long-lost son.

But as the door flew open, her eyes flew open too—in shock!

Standing in front of her, keeling over with a dozen grocery bags in hand, was Vivian. "I'm so sorry to come without informing you, but I thought you would be home, so . . ."

Mrs. Revathi almost fainted. Never, even in her wildest nightmares, had she imagined the trollop would land up at her doorstep!

"Where is Sankar?" she demanded.

Tathi Ma hobbled up behind her. "Who is it, *ma*? Everything okay?" When she spied Vivian, her heart leapt for joy. "Vivian! How lovely! Come in, please." But her daughter-in-law was still blocking the doorway. Tathi Ma seldom pulled rank, but in this instance, her voice was steely. "Revathi, move, please."

"You mean let her come *in*?" Mrs. Revathi continued to zealously guard the door.

"If you don't move, I will also walk out, like Sankar!"

Mrs. Revathi hesitated. She knew her mother-in-law was perfectly capable of packing her bags and walking out to be with her grandson. Vivian was already there to take her. She'd be all alone then, with no one on her side. It would be too awful to manage her life completely on her own. So she stepped aside and went back to her TV-watching spot on the sofa. "Do as you wish. I can't be bothered!"

Vivian had gained entry into the hallowed threshold! As she put the bags down, her eyes went to the pile of wet tissues. Wow, surely his mom wasn't still crying because Shanks had left? That would be a lot of trees being sacrificed for their cause!

"She cries when she's watching TV," Tathi Ma explained. "Come, come, dear, sit down. So how is Sankar?"

"He doesn't know I'm here. I don't think he would have let me come, because he feels . . . he's feeling bad." She paused. "Umm, I thought I'd bring you some groceries, so you wouldn't have to go shopping." She smiled at Tathi Ma. "Shall I take everything out in the kitchen?"

She started to unload the stuff onto the counter. Tathi Ma followed her in. "I couldn't get the, er, *natangai*? Is that how you say it?"

"*Nartangai!*" Tathi Ma exclaimed. "You know about *nartangai*, the salted lime pickle!"

"Oh, my friend Latha, she helped me, she's Tamil, from Sri Lanka," Vivian explained.

"You must bring her home sometime," Tathi Ma smiled. Then she said, "I'm thinking, why don't I make some coffee for us all?" Even though Vivian had just had a cup, with Latha, she couldn't refuse. She continued to unload the stuff, while Tathi Ma got the coffee started.

Mrs. Revathi had been watching the proceedings from the corner of her eye. But when Vivian came up to her with a cup of coffee, and politely placed it on a table by her side, she suddenly became so immersed in her TV soap that she couldn't even spare her the courtesy of a "thank you." Later, when Vivian and Tathi Ma joined her in the living room, she simply looked the other way. For Vivian, it was all very disconcerting. And depressing.

Tathi Ma's warm welcome was the one saving grace, reflected Vivian. The old lady sat down next to her, and patted her hand reassuringly. "We are very happy you came to visit us, and not just for the groceries, *ma!*" she cackled. "You must tell us about your family and everything."

Vivian spoke to Tathi Ma about her parents, her younger brother, and her hopes and dreams. To all appearances, Mrs. Revathi was still caught up with her TV soap. (Although she had turned down the volume a bit.) She didn't so much as glance in their direction—not one single time—thereby confirming that she was listening to every word.

"Shanks . . . I mean, Shankar and I, we very much want to take you out for a Broadway show or to Central Park. So when is a good time?"

That was when Mrs. Revathi finally swivelled her head. "You can say all this, but actually, you know he doesn't want to meet us! You have taken my son away from me and now you came to take me to Central Park! What do I care about Central Park! You think you can just walk into this house, bring some food, and pretend to be—"

"Enough!" Tathi Ma interrupted sharply. "Let's hear no more of this! Vivian is here to help us. She is trying to compensate for

Sankar's absence. If you can't be nice to her, Revathi, you will not abuse her. I forbid it!"

Mrs. Revathi sprang up from the sofa. "You can say anything you want, *Amma*, but you cannot make me accept this girl!" After delivering her piece, she turned on her heel and slammed the bedroom door shut behind her.

Vivian turned to Tathi Ma in distress. "Oh my God, I should never have come! I was hoping that if I tried to talk to her, reason with her, she'd see I'm not some kind of a . . . a . . ." Now, Vivian started attacking what was left of the depleted tissue box.

Tathi Ma firmly caught hold of her hand. "*Kanna*, don't cry, dear, everything will be all right in the end. I'm speaking from experience. Nowadays, I see so many young people like you and Sankar, in the exact-same-type situation." She smiled. "But why worry about all that now, ah? We got all those nice vegetables, *illiya*? Let's go into the kitchen. I'm going to teach you to make *thoran*, come."

Vivian soon discovered that Tathi Ma was very agile when it when it came cutting vegetables, and using her mixer grinder. She showed Vivian how to squeeze tamarind juice and crisp-fry curry leaves. The *thoran* turned out to be a great collaborative effort and very delicious indeed. "We'll pack for Sankar," Tathi Ma said. So Vivian packed her first attempt at Tamil cooking for Shanks to sample, while making sure there was enough for his mom and grandmom to enjoy too.

From inside her room, Mrs. Revathi had heard the pots and pans, the mixer, and the laughter in the kitchen. She was not happy to be confined to her bedroom space, but pride wouldn't allow her to make an appearance. She was the injured party, so it was important to keep up the hostility. There was no question of a truce with the trollop!

At the same time as the on-going drama at Shanks', there

was another, equally riveting theatre-of-the-absurd being played out with Shri. It all started with Shefali's cell phone ringing. It was Shri's mom, calling her from Atlanta. After a brief hello-how-are-you to Shefali, Mrs. Godbole got down to the business at hand. "Shefali, *beta*, Shri is not picking up his cell phone. Few times I've tried, no response, so I'm calling you to ask . . ."

Shefali knew perfectly well why Shri wasn't picking up his cell phone. The phone belonged to the bank, and they had made sure all the "pink slip-ers" had handed in their cell phones before leaving the office premises. She wanted to *kill* Shri for not telling them what his real situation was. Now she was stuck in a position where she'd have to withhold even *more* information than she already was. "Oh," she said, "I'm sure it's some connection problem."

"You see, we're coming to New York tomorrow," Shri's mom continued. "His father decided, last minute, to attend a conference there, at the Plaza. So I decided to come also. I can go to his apartment and spend my day there and meet him . . . and meet you."

Shefali could hardly tell her that Shri didn't have that apartment anymore, because he'd given it up to move in with another guy! She hesitated. "Umm, I'm not sure that would work. You see, Shri's really busy during the day, so I insist you come to my place first! Why don't I pick you up from the Plaza? What time are you arriving?"

They chatted for a few minutes more. By the time Shefali disconnected, her palms had turned clammy. "Damn you, Shri, you bloody idiot!" She stared at the wall ahead. His parents would fly in tomorrow, not knowing that their son had lost his job and was living with another man. Short of hearing that Shri had had some sort of fatal accident, she couldn't imagine how life could get any worse for them.

She called him, aware that he would still be at Neel's, doing the Thursday thing. He was. He saw the caller ID and smiled. "Oh, Shefali! Maybe she decided to come after all," he said and put her on speaker, for healthy group participation. "Hey, we're all here, wassup."

"Oh nothing much, only your parents are coming to stay with you tomorrow."

There was a stunned, stupefied silence.

"Hello, anybody home?" Shefali sounded irritated.

"What am I going to do!" Shri was trying to breathe.

"Darling," came the sarcastic rejoinder, loud and clear, "you're going to tell them the truth, and if *you* don't, *I* will!"

She was greeted with a longer, even more stunned silence.

"You can't do that!" That was Neel, sounding shocked.

"Try me, baby!"

"Shefali! Hi, this is Shanks." Like she didn't know. "Listen, let him say it in his own way."

"Guys, what the hell's the matter with you!" Shefali was thinking of Shri's wonderful parents and her own horrible part in deceiving them. The subterfuge had to stop, and soon. "Haven't we lied to them enough? Shri, tell me, don't they deserve to know what the hell is happening in your life? Do you *never* plan to tell them?"

They looked at each other, unable to come up with an answer. Sure, his parents had to be informed, but there was a time and place for everything. Shri had not intended full or even part disclosure anytime soon. He had hoped, in fact, to find another job before having to tell his parents he'd lost the last one. And as for his sexual leanings, or his relationship with Paolo, he wasn't sure he'd *ever* announce that!

"Is Paolo there?" Shefali wanted to know.

"No, he's in Rio. Business trip."

There was an exasperated sigh at the other end and

something that sounded like "Men!" but they couldn't be sure. The Gang exchanged uneasy glances. Things were looking dicey. In a situation as tricky as this one, the last thing they needed was a combative, non-cooperative Shefali.

But once again, Shefali proved that despite her misgivings, her loyalty trumped all else. The next day, while Shri's father was busy at the conference, she hired a limo and personally landed up at the Plaza. She picked Shri's mom up, ferried her back to her apartment, and served her lunch. When Shri called around three o'clock, to speak to his mom, Shefali informed him that his mother had had a good lunch and was presently taking a nap.

Shri was rendered speechless. A knot had formed deep in his throat, and it wouldn't go away. Here was this courageous, compassionate creature—his dear, dear friend—fighting for his cause once again. She was his Rani of Jhansi, his warrior queen, facing all kinds of life-threatening situations, but battling on, for his sake! (And neutralising the enemy each and every time.) How could he ever thank her?

"Shef," he whispered, "I owe you sweetheart, big time. I'm never going to forget this one, ever."

"Not to worry my love I won't let you," she informed him silkily. "I'm banking all my favours for future use . . . and I'm sure as hell gonna call 'em in."

That very evening, her "bank balance" was going to be further bolstered—the Godbole family reunion was scheduled to take place at her apartment, where all the Godboles were expected to congregate for dinner. A short while earlier, Shri's mom had surfaced from her siesta, and enjoyed a masala chai served along with some fabulous Gujju-style *farsan*.

That evening, once the little party had settled down, the conversation inevitably gravitated towards the Citi group story. Mr. Godbole turned to his son. "I read about all those lay-offs," he said. "My goodness, thousands of employees fired, just like that! Anyone you know?"

Why was it, Shri wondered, that they always assumed bad things happened only to other people? Why did they put the pressure on him, however unintentionally, to be the Good Son every single time? Shri swallowed convulsively. "Yes *Baba,* someone I know. Me."

Shri's father leaned forward in utter disbelief. "Can't be . . . can't be. Are you sure?"

Shri's voice went up a few notches. "Of course I'm sure, *Baba,* it's called a pink slip."

Seeing his father's shattered expression, Shri knew he should feel some remorse. But he couldn't. He was done pandering to the whims and fancies of his parents. Living up to their expectations had caused him so much grief that he wasn't about to put himself through the wringer yet again. He'd also come to the conclusion that his parents needed to hear about his "hidden life" asap. He'd actually been tempted to make the announcement that evening itself, but had refrained. They needed time to absorb the first shock, before he sprung the second one. The double whammy might seriously derail their mental equilibrium forever!

"Yes, yes, I have to say, I'm too shocked, too shocked," his father was still in denial, "I was sure that you'll be getting a promotion soon, and a better salary. I was thinking . . ." His father shook his head, unable to continue.

It was so unfair, reflected Shri bitterly. As long as life was on a roll, as long he was delivering the goods, his father waxed poetic about his achievements and his mother sang his praises to friends, neighbours, relatives, the household help, in fact anyone who was willing to listen.

But now? Now that the Good Son had morphed into the Good-For-Nothing Son, they didn't quite know how to handle it.

16

When Vivian placed the plate in front of him, Shanks' eyes widened in surprise. It was redolent of his childhood—the *thoran* and rice his grandmother used to make. It smelled divine.

"Wow," he said, after the first mouthful, "no way this came from a restaurant! It's completely authentic, it's—" He took in another heaping mouthful.

"You like it?"

"*Like* it? I'm telling you, it's brilliant. I haven't eaten *thoran* like this since—" He paused. "Where did you say you bought this?"

"I didn't say." Vivian paused. "Shanks, I made it."

"Yeah, right." Shanks was so taken aback that he actually stopped eating.

"I truly did, you know." She dimpled and perched herself on his lap.

He stared at her. He wasn't always perceptive, but he wasn't crazy enough to imagine Vivian had suddenly started cooking like his grandmother. "So you went to see them?" His eyes were searching hers, incredulous.

"Yes, I . . . I went to see them."

"And?"

"Okay, your mom wasn't very welcoming, but your grandma? Tathi Ma? She was amazing! She's the one who taught me how to—"

"Viv, why did you go?" Shanks was torn between admiration and annoyance. It was great that Vivian had fearlessly chosen to step into the lioness's den, but he wished she had told him about it.

"I wanted to reach out, that's all."

Shanks forgot all about his rice and *thoran* dinner. The lump in his throat expanded, as he drew her close, and held her tight. "I love you so much." Vivian sighed, and sank into his arms. It was moments like these that kept her going, she told herself. But it was all very hard, and all very hopeless! Soon, Shanks found his shoulder had become quite damp. He looked up in surprise. "Hey! You're crying!"

"I'm not sure she'll ever accept me . . . I don't know what we'll do!"

"We'll get married, that's what we'll do!" Shanks said with conviction. "We don't need anyone's permission, right? Remember we spoke about Skyping your family? Let's do it and get on with our life. I'm not going to wait for my mother's blessings forever!" His pep talk cheered her up no end, and seeing her smile made him smile too. "Think about it, we might be the first ones to get married! Among our friends, I mean. Unless Shefali and Ryan decide to—"

"Shefali's not marrying Ryan."

"She told you?" Shanks never ceased to be amazed how girls shared these personal confidences so readily.

"Oh, no, but I know!" Vivian seemed quite certain.

"How?"

"She's still in love with Neel. You can see it from a mile away."

Shanks could see no such thing. What he *had* seen was Shefali getting cosy with Ryan. And he couldn't fathom why she would be kissing another guy if she still loved Neel. He asked Vivian about this.

Vivian smiled mischievously. "Hey, don't even try to figure the workings of the female mind. You'd take a lifetime and still not know what we're thinking!"

Shanks had to acknowledge that she was probably right. He had grown up with an elder sister who still remained a complete mystery to him. He had long given up trying to figure his mom out, or even Tathi Ma. Now, Vivian was the new puzzle in his life. A fascinating, multi-dimensional, and deeply intricate puzzle that made algorithms look easy.

"Oh, by the way, she's invited him for her birthday." Vivian told him. "So both Neel and Ryan are going to be there."

Shefali was planning to celebrate her twenty-fifth birthday in style. She had booked a dinner table at the famous Russian Tea Room. Her father couldn't be there himself, but he'd wired a very generous sum into her account. "Get yourself a nice gift and go celebrate with your friends," he said over the phone. She had absolutely no trouble following fatherly advice of that kind! The very next day, she swept into Tiffany's, and picked a magnificent ruby and diamond necklace, with matching earrings. She resolved to send her dad selfies, with her wearing the pieces, to let him know how spectacularly well his money had been spent.

Her party list was a no-brainer. The Gang would all be there, of course, Neel included. Although she hadn't precisely *forgiven* him yet, she'd come to accept that he was a part of the larger circle. If only she could learn to treat him as just another friend!

While it appeared that Layla was out of his life, Neel didn't seem to have hooked up with anyone new. For all she knew,

Shefali mused, he might want to rekindle *their* liaison. It wasn't such a far-fetched possibility. (On a lighter note, as of now, she could classify him as her ex almost-boyfriend, if there ever was such a category!)

Having an "ex-almost" was crazy enough. But the make-believe boyfriend, Ryan, was a myth even *she*, with all her play-acting skills, was finding hard to perpetuate! She sensed the Gang was getting curiouser and curiouser about her scene with him, and soon, they'd want some clarifications on her status.

Not that there was much to tell. They hadn't met since the Hamptons, but they were in touch digitally. She liked Ryan a lot—what was not to like? He was charming, good-looking, and could kiss with a passion that took her breath away. But the truth was, she hardly knew him. One weekend—that too under false pretences—was barely enough to even get acquainted.

And yet, how could she forget the way he'd sportingly helped her out in her time of need? She also loved the way he'd bonded with the Gang, with no baggage and no hang-ups whatsoever. So she'd decided that, along with the Gang, she very much wanted Ryan to be a part of her birthday celebrations. For her quarter century milestone, she was determined to surround herself with friends who really meant something to her.

As she called Ryan, she wasn't sure what to expect.

"Hey, Shefali! How're you doing?" Ryan sounded enthusiastic, happy that she had called.

They caught up on the current events in each other's lives for a couple of minutes, then she extended her invitation. "Hey, by the way," she said, tentative, "I especially called to invite you for my birthday, the coming Friday, at The Russian Tea Room. It's the usual suspects, so it would be great if you could—"

"Neel still giving you a hard time?"

A pause at her end. "I don't know what you mean."

"Yeah, you do." She could almost see him smiling. "You're not over that guy, are you?"

"Maybe not, but that's not why I'm inviting you!" Shefali was indignant.

"Are you sure? You are not doing it consciously, but—"

"Okay, so now are you going to psychoanalyze me, or are you just going to come?"

He was laughing. "Sure, I'll be there, but—" he hesitated "—there's something I have to tell you."

Now what? she wondered.

"If I see you again and again . . . I might start getting serious."

"I might too," Shefali murmured.

Ryan appeared to take her at her word. He showed up for her birthday in a smart suit and carried an armload of blood-red roses. The red roses made Shefali go all pink. She accepted the flowers and glanced up at him almost shyly. The Gang couldn't help noticing the super-hot vibes—looked like the romance was blooming all right!

Neel was looking heart-stoppingly handsome too, in a dark suit. Shefali couldn't help secretly moaning the unfairness of it all. Here she was, entertaining two amazingly attractive guys, both assuming they were rivals for her affections! And the reality was that she was still as single as a nun!

That evening, both her admirers were looking at her with new eyes. She was the perfect hostess, vivacious, effusive, and totally in her element. The sparkle in her eyes and the smile on her lips added a whole new dimension to her beauty. In fact, Neel, who'd been casting sidelong glances in her direction, couldn't help comparing her to one of those old-world Bollywood beauties. *Like a Raj Kapoor heroine,* he mused, although he couldn't precisely remember which one. A beautiful star-crossed maiden ruing her fate as she sang her song, caught as she was, in a love triangle of destiny.

However the reality on the ground was somewhat different. There was no love, no triangle, and certainly, Neel and Ryan weren't about to burst into song anytime soon.

Since Neel was off alcohol, Shefali had decided, in consultation with the F&B manager, to cut out the alcohol completely. She had requested they serve mocktails instead. So when the first round of mocktails arrived at their table, with exotic titles like Cranberry Clown and Lychee Lovers, Neel turned to Shefali in a state of shock. "You gotta be kidding me! No booze? Because of me?"

She couldn't help smiling at his horrified tone. "It's okay, we'll survive. It's just one evening. And they promised us we won't miss it. They've got some more great stuff lined up— mock this and mock that."

"Shefali! You can't do this!" Neel was feeling super guilty about spoiling the party. "It's your twenty-fifth. You should be celebrating with champagne! At twenty-five, you're not even supposed to be sober!"

She touched his hand lightly. "Neel, that's really sweet of you, thanks for your concern, but let's not mock the mocktail!" She looked around. "We're all doing just fine. Right, guys?"

There was a chorus of assent as everyone raised their mocktails. Neel reluctantly did so too. Shefali held up her glass, very emotional. "Guys, thanks for being around. Having you all here . . . I'm gonna be high on the company!"

Shri felt things were getting out of hand. "Oh hello, let's not push it, okay? You're getting too senti. I don't think it's fair to use us as a booze substitute! I don't want to be a booze substitute!"

Despite the alcohol ban, it turned out to be a really animated party. After a long spell, the Gang was lightening up and really having fun. Although the problems hadn't resolved themselves, they were on the back burner, for that night at least. And quite surprisingly, Neel and Ryan, who were seated next to each other, found several interesting things to talk about.

"Tell me more about what you do," Neel said. He was genuinely interested in the Giffords Trust, which was doing some great work in the field of global warming.

"Don't start me off." Ryan laughed. "You won't get me to shut up."

"Hey, you got some great stuff going on." Neel smiled. "Seminal work happening. Our portfolio's already big on hydro, bio, wind, so any pearls of wisdom coming from you, you bet I'm gonna be listenin'!"

Apart from the mind-expanding merits of the conversation, Neel wanted Ryan to continue talking for another important reason. He needed a distraction. On occasions like this, when he was habituated to steady drinking, it was very hard to hang on to lychee juice all evening, even if it did have an exotic name.

His AA sessions had been difficult, and demanding. The toughest part—to actually accept he was an alcoholic—was a start. Now that he had crossed that initial hurdle, watching for the trigger points was the next big challenge. It took just one evening like this one to reverse all his good work. Fortunately for him, he had sensitive friends like Shefali looking out for him all the time. When she'd said "don't mock the mocktail," she was offering him her support. Gratefully, he sipped his fresh refill of lychee whatever.

As the birthday girl put on her best smile and partied through the evening, no one would have suspected how low-spirited she was actually feeling. It was hard for her to accept that she'd hit the quarter century mark and was still pathetically, painfully single! Like a solitaire that wasn't finding a setting. Was there no one in the whole wide world whom she could have in bed that night? Vivian had Shanks, and Shri Paolo. She wanted someone in her life too. Her dad, a great believer in astrology, had told her there was a time for love. Maybe her love was destined for some future date, and not at The Russian Tea Room right now.

But Shefali had made a birthday resolution. Even if love eluded her, there were other, equally important aspects of her life that needed urgent repair. And she was counting on some help from her friends. She turned to Shri during the dessert course. "Hey, I could use some advice."

Shri raised his eyebrows. Advising Shefali, especially where it concerned her love life, could be quite a balancing act. "Like, what kind of advice?"

"Umm, my new resolution, birthday resolution actually, is to find a job."

Shri's eyebrows shot up to his hairline. "Really?" he said, genuinely amused. "And what kind of *job* d'you have in mind?"

"Stop being such a hater, and listen. I'm looking at fashion, fashion journalist, writer, columnist . . . something in that space."

He stared at her. He'd give her full marks for optimism, if nothing else! Getting a break in the fashion industry was notoriously difficult. She would have to start at the entry level, as a general gofer, and work her way up. In the present economic uncertainty, she'd be lucky to get even that. Her qualifications were basic, and work experience non-existent. But he could hardly tell her so. "Why don't we first get your résumé in order . . . and take it from there. Tomorrow morning?"

She was serious enough to land up at Paolo's place the very next morning, at ten sharp. Shri opened the door, and stood transfixed. He couldn't believe his eyes. Shefali, up and about at this unearthly hour! And that too after a late night! He hadn't actually been expecting her till noon. So obviously, she had to be serious about this job business, he told himself. A fellow job-hunter had joined the ranks.

"Some coffee before we get started?" he asked her.

"Sure, I'll make it." She headed to the kitchen. "And hot chocolate for you?"

He blushed. "Umm, actually, I'll have coffee too."

"No!" She stared at him. "No way!"

"The thing is, Paolo's real big on coffee. He introduced me to some great beans, you know, specialty java, and now I'm hooked!" He followed her into the kitchen. "And I've discovered coffee's a great stress-buster, it's—"

"Welcome to the real world!" Shefali rolled her eyes.

It was strangely comforting to sip hot java and hunt for jobs together. Of course, being jobless was no fun, and in Shri's case, it was almost a health hazard. But coping was easier when you had a companion to share the gloom-and-doom moments. They browsed Monster, Glassdoor, and some other job search sites that Shefali had never heard of in her life. For her, it was a learning experience.

"Keep in mind," Shri instructed, "that LinkedIn is your most important tool. You need to keep expanding your LinkedIn contacts, to connect to the universe out there. Unfortunately, my contacts are mostly in the banking space, not much use to you." Suddenly he inhaled sharply. "Oh, oh my God, why didn't I think of it! Not too long back, Neel used to date this fashion-model-turned-editor. I'm forgetting her name, something with B, I think—"

"I'm not asking Neel's ex for a job." Shefali stared at Shri like he'd lost it.

"Hey, we help each other out, that's what we do, remember? Neel gives you her contact, you follow up it with a phone call and—"

"Shri, stop! I can't do it." She was almost in tears.

"Oh my God, I'm sorry, Shef. Really I . . ." He paused. "Seriously, I thought you were over him!"

"I thought I was too! But I just can't seem to—" She stopped. God, she was really tying herself in knots. She didn't want to talk about it, not even with Shri. It was weird to be in this transition phase of her love life. She still had feelings for Neel, but she was also attracted to Ryan. She was not sure how that worked, but she was hoping that if she stopped thinking about either of them, it would sort itself out.

". . . so where does Ryan figure in all this?" Shri was asking. Like the rest of the Gang, he wasn't party to her transactional deal with Ryan. Shefali had been a bit too ashamed to divulge the details at that time. Now, it seemed redundant anyway.

"Shri, I like Ryan, I like him a lot," Shefali tried to explain, "but I'm so confused." She looked at him pleadingly. "It's complicated."

Apart from the make-believe boyfriend story, there was another story, a sequel, that she conveniently omitted to mention. After the birthday bash, Ryan had insisted on them having a drink together. A proper cocktail, he'd said, with real alcohol in it! He'd taken her to an exclusive, members-only bar, where the celebratory champagne had gotten way out of hand. They'd landed up at her place, then they'd had sex. This was the very first time, since coming to New York, that she had had a guy in her bed. She was glad Ryan had been that guy, a sort of a twenty-fifth birthday gift to herself, wrapped up in her 1000-thread-count Egyptian cotton sheets!

"You were pretty amazing, but you already know that," Shefali had told him. He was next to her, holding her close, and they were both still breathless from all the exertion.

They had agreed it was too premature to predict what could

happen next. He disliked New York City and preferred to live in the relative isolation of the Hamptons, only about a hundred miles away. In complete contrast, she adored Manhattan, and the lifestyle that came with it. But the real issue was, if she did get a job, it certainly wasn't going to be in the bucolic suburbs of Long Island.

"I don't want you on the rebound, you know . . . confused or guilty," Ryan had said. "So, if we take things slow . . ."

"I'm with you there," Shefali had replied. "And Ryan?" She smiled. "I'm not sure how things will go but whatever happens, I'd like to be friends, always."

They both knew that her feelings for Neel also had to be factored in. It was not something that could be wished away, overnight. It was ironic, in a sense, that it was her Neel obsession that had brought Ryan into her life. Ryan, too, had had broken relationships but, like he told Shefali, he'd moved on.

"Cynthia was special," he reminisced, "but at that point, I had to be in Indonesia for a year, and she just couldn't handle the whole long-distance thing. We're still friends though."

"And no one in your life since then?"

"Umm, no, not really, just casual sex, I guess."

She hoped she wasn't going to be the next casualty on his casual sex list. But there was no point dwelling on Ryan's non-committal approach to his love life. She needed to get her own stuff in order. Her mission right now was to concentrate on getting that job. She wasn't planning to sit around waiting for guys to happen.

The ad on her MacBook screen, therefore, deserved her dedicated, undivided attention. *Committed, hard-working, with a burning desire to succeed.* That was what this particular advertisement wanted. Did she really have that kind of diligence? It wasn't just about a list of random academic accomplishments anymore, she realised. Most employers wanted the perfect amalgamation of qualifications and qualities. For starters, she'd have to re-orient her priorities. No late nights, no more sleeping in.

If she got a job, she'd have to be up and about at the crack of dawn, probably taking orders from a boss like Meryl Streep in *The Devil Wears Prada*. But it was all worth it. She was going to be a working girl, an independent woman who could earn her own salary and be her own person. With Shri's guidance, she shortlisted her wish list options. Then she conscientiously sat scanning, listing, filing, writing, and re-writing her material.

When he suggested lunch, she murmured "in a bit" and continued to frown into her handwritten notes. By then, his addled brain needed a carb fix to function. He reached for his phone, and dialled out for pizza.

17

Neel was gazing out of his bedroom window, staring at the most-filmed and the most-photographed skyline in the world—Manhattan. It was a beautiful fall evening. The setting sun had left a rosy glow over the skyscrapers. This used to be his "happy hour," the time when he headed home and slouched on the sofa in his boxers, drink in hand. Other times, he'd go out to a bar to meet someone, usually a beautiful woman, and make out over a drink.

The booze ban had stymied his social life. Now, he desperately needed something to fill up his evening. A distraction was what he needed—something like yoga, or bridge, or salsa dancing. At AA, they highly recommended that you find an activity, such as community work, to manage the difficult moments. But Neel wasn't a soup kitchen kind of guy. Golf, he told himself, would be more his thing. Golfing also came with a built-in perk: he could get his business networking skills into play!

He sipped his jasmine tea and pulled out his MacBook. There were some beginners' classes in the vicinity. Chelsea Piers, at walking distance, might be worth checking out. Just as he'd begun browsing through their programmes, the doorbell rang. Neel knitted his eyebrows. He wasn't expecting anyone, but then the Gang didn't stand on ceremony. They often dropped by without an invitation. It had to be Shri, Neel told himself, looking to pick his brains on the job hunt.

But when he opened the door, he almost passed out. Standing in the doorway was the last person he thought he'd see. "Layla!" She looked as sultry and seductive as ever. Her musky perfume only underscored what he already knew—that she was the sexiest woman alive!

"Aren't you going to invite me in?" She was looking directly into his eyes.

"Umm, what is this regarding?" He knew he had to stand his ground. Otherwise, he'd be a lost cause.

"*Regarding?*" Her face twisted into a smile. "This is *regarding* some unfinished business we have." And her tone suddenly turned businesslike. "Neel, I need to talk to you."

He stepped aside to let her in. He might as well let her say her piece, and leave. She sashayed in and sat down. "Hmm, I can see my mom has work to do!" The place was a mess. He'd always tidied up before she came, so naturally, she had never seen it the way it mostly was.

"So, do I help myself to a drink or—"

"All I can get you is some tea. Or coffee." He paused. "I've stopped drinking."

Layla's eyes flew open. "No! Seriously?"

That was when Neel realised that she had no idea about what had happened after she'd left. She didn't know that he had almost binged himself to death because of her. Okay, he corrected himself, he couldn't entirely blame her for it. But certainly, the showdown and her stormy exit had been the trigger points for his boozed-up blackout.

"If you'd answered my calls, spoken to me," she was frowning, "I'd have known you've stopped drinking, right? But now, never mind all that. Here." She was holding out a gift-wrapped package. "I want to make it up to you, Neel, and this is my peace offering. A single malt, from a boutique distillery, I was told."

"And *I* just told you I've stopped drinking. You should take that back."

She was staring at him, trying to gauge his mood. She had never seen him like this, so distant, and so aloof. She had hoped her peace offering, the malt, would thaw the rift between them. Not that she needed an ice-breaker to seduce a guy. She had complete faith in her own powers of seduction.

"Layla, you shouldn't be here."

"I came to apologise, to tell you how sorry I am." She looked so contrite that Neel couldn't be indifferent. But he made sure his face remained a mask, cold and unapproachable. He wasn't about to let his heart hang out, ever again. She drew a little closer. "I also came to tell you I'm through with Jonathan—done and dusted. I'm never going back again."

"Good for you." Neel had never needed a drink so desperately. He had to do something, make use of his hands, and keep busy. "I'm getting myself some more jasmine tea. Would you like some?"

"Sure, I could make it, if you like." She followed him into the tiny kitchen space. The very spot where he had offered her coffee and biscotti and looked at her with bedroom eyes, all those months ago.

"Neel," she hesitated, "if there's someone else . . ."

What could he tell her? That she was still haunting his every waking moment, like a bad dream? He wanted to let go and never see her again. So far, he had managed admirably, by cutting off her calls and not responding to her emails. But seeing her in person was completely different. Her sexual energy was so potent that just having her there made him feel on top of the world.

"You know, honestly, I don't think we can make it work." He looked at her, and held his gaze. "We're two very different people, with different expectations." He wanted to say he'd never trust her, not after what she had put him through. There would always be men lusting after her, and there was no way he'd be able to stop them. The 24/7 tension of getting Layla "exclusive" was not something he was prepared to take on.

"What? So we just say goodbye and never see each other again? Is that what you want, Neel?" She was giving him an ultimatum. She'd walk out of the door and there would be no second chances. She placed her hand on his thigh. "Neel? Forgive me, please? Let's kiss and make up . . ." she smiled naughtily, "in bed! I bought this amazing new lingerie set, black Chantilly lace, from—"

Neel didn't even wait for her to finish. His lips were crushing hers with a passion he hadn't believed himself capable of. He gathered her in his arms and made his way to the bedroom. He barely noticed the fancy lingerie as he pulled it off her and gave himself up to her soft curves. She responded with the same fervour, letting his tongue explore her body and stray anywhere he pleased.

The frenzy built up to fever pitch. Fulfilling her most intimate demands, and his own, it was the most unbelievable sex he'd ever had. Later, when he stepped into the shower to cool off, he couldn't believe what had just happened. He'd been incredibly stupid, and shortsighted. In a weak moment, he had allowed Layla to control him, with sex. How could he have been such a wuss! He should have exercised some self-restraint, and stood up to her!

He emerged from the bathroom to find Layla still reclining in bed, only partly covered by the crumpled sheets. Her sultry-eyed gaze was doing nothing, absolutely nothing, for his self-control. But this time round, those feminine wiles were not going to work. He wasn't going to be tempted, or trapped into submission. Nope, he was going to show her once and for all who was boss.

After their tumble between the sheets, Layla had pretty much assumed that they were back on track. Neel's no-holds-barred performance in the bedroom had demonstrated, very emphatically, that he was just as crazily, madly, insanely in love with her as he'd always been!

He'd desired her—body and soul—and now, as she basked in the afterglow, she couldn't help feeling a trifle smug. She'd always known she could have him where she wanted him—in bed!

"Layla, I'm not sure what you had in mind, but I think you should . . . leave."

Layla's eyes widened in disbelief. Was this really Neel speaking? What on earth had come over him? "Neel, that's no way to speak to me. I can't believe you just said that!"

"I meant it."

Layla drew her breath in sharply. This was beyond real. He was actually giving her the boot, asking her to get out of his home, and his life! "You think I'm some kinda one-night stand, think again! I'm not like your Shefali, to be used and then discarded like an old sock!" She was grabbing her clothes. "I'm so outta here, Neel," she raged. "I never want to see your face again!"

As soon as she was dressed, she ran into the living room and got her sandals on. By the time Neel followed her out, she'd picked up her handbag and opened the front door. In the doorway, she turned back for a couple of seconds, and glared at him through her mascara tears. Then, she slammed the door with such force that the china rattled.

Neel slumped onto the sofa, feeling rather rattled himself. Why was his life such a huge frigging mess? He needed someone to talk to. Shri would have been his first phone call, but he knew Shri was seldom free these days. Paolo had just got back from his Rio de Janerio trip and, obviously, they'd want to spend some quality time together. Shefali was out of bounds too, for obvious reasons. And Shanks, well Shanks just wasn't the go-to guy when you needed solace and succour.

He picked up his cell phone. He could call AA, where he'd get anonymous advice from an anonymous volunteer at an anonymous location. Or, he reflected, he could simply dial Dr. Natasha Singh. She might not be available but it was worth a try.

She picked up on the second ring. "Hey, Neel, how're you?"

"Umm, surviving, I guess." He paused. "Hope I'm not catching you at a bad moment. I know it's pretty late, but I just couldn't sleep so—"

She interrupted, laughing. "You must know, doctors don't sleep much either!" Then her tone changed. "Neel, not to presume or anything like that, but . . . we're friends, right?"

"Yeah, sure."

"Are you having a problem right now?" He heard her take a deep breath. "Is there something you want to share?"

"Well, no, not really, I mean, it's hard, it's really hard, but I took your advice and I'm very regular with the AA meetings, so that helps," Neel replied. "I think I'm on track . . . but of course, it's early days."

"Every day counts, you know. I've seen—" She was interrupted by the sound of another voice. "Yeah, coming!" she called to the other person, and then reverted to Neel. "Umm, I gotta go," she said. "That was my emergency call. Looks like a long night ahead." She paused. "Oh, by the way, I should tell you, my fellowship's come through. I'm going to be based in *your* city very soon!"

"New York! That's fantastic!" Neel said, and meant it.

"Be well, Neel, and try to get some sleep. And let's catch up, like, soon, okay?"

"Sure, great idea! Let me know when you're in town, and—" he almost said *and it's a date*, but stopped himself just in time, finishing smoothly with "—and take care."

As he disconnected, he suddenly realised that if she had a long night ahead, so did he. With a sense of shock, he realised that Layla's "peace offering" was still on the sofa, exactly where she had left it. A ticking time bomb, a clear and present danger.

But Neel didn't quite see it that way. Like a man in a trance, he moved forward to inspect the gift. It was, just as she had said, a very premium bottle of single malt. He held it in his hand, and weighed his options. He'd been very good so far, but the fall-out with Layla had shaken him to the core. He needed a reprieve. In any case, it would be a shame to pour something this worship-worthy down the kitchen sink.

So he made up his mind to have one drink. A single drink couldn't hurt, he told himself. To truly enjoy the finer aspects of the malt, he pulled out one of his special Riedel glasses. It was thistle-shaped, with a short, truncated stem—considered to be the connoisseur's way of savouring the best malts. He took a deep breath, opened the bottle, and poured himself a generous shot. Neat.

A couple of hours later, he'd gone through the entire bottle. He staggered into his bedroom, crashed face down onto the floor, and passed out.

The next morning, when Shri tried to call him, the call went to voice message. But that didn't bother him. He assumed Neel was already caught up in meetings, with his cell on silent. So he texted him, asking him to get back when he had a moment. There were some more job options he'd shortlisted, and needed to run them by Neel.

However, about half an hour later, Shri received a call from Neel's office. A common acquaintance was on the line, trying to locate Neel. Apparently he hadn't come in to work at all. Nor could he be reached on his cell. Would Shri know where he might be? The colleague was trying to cover for him, hoping to track him down before the bosses discovered that he was AWOL.

The phone call immediately got the alarm bells ringing inside Shri's head. He knew he had to rush to Neel's, to make sure everything was okay. Fortunately, the spare keys were still with him, just in case! As he hailed a cab and jumped in, he told himself that he was probably overreacting. But his sixth sense was telling him otherwise. The pit in his stomach—what he called his gut instinct—was making him physically sick.

When he reached Neel's, he rang the doorbell to alert him. Then he entered the condo with his key. "Neel? Neel?"

There was no sign of Neel. Shri stepped towards the bedroom. Even before he fully entered, his eyes became as big as saucers. And he staggered back in horror. Lying prone on the floor, sprawled exactly like he'd found him in the Hamptons, was Neel Sawhney.

The déjà vu flipped him out. It was unreal. Only this time, there was no one to call for help. Shri felt the familiar palpitations taking control of him again. Why was *he* always the one to discover Neel comatose like this? What about his own state of health? Was anyone worrying about *his* heart condition?

But like it or not, he'd walked into a situation. As emergency first responder he needed to do his shit, and do it quickly. With his heart pounding out of his chest, he bent over Neel's prone body, and shook him lightly. "Neel!" No response. He prodded him again, more urgently this time. "Neel, bro, get up for God's sake! *Neel!*"

Neel stirred slightly, and coughed. Then he opened his eyes with an "Ouch!" and shielded the light out with his hands. Shri was just so thankful to see him alive, that he couldn't rant at him the way he'd have liked to. He got busy cold-towelling Neel's face and made him drink a few sips of water.

Soon, Neel was able to prop his head up.

"Oh my God, what time is it!"

"What time is it! What time is it!" Shri was in a state of near-hysteria. "You should be grateful you're alive, asshole!" The high tension of search and rescue had almost killed him. And here was Neel, roused and rescued from death, airily asking what o'clock it was! Blasé, *bindass*, like it was no big deal!

"I'm sorry, bro, I-I don't know what happened last night." Neel managed to get up, shakily. "I have meetings. I gotta get to work, I . . ." With slightly unsteady steps, he headed towards the loo.

"And where d'you think you're going in this condition, hah? You're reeking, you're totally hungover, you're . . ."

Neel popped down some Alka Seltzer he found in his bathroom cabinet. Then he held up a bottle of Listerine and opened the cap. "Listerine *ka kamaal*." He started gargling, then turned to Shri. "Works like a charm." He took in another mouthful.

Shri turned away, fed up. There was only so much you could do for a friend. But if the friend willfully refused to obey all instructions!

"Dood? Pleasshze, pleasshze, fixsh me an OJ?" Now, Neel was busy brushing his teeth.

"Dude, orange juice won't fix you. You need a doctor!"

Neel stuck his head out of the loo. "No time." And next thing Shri knew, Neel had shut the bathroom door and started up the shower. Shri shook his head in despair as he went to the kitchen to fetch the juice. He toasted a couple of slices of rye bread too, just in case, and left everything on Neel's bedside table. He tapped on the bathroom door. "Hello, OJ's here, and I'm out, okay?"

"Thanks man!" Neel yelled back from the shower. "Catch you evening, okay?"

So that was that. Neel managed to work through the rest of the day without any untoward incident. And, just as he had promised, he was back home by seven in the evening, to spend time with Shri. They'd scheduled that particular meeting at Neel's well before the morning's incident. The idea was to sit together and work on Shri's job options.

The evening programme also included dinner. The entire Gang was supposed to land up at Neel's place directly after he and Shri were done with their one-on-one session. So despite the morning fiasco, Neel saw no reason to ditch the original plan. He ordered Indian Chinese, or "junglee Chinese" as he liked to call it. The hybrid Indian-Chinese junk food was always a big hit with the Gang, particularly the chicken chop suey that came with the most horrendously delicious orange-coloured sauce on top.

When the rest of the Gang arrived, Shri hadn't planned on telling anyone about Neel's morning saga. It didn't seem cool. However, shortly after the Gang had demolished their starter round of shrimp pepper salt, and vegetable spring rolls, and were busy chomping down the chop suey, Neel called for everyone's attention. "Hey, guys, just wanted to share with you, I had a relapse last night."

There was a shocked silence. What were they supposed to say?

"In my AA group, we're supposed to talk," Neel explained. "It's important to acknowledge that I made a mistake, so that I become more aware the next time I digress."

Shanks said, "The next time? What d'you mean, next time? Like, you'll go out again, and—"

"The scotch was a gift. From Layla."

Bombshell after bombshell. It was as if Neel had taken it upon himself to keep them on the edge of their seats all evening.

"So, you guys . . . you're back together?" Shri was tentative. He hadn't heard this bit before. He wasn't sure if disclosure on romantic entanglements was also part of the new-found AA camaraderie.

Neel fidgeted. "No, no, we, umm, we called it off." Then, obviously keen to change the topic, he delved into the brown paper bags. "Hey guys, who's up for the fried rice? Chili chicken? There's still tons of stuff here, and—oh!—fortune cookies!"

No one was interested in the food anymore. They were all trying to digest what he'd told them. He had been drinking again, and Layla had presented him with the booze. The temptress and the temptation, rolled together into one irresistible package.

Shefali realised, at that point, that Layla would always be Neel's big passion. She wasn't just a passing phase. She was permanent. Just as well it was out in the open, she reflected. Now, she could seriously think of moving on.

After Neel's latest meltdown, the message was loud and clear. No way he could be left alone—not even for one single night. Shanks spoke to Vivian and then turned to Shri. "I'll stay over tonight."

Shri tried not to look too relieved. Paolo was off again, the following afternoon, to Peru. Before that, he wanted to spend as much time with him as he could. (And besides, another search and rescue might be too much for his weakened heart to take!)

Predictably, Neel kicked up a fuss about being baby-sat, but when Vivian turned on her most charming smile and pleaded, he couldn't say no. So Shanks settled on Neel's couch for the night. He told himself he'd better get used to it. Rotating on assorted beds and sofas and air mattresses around Manhattan seemed to be carved into his destiny. He hadn't checked the fortune cookies that evening, but he wouldn't have been surprised to read something like, "Hobo, with nowhere to go, looking for succour, yet life is status quo."

18

Mrs. Revathi was on her computer, wondering how to say it. She had decided it was beneath her dignity to ask Shanks to come back. But the face-off had dragged on long enough, and she wanted to send out a feeler. Initially, she had assumed that after sulking for a couple of days, Shanks would be knocking at the door. But that hadn't happened. He hadn't even made a phone call. True, Vivian had come by in his place, but now, even she was incommunicado.

The only sign that Shanks cared at all was his envelope in the mail. It arrived every week, always stuffed with generous sums of cash. But Shanks' generosity meant nothing unless *he* was around— not just giving them the benefit of his cash, but also his company. They hadn't come all the way to New York to sit and watch TV all day!

She had tried to be open-minded, Mrs. Revathi told herself. But the prospect of a Chinese daughter-in-law was driving her up the wall. She didn't even want to imagine how the non-vegetarian grand-children would turn out. Eating that sweet-and-sour pork and making fun of her, in Chinese. (She had no idea that Chinese wasn't a language and that

Vivian, being from Hong Kong, spoke Cantonese.)

She started off her letter with a "Hello Sankar," then deleted it, sniffing audibly. This was proving harder than she'd expected. She settled for "Hello My Dearest Sankar" and started writing to him about how much he was being missed. Tathi Ma, who sat nearby, pretending to read a book, was watching her closely.

"So you decided to write to him, *ah*?"

Mrs. Revathi looked up with a little start. She quickly deleted whatever she had written. "No, no, not to Sankar. I was simply writing to Pushpa, you know, Pushpa in Chennai, asking her to check if the building repairs had started. Once they finish the wiring work, they—"

"That you did yesterday. You wrote, asking if the workers were pinching things from our balcony."

Mrs. Revathi was crying for real now. "Why do you always make me feel bad?"

"I'm not, *ma*. I'm sorry, but," Tathi Ma hesitated, "but if you don't get in touch with him, it will become more difficult later."

Her daughter-in-law heaved her chest. "So what, you think we should simply accept? Not say anything? Let Sankar do whatever he wants?"

"He is going to do it anyway, *illiya*," Tathi Ma said quietly.

"I will be all alone in my old age. No one will bother about me, no one with me, even if I'm dying . . ."

Tathi Ma secretly thought she was watching too many TV serials, where the mothers-in-law enacted their daily dose of high drama, accompanied by screechy sound effects. She had to be made to realise that Shanks didn't need her, that *she* was the needy one. If she wanted to have any kind of relationship with her son, she had better put her pride aside and learn to adjust to the twenty-first century.

"You want me to call them, I can do that," Tathi Ma

volunteered. If Revathi was squeamish about making the first move, she, Parvathi, had no such issues. But Mrs. Revathi couldn't allow Tathi Ma to "stoop down," even if it meant stooping to conquer.

"No, no, our Sankar has been taught, from an early age, to respect his elders. Let's wait a little longer, *Amma*. I'm sure he will not forget his duty."

Tathi Ma decided not to push it with Revathi. It was clear that she had no intention of getting off her high horse, at least not just yet. But meanwhile, their stay in New York was fast concluding. The time to act was *now*. So, the very next day, when Mrs. Revathi was in the shower, she called up Shanks. All she got was his voicemail at the other end. And she couldn't follow a word of it! He had put on some strange American accent, obviously switched on for the workplace. After a few attempts, Tathi Ma abandoned her initiative. It was too complicated understanding which button he was asking her to press for what.

Instead, she decided on a bolder move. She'd go to Sankar's office to see him in person. Aware that Revathi was setting out for groceries later that morning, she felt it would be the perfect time to sneak out.

When Revathi emerged from the shower, she'd obviously overheard some part of the voicemail. "Sankar was calling, by some chance?"she enquired eagerly.

"No, no, he didn't call," Tathi Ma replied truthfully. "It was the phone, making funny noises."

Mrs. Revathi had started flick-drying her long wet hair with her towel. She told Tathi Ma she was off to the little mom-and-pop shop, which was quite a distance away, but more reasonably priced. It was criminal to spend three hundred rupees on a kilo—or rather—a *pound* of potatoes, she explained virtuously. Then she disappeared into the bedroom to get dressed.

It gave Tathi Ma the opportunity to quickly go through the transportation leaflets that Shanks had given them. When they'd first arrived, he'd wanted to acquaint them with the main bus and subway routes. "In case you decide to go to check out the Farmers' Market, or Battery Park," he had said. Tathi Ma used the maps to chalk out her route. She'd be taking the crosstown bus to Shanks' office. It wasn't very far, she discovered. A younger person could easily have walked.

Tathi Ma waited till Mrs. Revathi had picked up her shopping bag and was safely out of sight. Then, *she* headed out too, towards the bus stop. Less than half an hour later, Shanks was informed that a Mrs. Subramanian had come to see him. When Shanks heard the news, he blanched, and his blood ran cold. The thought of his mom storming into his workplace had to be the ultimate nightmare!

However, upon entering the reception lounge and spying Tathi Ma in conversation with the friendly Hispanic receptionist, Shanks was stunned senseless. "Tathi Ma!" Shanks was rooted to his spot. "Is everything okay? Is—"

"Yes, *kanna*, everything fine," she replied, coming forward and taking his hand. "I just needed to talk to you."

Shanks quickly completed the formalities to cut his day short and checked whether Vivian would be able to do the same. She informed him that she could spare an hour, but no more.

Soon, they were sitting at an Indian restaurant in Chelsea, and Tathi Ma was updating both of them on "the mood." His mom, apparently, vacillated from extreme pessimism, when she cried buckets, to irrational optimism. During her up phase, she imagined Shanks would ditch Vivian overnight and rush back, repentant and remorseful, into the family fold.

"I was thinking, if you tell her you're getting married soon, she will have to accept," Tathi Ma advised. "Tell her that you are going to run away and get married in Las Vegas. I saw it in a movie long time back, you know, the couple, they have a romance, then after that, they drive to Las Vegas and marry there . . ."

They stared at her, stunned. Shanks knew his grandmother was a radical thinker, but this was a bit too drastic, even for her! Vivian had visions of herself in a cheesy wedding dress and Shanks in a hired tux, posing for wedding photos along with Elvis and Cher lookalikes.

"Oh God, I don't mean actually," Tathi Ma clarified upon seeing their frozen faces. "This is just to scare her, little bit. If she thinks you will get married without her blessings, no priest, no guests, nothing, she'll have to accept . . ."

Shanks was getting the drift. They were plotting to blackmail his mom into accepting Vivian. The rationale was that anything would be better than him "eloping" to Vegas! It was certainly worth a try. Vivian, however, wasn't so bullish. From what she'd seen of Shanks' mom, first hand, the lady was a tough nut to crack!

Nonetheless, they decided to go ahead with Tathi Ma's little ploy. Either way, they had nothing to lose. So that evening, when the doorbell rang, Mrs. Revathi stiffened. She sprang up and turned to Tathi Ma in excitement. "Sankar!"

But when she opened the door and saw that Shanks was accompanied by Vivian, she put on her best funeral face. "Sankar, I'm glad you found some time to come and see us," she said. "I was beginning to think you forgot you had a mother."

Shanks wanted to tell her that that would be very hard to do, but refrained. "Sorry, I've had a lot on my mind," he said tersely.

They came in, and sat down like guests in their own home. Shanks felt like he'd been away for eons, while actually, he realised, it hadn't been all that long. He knew he wasn't particularly welcome. His mom was still waging her lone war and continued to be vengefully anti-Vivian.

But typically, Shanks had misinterpreted the situation. His mother *had* been studiously avoiding all eye contact, or conversation. And yet, she was on the brink of an emotional ceasefire. Was he here to announce his return? Should she make the first move? Given the slightest encouragement, she would have rushed forward and welcomed him back with open arms.

Shanks, meanwhile, figured he might as well cut to the chase. "Ma," he began, "I'm prepared to come back right now." His eyes rested on his mother, and softened. She had obviously been hurt, very hurt, and he didn't want to put her through any further pain. "If only you agree to our marriage."

For the first time, Mrs. Revathi was seeing Shanks and Vivian together, as a couple. Her instinct told her that from now on, she'd always have to relate to her son in that context. He would always have Vivian by his side, and all the tears and tantrums in the world weren't going to change that. The thought of Shanks turning his back on her, and walking out once again, was too distressful to contemplate. She took a deep breath.

"I have a condition," she said. "It has to be a proper Tamil ceremony, with a priest, in a temple."

Shanks stared at his mother till his eyes popped right out of their sockets. She had just passed the most historic judgement of her entire life with no histrionics, no bosom-heaving, and no screechy sound effects. She hadn't even invoked his dad's memory to make her point. It was unreal. Blinking away his tears, he turned to Vivian, who was looking equally teary-eyed. He took her by the hand and led her forward. "Ma, we want your blessings, please."

He bent down to touch his mother's feet, and Vivian, hesitantly, followed his cue. Next, they went over to Tathi Ma to pay their respects. The old lady blessed them whole-heartedly, very thankful they hadn't had to resort to the Las Vegas scheme after all.

By then, Mrs. Revathi's tears were breaking all records. So overcome was she by her own largesse, that her tears flowed in full spate. Even after her emergency tissues ran out, she was still weeping buckets, and had to resort to her *pallu* to mop up. "I'm so happy, so happy to see you both together. Sankar, this will be a *gandharva* marriage, where the bride and groom find each other and fall in love . . ."

Once the hugging and crying cycle was complete, Shanks sank into the sofa, emotionally spent. He still couldn't believe his mom had actually capitulated. The condition that she had put forward was merely an excuse, a face-saver, and he was only too happy to concede to it. Both he and Vivian had already decided they were fine with any kind of ceremony, even a civil marriage was cool.

Mrs. Revathi turned to Vivian. "I should be giving you some gold, as a gift, you understand, a piece of jewellery, but since I was not expecting all this . . ." She pulled off a pair of shiny gold bangles from her hand. "You may please accept these."

Vivian extended her slender wrist, and Mrs. Revathi slipped the bangles on—glittery gold circles that dangled around loosely. It was not a moment to be forgotten. Shanks instantly whipped out his iPhone. "Ma, repeat please, for the camera."

Even as Shanks-the-photographer was getting his lighting and angles right, Vivian was thinking of the bigger picture. Here, for the first time ever, she and her future mother-in-law were bonding—a truce had finally been declared. When Shanks told them to smile, they smiled as much for the happy moment as they did for the photograph. But one thing was certain. This particular photograph would go down in the annals of Iyer history as a template of sorts for future generations!

A short while later, they were sitting down to dinner. As they sat down at the family dining table, as a family, and Shanks tucked into his *sambar*-and-rice heaven, he reflected that this was how it should have been, right from the beginning. A family dinner, with three generations sitting together, all warm and fuzzy as they partook of the simple repast.

The next big hurdle would be Vivian's family. Her Hong Kong-based parents did not even know Shanks existed. But both Shanks and Vivian had decided to take it one step at a time. They had just crossed one seemingly insurmountable barrier. With patience and perseverance, they would overcome other obstacles too.

Later, when Vivian called Shefali, she couldn't keep the excitement out of her voice. "Hey, guess what!"

"Oh my God, it's happened!" Shefali, at the other end, didn't need ESP to decode Vivian's elation.

"Yeah, she's agreed, and even gave me two gold bangles to seal the deal!"

"Oooh, I'm so, so, so excited for you!" Shefali squealed. "When's the wedding!" That was the question they got from everyone who heard their news. No one had thought Shanks might be the first guy to be walking up the aisle, but certainly, it looked like a strong possibility.

The immediate outcome of the truce was that Shanks decided to move out of Neel's place that very same night, and head homewards. His hobo-like existence was finally coming to an end. His air mattress beckoned! Fortunately for him, Neel had recovered sufficiently from his post-Layla digression and didn't require assisted living any more. So, in that sense, Shanks' return into the family fold was perfectly timed. The prodigal son was going home.

He was particularly delighted to be reuniting with his

grandmother. Tathi Ma had made the arduous journey to the US only to see him. For no fault of hers, she'd been caught in the crossfire between mother and son. Now, he wanted to spend more time with her, and shower her with all the love and affection she so richly deserved.

19

Neel was headed home after a long day at work. After the recent Layla episode, he had become very careful about setting himself an evening routine. That way, he could keep his mind occupied and still have a pleasant, tension-free evening. This particular evening, his plan was to complete the golf enrolment formalities, grab a bite, catch the nine o'clock news, and get to bed.

When he let himself in, he was surprised to see that the living room light was on. He didn't remember leaving it on. He was usually very careful about wasting electricity.

Then, he saw Layla.

She was sitting with her legs up on the couch, like an artist's model. Her eyes were fastened upon him.

Neel's head reeled. For an awful moment, he thought he was hallucinating under the influence. He shut his eyes, hoping the illusion—delusion was more like it—would vanish into nothingness. But it didn't. When he re-opened his eyes, she was still very much there.

"Hi." Layla said.

Neel gripped his buzzing head. "How on

earth—" He stopped short, realising that she must have used Lida's key.

"Yeah, you guessed it. I used my mom's key to get in, and surprise you." She narrowed her eyes. "Hey, I was expecting a warmer reception than this! I mean, after our last time . . ."

"It's illegal to break into someone's apartment, you know that, don't you?"

"You're not 'someone,' and I didn't break in. I had a key, remember?" She got her feet off the sofa, revealing almost all of her long, shapely legs. Neel looked away. He didn't need this, not now.

"Please leave, Layla, please." How he wished Shanks hadn't gone back! If Shanks had been there, in his role as nanny-in-waiting, he'd have made sure that Layla was barred from entry. She wouldn't have been allowed even a toehold in!

But as of now, she was well ensconced on his favourite sofa, looking at him with something like amusement. "You're really nervous, aren't you? I don't bite, you know, unless you want me to!"

Neel was about to reply, when his cell phone rang. It was Natasha. "I have to take this," he said and headed off to his bedroom. He really didn't want Layla listening in as he spoke to Natasha, so once he was in the privacy of his bedroom, he firmly shut the door behind him.

When he emerged a couple of minutes later, Layla was pouting, and put out. "So? A new girl in your life already?"

Neel gazed at her. She was beautiful, very beautiful, but really, she was quite one-dimensional. All she obsessed about was her sex life! She had never showed any interest in the larger world around her, like current events, or animal rights, or global warming. Nor could he recall a single instance when she had taken an interest in him as a person. She had never enquired about his hopes, desires, home life, or even his hobbies. It probably stemmed from always being the centre of attraction: perhaps she found it too tedious to divert her attention elsewhere.

"Layla, I'm kind of busy tonight, so it's best if you—"

"Neel, how many times do I have to say I'm sorry?" There was a catch in her voice. "I've told you I'll do anything! I'll make amends. I'm ready to move in with you, if that's what you want."

"No, no! Look," he paused, trying to get it right, "this isn't about forgiving or anything like that. Just that I've moved on, you know."

"Moved on to another woman, you mean?"

Neel frowned. After her acrimonious goodbye, he was surprised that she still chose to come grovelling back in this unseemly manner. In fact, the whole thing was getting very repetitive and tiresome. He felt like a drink. His throat was parched, and he realised he was quite hungry too. He'd have to find a way to get her out of the door, quickly, before—

The doorbell rang. Neel's eyes slid towards Layla, but there wasn't much he could do. He hurried forward to get the door. Before him stood Dr. Natasha Singh, carrying a really enormous take-away parcel.

"Here I am, with so much food, you're not going to believe it!" she said.

"I'm glad you took the detour!" Neel responded, as he let her in and helped her with the packages.

What had happened was, minutes earlier, Natasha had called Neel to say that she was passing by his place. She'd ditched a colleague's party, because she was detained by a last-minute emergency, but the co-worker had generously packed her tons of take-away pizza, chicken, and salads. The quantity of food was so substantial that she'd figured Neel, who lived enroute, might want to share some. She'd called to check if he was available, and if she could drop by.

For Neel, Natasha's call had been an absolute godsend. His only concern had been to somehow get Layla to leave, before she showed up. But now, it was too late. Natasha had already arrived! When he saw Layla sizing her up through slitty, suspicious eyes, he hoped the situation wouldn't turn Jerry Springer-ish. He knew Layla was perfectly capable of a catfight if the need arose. Never in his life as a serial dater had he dealt with a situation like this one: two separate women landing up at his condo at the same time and exhibiting the iciest vibes between them.

Amazed that Neel had moved on so quickly and snagged such a hot prospect, Layla was giving Natasha an openly hostile once-over. She had her grading system down to a T, and was critically checking out Natasha's plus and minus points. Usually, few others measured up to her own score of a perfect ten, but this one was close, very close—tall and classic-featured, with waist-length hair that fell about her like a curtain.

Neel wasn't surprised at Layla's confrontational stance. Natasha was looking quite spectacular, and Layla was obviously viewing her as a rival in his bedroom.

"Hi, I'm Layla," she said to Natasha, without holding out her hand.

"Hi, Layla. Natasha."

Meanwhile, Neel was wondering how to get Layla to exit, peacefully. Although she hadn't bared her claws yet, he was quite sure she would. The only way to avoid a confrontation was to evict her from the apartment, asap, with minimal collateral damage. But easier said than done!

"I'm guessing you didn't have a threesome planned, at least not intentionally?" Layla was curling her lips nastily.

He'd have given anything to murder her smiling face. Natasha was so going to assume this sort of thing was the norm in his apartment. A happy free-for-all—all entries entertained.

Then, quite out of the blue, Layla snatched up her handbag and snarled, "I hate you, Neel, hate you, hate you!" and came at him with the bag. He managed to grab her wrist just in time, to stop her from actually slugging him with it. But it had been a pretty close call!

Natasha gaped in surprise. Wow! This girl was unbelievable! Her little handbag manoeuvre smacked of real desperation. But taking a swipe at Neel, and that too with her handbag, wasn't going to help her cause. Surely she could see that? Her tirade towards Neel, vicious and vitriolic, was guaranteed to push him away even further.

"Good luck to you and your slut out there!" Layla was going down fighting, but this was taking it too far. Neel opened the door and pointedly told her to leave, right away. Before stepping out she turned to Natasha to deliver her final salvo. "Have fun, honey, but do keep in mind it's a revolving door around here. I suggest you keep your options open!"

When he finally shut the door behind her, Neel was a total wreck. He turned to Natasha, mortified. "Hey, look, I'm so sorry about all this, I really don't—"

To his utter astonishment, Natasha sank onto the sofa, giggling. "That. Was. So. Funny!"

Neel really couldn't see the humour in it. He had never considered Layla a source of amusement.

"She actually thought I was competing for your bed." Natasha was still giggling.

Neel was discovering a whole different side to Dr. Natasha Singh. Out of her lab coat, she had revealed herself to be a very desirable woman. But that he already knew. The *other* revelation— her whacky sense of humour—came as a total surprise. That seemed to be part and parcel of her non-doctor avatar. Only Neel wasn't sure whether it was *him* she was laughing at. He smiled a little self-consciously. "Okay, I haven't exactly signed up to feature on Comedy Central, so if you could tell me what the joke is—"

"Oh my God, it's not you, it's your Layla!" She wiped away a tear. "What a drama queen! Revolving door, indeed!" Natasha was making an effort to sober up. "Is that *true*, Neel?"

"Obviously, finding you here, that's how she sees it. As you probably figured, she doesn't like competition."

"Really, she thought I was the competition? So now you don't see her anymore?" She had begun to unpack the pizza boxes.

"We've been on and off—more off than on now."

"So is that why you . . ." Natasha paused delicately. She'd concluded that Neel's on-and-off scene with Layla had to be linked to his mega binge at the Hamptons. While he had never given her the specifics, she was smart enough to connect the dots.

"Umm, yeah, more or less," he admitted.

Natasha pondered Neel's problem. If he really wanted to distance himself from Layla, it was not going to be easy. While he appeared to be happy to get rid of her, she couldn't be sure what his deeper feelings were. "So you think you're still involved with her?"

"Why does everyone keep asking me that?" Neel was losing his cool. "I mean, I just said I'm through with her. I've been saying that to my friends too, but no one seems to be listening!"

He wasn't completely over her yet, Natasha reflected. He was probably in the transition phase. From the little she had observed some minutes ago, she could see that Layla had a way of getting under his skin. In a sense, she was probably as toxic as the alcohol habit he was trying to kick.

"You didn't like her, did you?" Neel asked, reading her thoughts.

She looked up at him. "Neel, I don't have to like her, you do!" Then she got serious. "The only thing I have against her is that she somehow connects to your drinking. I guess it's the tension she creates."

He had to agree. Like all his other friends, Natasha was basically telling him to delink Layla from his life. Well, it was good advice, and he was on the job. His next move would be to get the condo keys back from Lida. That would cut off any such surprise visits in the future. Lida would simply have to come in when he was available at home. If she still wanted the job, that is.

But here and now, his priorities were somewhat different. He was finally alone with Natasha and he intended to enjoy what remained of the evening. So he made her comfortable on the sofa and offered her an orange juice. Then they opened up the cartons of food, and chatted, as they devoured the assorted spread. After a long time, he was having a really chilled evening without missing a drink by his side.

"Now, how about some dessert?" Neel asked, after the dinner. "Ice cream? I've got Häagen-Dazs chocolate chocolate chip."

"You're talking to a chocoholic, no sell needed," Natasha replied. "By the way, does repeating it twice mean *more, more* chocolate?"

Minutes later, they were sitting on his couch again, digging into sinful portions of the fast-melting chocolate chocolate. In normal circumstances, Neel would have made his move by now. He was on his sofa with a stunning woman, consuming large quantities of chocolate ice cream. But he was unsure about the doctor-patient protocol. Technically speaking, he was no longer her patient. So did their evening qualify as a date? He had to know. "You think I'm sending subliminal signals? You know, with the whole chocolate-as-aphrodisiac equation . . ."

Natasha was shaking her head and looking like she might go into giggles again. "Is that why you offered me the chocolate chocolate?"

"Okay, gimme a break, it's all I had in the freezer!"

"Just so you know, there's no proof, no studies to support the chocolate theory. Chocolate contains phenylethylamine—PEA—a chemical that creates euphoria, it makes you happy, but that's about it. The other thing is, it's digested pretty fast, which means it doesn't affect your—"

"You're breaking my heart, doc! You're telling me chocolate and love aren't connected!"

"Sorry to kill the romance, but even for chocoholics, it's psychological, not physiological." She paused and her eyes were laughing. "But hey, you tried!"

"Meaning what exactly?"

Natasha put aside her ice-cream bowl and leaned forward. "Meaning you can kiss me, if you want to."

Neel dumped his own ice cream on the coffee table and let the chocolate chocolate melt as he swooped down to oblige her.

20

As Neel's love life was taking new twists and turns, Shefali was shifting away from romance to other more important life goals. Getting hired was right on top of her to-do list. Her stint as a jewellery designer in the family business was all very well, she told herself, but securing a *real* job was far more challenging! So far, the job hunt had yielded mixed results. She did have a couple of interviews lined up, but her chances were looking pretty slim. So slim, in fact, that the upcoming appointment was making her very, very nervous.

It was going to be her first interview ever. And, although she desperately needed moral support, she didn't want to share her insecurity with the Gang. That would only get her more keyed up than she already was. The one person who could calm her down and contribute in a positive way was Shri. She called him up. "Hey, you busy?"

He'd been watching *Mission: Impossible III* with Paolo, and they were halfway through a thrilling car chase scene. But Shefali sounded a bit urgent, so he motioned to Paolo to put the movie on pause. "Never too busy for you, my *jaan*. Wassup?"

"Shri, my interview's for ten tomorrow . . . and I'm dying!"

"You mean the Harper's?" They had worked on that application together.

"Yeah."

"That's amazing! Now, remember everything I've told you. Be assertive. And don't grovel," Shri instructed.

"I will grovel, because I really want the job!"

"That's not how it works," he repeated. "You got attitude, right? Your diva fixation? This is where you get to flaunt it!"

"What? I give Lisa Labatt attitude? She'll throw me out on my butt!" Shefali was wondering if asking Shri for advice had been such a good idea after all.

"No, my dear girl," Shri went on, "she won't. On the other hand, if you sound like a newbie who's over-awed by the business, she'd pick it up immediately and think twice about hiring you." He paused. "In any case, being servile goes against your grain, so you should have no problem at all." Shefali could almost see him smiling at the other end of the line. "Just be yourself, okay?"

"O . . . k." Although not convinced, Shefali trusted his judgement. "And Shri?"

"Hmm?"

"Don't tell anyone about this interview, because I haven't."

"Okay. Call me as soon as you're out. The suspense will be killing me!"

The next day Shefali was up bright and early. She dressed up carefully, in a fitted electric-blue skirt and a beautifully cut black Chanel jacket. She wore her brand new Jimmy Choo pumps and finished off the ensemble with a really pricey Louis Vuitton bag. She gazed at herself in her full-length mirror, and broke out into a self-satisfied smile. Could anyone say she didn't fit the job?

But when she reached the Harper's office, her self-confidence took a bit of a hit. There were other candidates—several other candidates—waiting in the lobby, looking every bit as glamorous as she was. By the time it was her turn, Shefali was all aflutter. To think that she was finally coming face to face with the much-admired and much-photographed Lisa Labatt! She *knew* she was going to trip over her heels or smudge lipstick over her teeth or *something!* Easy, she told herself, easy. Now was not the time to fall apart.

So she entered Lisa Labatt's sanctum sanctorum with her customary head toss and seated herself with her usual poise. Unfortunately, Lisa Labatt appeared not to notice. She was frowning down at some notes and marking something in an absorbed manner. Known in some circles as the "The Presence," the moniker seemed very apt indeed. She hadn't even glanced up to acknowledge Shefali yet. At least, that's what Shefali thought.

What she was actually getting was an "unflappability test." Ms. Labatt liked to pretend she was busy while she secretly observed the candidate, as reflected on her shiny glass-topped table. For the moment, she actually liked what she saw. A very good aesthetic, she noted, plus her papers indicated she'd studied fashion in Europe. The girl was impeccably, yet interestingly dressed. Lisa Labatt hated boring people, and the one thing Shefali did not come through as was boring. Nor did she fidget or frown when she was being ignored. She just waited, with her legs crossed and her head held high.

"So why do you think you can write?" Lisa Labatt asked Shefali abruptly.

"I think I know fashion and would like to learn to write about it."

After answering a few more questions, Shefali's bratty side got the better of her. She decided that *she* wanted to know a few things too. So she asked Lisa about cutting-edge fashion forecasts and the expanding developing-world markets, particularly the highly fashion conscious Asian markets. She enquired if there was scope for her to find a niche there.

On the surface, Lisa Labatt seemed noncommittal. But she couldn't help being impressed. She liked independent-minded employees who could do their own thinking, even if this one *was* rather pushy. Quite a piece of work, in fact! However, throughout the interview, she didn't smile even once. And when she terminated the session, she deliberately sounded distant, almost dismissive. "We'll let you know. Thank you."

Shefali had to make a huge effort to not burst into tears then and there. She had obviously been a complete, unmitigated disaster. She wanted to crawl out of Lisa Labatt's presence as fast as her legs could carry her. But she remembered Shri's strict instructions. No grovelling, no giving her the upper hand, he had said.

"Thank you for your time," Shefali said, and smiled politely as she rose to go. Then with a light nod, as if *she* were dismissing Lisa Labatt, she walked out with measured strides.

As soon as she was out on the street, she called Shri. "Oh my God, I think I blew it!"

"Meet me in half an hour. Usual place—Starbucks on 23rd," Shri said. Now that he was a converted coffee lover, he had become a regular at all the java shops in the city.

Half an hour later, Shefali was pouring out her first interview experience before Shri. She looked at him anxiously. "So? What d'you think?"

He laughed. "I can't answer that! You'll just have to be patient. And don't forget, this was just your first one. There are more to come."

"Oh God, if I don't get this, what will I do!" Shefali wailed.

"You'll do just fine, on your very generous allowance," Shri said dryly. That was when she realised how selfish she was being.

He had made the time to help her with her job search and, even now, he was being so supportive for a job she didn't really need. And here she was, not even enquiring about his status.

"Oh my God, I'm so sorry." She got up and circled her arms around him. "I'm being my usual self-obsessed self!"

"Hey, it's okay," he said, touched. "We help each other, right?"

"Right. Only I haven't done much helping so far."

"I'm getting by, but . . ." Shri was finding it difficult to continue.

Shefali held him even tighter. "Hey, I'm here for you."

He nodded wordlessly. His jobless status and the humiliating job-hunting process, with all those endless rejection letters, made him want to hang his head in shame. He worried about what Paolo would think of him. Would he see him as a wasted, washed-out shadow of a man, with no future ahead of him? With Paolo, it was hard to let his defences down, because he always felt he had an image to uphold.

But Shefali was different. With her, he could let it all hang out. She was family, the little sister he'd never had. He squeezed her hand gratefully. "I'll be honest with you, I'm pertified," Shri confided. "So petrified, some days, I can't get out of bed, can't function at all, you know. I'm like, blanking out, Shef, I'm forgetting things. Losing track of time."

She could see that he was going off into the deep end again. She'd never seen him so despondent, and didn't know how to respond. "Don't fret too much," she said comfortingly. "Something's gonna work out, you know it is."

"When? And what happens till then? I'm illegal, I'm an alien, right? I mean, technically they can put me behind bars anytime. I could be held in custody or deported or—"

"Wasn't Neel supposed to be helping out?" She could not

allow him to rant on.

"He's doing what he can, I suppose," he admitted grudgingly.

There was no point in discussing his future any further. His tension was only escalating. So she decided to change the subject. "Hey listen, why don't we do Thursday at my place this time?"

Shri did a silent *oh!* "I was supposed to tell you! Completely forgot. Neel says, enough of this stay-at-home business. We should all step out and enjoy the fall season, and have—"

"No way, he's not ready to go bar-hopping just yet!"

"Not bar-hopping, no, what we had in mind was a dinner place, where anyone who wants to drink can drink."

Shefali nodded. That sounded good. Of late, she'd gotten a little more comfortable about being around Neel. Considering how frequently they met, she knew she'd have to find an equation where they could be just friends.

So the following Thursday, after a long gap, it was not the usual take-out in someone's home. They were meeting in a proper restaurant and Neel was hosting the evening as his "coming out party." He'd picked a trendy new Moroccan place, where the menu—as listed on their website—looked just awesome.

Once they were all seated around the large round table, Neel raised his non-alcoholic beer glass. "This is a double celebration," he said. "First, let's congratulate Shanks and Vivian for being officially Iyered! Woohoo!"

Vivian held Shanks' hand and smiled, to general applause. "Thanks, people, we couldn't have done it without you."

Then, Shri held up his glass. "And Neel? To your second coming!" There was another vociferous round of cheers and claps. Neel bowed gratefully. "Whoa. I hear you guys, I hear you. Thanks!" He looked around, deadpan. "And hey, a special mention for my bodyguards here. Shanks? Shri? Take a bow. Thank you, *both*, for breathing down my neck with such enthusiasm. I mean, short of following me into the loo!" He smiled, shook his head, and continued. "Don't get me wrong, I'm grateful, very grateful. If I stand here today, it's only because of your merciless, cold-blooded, inhuman—"

By then, his bodyguards had overpowered him and forced him to sit down again, and shut up! It was fun. Finally, after a long dry spell, everyone was letting their hair down and having a good time. However, in all the merriment, Shefali was aware that she needed to think about Shri. So she waylaid Neel as he was heading back from the men's room. "Hey, need to talk."

She looked so worried that he was immediately concerned. "Everything okay at home? Your dad?"

"Yes, all's well there." She paused. "Neel, it's Shri. I'm really disturbed about his mental state, I—"

"Hell, me too!" He was startled to find Shefali echoing his own concerns. "*I'm* getting kind of anxious about him too. He seems . . . zoned out?"

"Zoned out is exactly right. Should we talk to Paolo? Ask him to do something?"

"What can Paolo do?" Neel chewed his lip. "Paolo and I, we're both trying our best to set him up, but it's not easy. We've lined up our contacts, pulled favours. Let's see where it goes . . . he's got a couple of interviews for next week." His expression lightened. "And how's *your* search going?"

"Not going," Shefali grimaced. She hadn't heard anything from the three interviews she'd done so far. It looked like she and Shri would be contributing to the current jobless statistics for a little while longer!

Then suddenly Neel said, "Oh. Just struck me, I knew someone in the fashion space, not so long back. So if you need a toe in, I could—"

"Oh don't worry about me. I'm doing fine so far." She

guessed it had to be the same former girlfriend that Shri had mentioned a few days back. She was happy that Neel had offered, but she wasn't still comfortable with favours of that kind from him. Until she had a better idea of where they stood with each other, she had decided to remain cautiously neutral.

But that didn't mean she couldn't look her best. She was young, attractive, desirable, and had every intention of letting Neel see it. Her short bandage dress hugged her curves quite enticingly and her light, no-make-up look was especially flattering. She knew she looked good, and from the way Neel was eyeing her, she knew he knew it too!

She'd read him right. In her clingy dress and hot new hairstyle, she did look quite ogle-worthy. But he was determined not to make any moves till he had his own head sorted out. Natasha was still a work in progress. While they had ended up in bed that night, after consuming copious quantities of chocolate ice cream, he was kind of confused about where it was all headed with his erstwhile doctor. He found it almost strange that she wasn't getting clingy, or asking for a commitment of any kind. Her work seemed to be her priority, which was all in its place, but—

"Neel, hello. Are you listening to a word I'm saying?" It was Shefali, sounding very miffed, and still very much on the Shri topic. "Pay attention, will you? What I'm saying is, he seriously needs to see a shrink. You think your doc could recommend someone?"

"*My* doc?"

"Yeah, Dr. Natasha Singh is your doc, isn't she?"

"*Was*." Neel emphasised. "But, yeah, sure, I'll ask her. And let's hope he agrees."

"Yup, let's hope," Shefali said. "I mean, he's a freaker-outer, but even he must see he needs help!"

So the time had come to introduce Shri to the S-word. Without hurting his sensibilities, they needed to convince him to see a shrink and start some sort of therapy. When they got back to the table, Neel waited for a suitable opportunity to broach the subject. But just when the moment seemed ripe his cell rang. "Natasha?"

Everyone had stopped talking. They all turned to stare at Neel, smiling away into his cell phone. Since when was he on "Natasha" terms with her! He was gesticulating towards them, checking whether she could join them too.

"Of course, Neel, call her." Shefali said, with a forced cheerfulness. She had considered the possibility of something between Neel and Natasha, but hadn't been one hundred percent sure. He didn't need to see her professionally anymore, so certainly, that left the personal field wide open. That Neel was attracted to Natasha was hardly a huge revelation. The doc was a very attractive woman.

What came as a revelation was her own reaction. She was *still* not over Neel. Her Neel-mania seemed to be alive and well!

Less than half an hour later, Natasha walked into the restaurant, looking quite different from business-like Dr. Natasha Singh they knew. She'd morphed into her doctor-off-duty persona, which was really like seeing a completely different woman. Even Shefali, who knew fashion made a difference, had never seen such a transformation, just for shedding a lab coat! The doctor's manner had changed too, especially towards Neel.

"Hi Neel, hi all . . ." She managed to squeeze herself next to Neel and, after getting settled, turned to the others. "I hope you guys haven't been waiting to order?"

They had been. Neel raised his hand for a waiter.

Meanwhile, like Shefali, the Gang too was wondering about his cosiness level with the good doctor. He hadn't mentioned being this pally with her. They were, therefore, quite unprepared for such a quick turnaround on Layla's replacement! Although they were dying of curiosity, and wanted to know more, asking was obviously not an option. His body language with Natasha seemed intimate, but unlike Layla, she wasn't falling all over him. It was hard to decode what was *really* happening.

A little later, when Natasha rose to go to the ladies', Shefali accompanied her. They were at the washbasin counter, doing all the girl things in front of the mirror. "Hey, I hope you don't mind. I wanted to catch you alone," Shefali began.

Natasha looked at Shefali in the mirror. "Oh? Is this about Neel?"

This girl was very direct, Shefali noted, almost amused. That could be a good thing, or a bad thing, depending on how you looked at it. "Oh, no, I'm sure you have Neel well under control." It was hard not to be just a little bit bitchy. "I wanted to talk about Shri."

"Shri?"

"Yes, we think he needs a shrink. So if you know someone . . ."

"Oh, I see." Natasha considered. "Okay, yes, I can get him in touch with Bethany, she's really good. She doesn't take new patients, but I can speak to her . . ."

When they got back to the table, Shefali gave Neel a speaking look. He needed to get working on Shri asap. Neel obediently steered the conversation towards stress levels in general, and even higher levels of tension for people who didn't have jobs. The jobless ones could get extremely depressed, and the sad part was, they often didn't realise they needed help.

Shri picked it up immediately. "Are you referring to me, by any chance?"

Neel said, "In a sense, yes. I mean, you have to admit, you've been kind of stressed lately . . . so it might be a good idea to see someone, you know, someone who can—"

"A shrink." Shri brought the S-word out in the open.

"I know someone really good," Natasha added. "I could put you in touch—"

"Why? You think I'm losing it? Is that what you think?" Shri glared at her. Then he turned to the others. "That's what you all think, don't you?"

"Now look, you're overreacting," Shefali said. "All we're saying is, you could use some help. So what's the harm in seeing a good practitioner who could—"

"I'm not seeing a shrink and that's final."

"Your call, bro," Neel said, soothingly. "No one's forcing you to—"

"Yes, you are! You, and your doc here."

That was the second time someone had called Natasha that. She wasn't *his* doc—why couldn't they get that straight?

"Natasha has nothing to do with this, and, anyway, if you're not interested, let's just forget about the whole thing, okay?"

But they couldn't forget, because Shri continued to bite all evening (and it wasn't just the food!). The Gang knew that until he found a job, they were going to have to put up with a wired, highstrung freaker-outer in their midst. They had to remind themselves that that was what friends were for: to smile and support and still be treated like shit.

Later that night, in the privacy of their bedroom, Shri reached out to Paolo. "I behaved like a total jerk tonight, I know. I'm sorry."

Paolo took his chances. "Maybe the shrink thing isn't such a bad idea, you know."

Shri nodded and drew Paolo closer. He decided to sleep over it. Little did he know that, by the next morning, things were only going to get worse. What changed was, the following morning,

236

Shefali actually landed herself a job. The confirmation letter was sitting in her inbox, awaiting her final response. So from that moment on, Shri was the sole job-seeking Gang member, with no takers for either his coffee, or his woes!

Shefali, meanwhile, was feeling quite self-congratulatory. Lisa Labatt had hired her! She was going to be a working girl! She grabbed her cell phone, to convey the good news to Shri. Then suddenly, she went all goosebumpy. What could she be thinking? Only last night, the poor guy had had a near meltdown, and here she was, gloating over her new job. Nope, no way she could tell him. She'd have to conceal the happy tidings, until he had something lined up too.

But she had to share her headlines with *someone!* She called Ryan, to announce her triumph. Depressingly it went to voicemail, so she left a brief message, assuming he'd call back. Then she texted Vivian, with strict instructions to tell Shanks to keep his mouth firmly shut. Not too surprisingly, within ten minutes, she got a call from Neel.

"I know I'm not supposed to know, but I hear congrats are in order."

"Shanks, of course?"

"Of course."

"Stupid old me, expecting that blabbermouth to shut up." Shefali's heart was doing its usual summersaults, as it always did when she spoke with Neel. She hated herself for being such a wuss. It was crazy to have feelings for a guy who was so very unavailable. "Anyhow, just as well I guess, and thanks for calling. Though I have to tell you, I still can't believe I got this . . ."

"You underestimate yourself," he said.

She wanted to say, "And so do you." Instead, she said, "You better be right on that one. I mean, I'm so nervous. It's a high pressure job, from the get-go."

"You'll do fine," he assured her.

If only, she sighed silently. Then, as they disconnected, she burst into tears. It was probably the relief of getting the job, she lied to herself. Because the truth was harder to face. "You'll do fine" was not what she wanted to hear from Neel. He sounded like her dad. And as for Ryan, the less said the better—he didn't even have a real voice, only voicemail!

Shefali might have been slightly happier if she'd known that, at that moment, Neel was thinking of her. He hadn't expected her to find herself such a plum assignment, so quickly. The fashion industry was still in the doldrums, but she had obviously made an impact, on her own terms. He couldn't help being impressed.

Then his thoughts drifted to Natasha. A super achiever, she was so career-focused it was scary. He hadn't gone public yet, but they were sort-of-dating. At least, he hoped they were. With Natasha, he never knew if it was a date or not. It just felt like time-squeezed-in before her next emergency call.

"I'm not sure, tonight looks iffy" was one of her favourite expressions. Although she'd moved into the city a month back, to pursue her fellowship, she was still renting a service apartment. Whenever she was free, she landed up at his place to spend time with him. But Neel wanted her in closer proximity. He wanted her to move in with *him*.

"What stops you from giving up that sketchy rental of yours, and moving into my nice, stylish condo, with actual closet space, and—"

"You won't want me sharing your place. I have stacks of books and notes and coursework files. Enough to fill up an entire bedroom!"

"Notes in the bedroom! Why!"

"Notes in *bed*," she clarified. "Because I study in bed, of course! If I'm not at the hospital, on duty, then I'm in bed, studying . . . and it will be far too distracting to have you in the same bed. Therefore."

Her "therefore" was delivered forcefully, and sounded final. He would be competing for her in bed, with her books. Neel felt he could deal with that. "So tell me, where do I fit into your Rolodex? If I do, that is!"

She had assured him he very much did. The little time they spent together was quality time. Coincidentally, she was really into golf too, which she'd started learning during her brief stint at the Hamptons. So when Neel mentioned that he'd recently enrolled for the game, she perked up. "Oh good, we should do a practice session together! And, hey, let me tell you, once you get started, you're gonna be hooked."

Neel discovered, as he got the hang of the game, that he had quite an aptitude for it. And Natasha was right. It was easy to get addicted to golf. Fortunately, it was an addiction he could live with, and not have to worry about the consequences. The other big bonus of being with her was the fact that she *was* a doc. Neel often teased her about it. "You know, you're playing so hard-to-get, I'm gonna have to invent medical emergencies just to catch hold of you!"

What he loved best, however, was the way she laughed, and made him laugh. Neel had never imagined he'd fall for a woman because of her sense of humour. But Natasha was that woman. The funny side was in addition to all her other plus points, of course. A guy like Neel wouldn't be caught dead with an average-looking girl, but with Natasha, even the lab coat Natasha, that would never be a problem.

"So do I get to be part of your Thursday club?" she had wanted to know.

"You already are, whether you like it or not."

"What about initiation rites? No tattoos, bloodletting, eating fifty *gulab jamuns* . . ."

Neel shook his head, smiling. "Sorry to disappoint you."

"I just hope they like me . . . I know they're an important part of your life."

"Yeah, they're family . . ."

"So tell me about your *real* family . . . any brothers? Sisters?"

Neel couldn't ever recall a girlfriend asking him such questions. Was it because he'd never dated an Indian girl before? He told her how, after his sister Manisha had got married, and moved to Sydney, he had seldom seen her. She had a set of two-year-old twins on her hands, so her life was pretty crazy. His parents had visited her from Delhi, but he still had to make that trip. What invariably happened was, every winter, he ended up going to see his parents in Delhi, so that took care of his annual leave.

Apart from immediate family, Natasha also wanted to know more about Shefali.

"Honestly, I don't know how to answer that one," Neel responded. "We were not exactly dating, but it wasn't platonic either . . ." He looked up. "But that's history, she's seeing someone now, at least, I think she is!"

"She's still in love with you, I hope you know that."

Neel was extremely uncomfortable discussing his relationship with Shefali. She was a very dear friend, and nothing or no one could change that.

"She's a great friend to have," was all he would say. So Natasha left it at that. She liked Shefali, and wanted to know her better. But right now, making new friends was a challenge, she barely had time for Neel!

Sometimes, when she was too exhausted to head back home, she'd fall asleep on his sofa, with her notes around her. The next morning, she would find he had already left for work. But her notes would be stacked in a neat pile and a duvet would be spread out over her. He also kept a thermos flask with fresh-made coffee by her side. Sometimes, there would be handwritten notes, about porridge in the micro, or organic waffles in the fridge.

So much sexier than text messages, Natasha would tell herself, smiling.

21

It was Monday morning in Manhattan. Striding forth in her brand new Blahnik heels, keeping up with the momentum of the surging crowds, was Shefali. She couldn't believe how many million New Yorkers were out of bed and on the streets. That such multitudes ventured out at this unearthly hour was quite a revelation. Now, she was one of them too.

She made her way into the swanky Harper's building and displayed her ID to the guard on duty. Security was crazy, she discovered. She'd need an extra five minutes every morning, lining up, just to make it into the building. When she finally reached the office lobby, a handful of other interns were already hanging about, waiting to be summoned. Feeling viciously relieved to see the newbies looking as lost as she was, she introduced herself around, and made polite conversation with some of the friendlier ones.

Soon, they were all herded to The Presence. And Lisa Labatt had exactly one minute to spare. "This week, you'll go through the departments, wardrobe, photography, studio, props, news desk, and see how we do things around here." She raised a non-existent eyebrow. "No coffee breaks, no water cooler conversations. And no—I repeat—no touching the racks without permission. Any questions?"

No one dared to open their mouths.

"You may go."

It was a bit of a downer to be doing peon-level jobs all day, but that was exactly what she did. By lunch, Shefali was in heel hell, Blahnik be damned! All she wanted was to kick off her stilettos and run around barefoot. Till late evening, she and the other interns busted butt as general gofers for a magazine shoot that was scheduled for the following day.

As Shefali finally emerged from the building, well past rush hour, she felt like extruded meat coming out of a meat grinder. She resolved to buy herself a pedometer, to clock how many footsteps she was logging on a daily basis. Ten thousand steps at least, she estimated, as she slipped thankfully into a waiting taxi.

She really wanted to share her day with Shri, but realised, very guiltily, that she still hadn't told him. It was unfortunate that Shanks had randomly gone and announced the news to everyone and now, Shri was the only Gang member who didn't know. She made up her mind to meet Shri, within the next couple of days, and talk to him in person. The other friend she still had to inform was Ryan. She tried calling him again, but once again, there was no response. Well, technically, there *was* a response—a digital one. She left another message, even briefer than her previous one.

Shefali wished she was thick-skinned enough not to care. She wanted to be the twenty-first century woman who accommodated men into her busy schedule and rationed time for multiple partners, depending on her mood. Her EQ level would be subpar, but at least she'd be having a good time. One of the hottish guys at work had already sent out feelers. Maybe she should check him out, no strings attached.

But there were more immediate matters to attend to! She reached for her handbag, placed beside her on the back seat of the cab, and plucked her cell out. She called Rachna Ben, instructing her to be ready with towels and a basin of hot salt water. She, Shefali, needed to soak her desperately aching feet.

Her new job continued to chew up all her waking hours. So all the way up until Thursday evening, she'd had no time to meet Shri. By then, her conscience was seriously beginning to bite, and she was thinking about ditching the Thursday do altogether. On the other hand, the evening offered her the opportunity to catch Shri alone. She told herself she needed to be there.

So by the time Shefali arrived for the get-together, she was carrying a lot of baggage. A whole week's worth of guilt was sitting heavy with her! Her gameplan was to slink in quietly, seek Shri out, and explain the situation to him right away. But that didn't happen because, as soon as she walked in, she got the usual noisy Gang welcome, with cries of delight from everyone. Everyone except Shri. He was eyeing her strangely. "All formal today," he said. "Did you have an interview or something?"

She froze. "No, I . . . actually . . ."

"Don't tell me you've started working." Shri's frown was a storm cloud, threatening to wreak havoc on humankind. Now he knew why she'd been avoiding his calls. Now he knew why she had come in late, dressed in a smart working suit.

Shefali lowered her eyes. "I didn't want to tell you because—"

"—because poor Shri, how can we tell him? He *still* doesn't have a job!" Then his voice turned dangerously quiet. The calm before the storm. "Am I the only one who doesn't know? Am I?"

The loaded silence was all he needed. Shri leapt up and went completely ballistic. "Shef! How *could* you! How could you after everything we've been through together!"

"Shri, it's not like that, please understand . . ." Shefali was in tears.

"You, all of you, call yourselves my friends, but except for Paolo here, no one, *no one,* really cares about me or my feelings! You think any of you know what I'm going through? Do you have any idea what it's like to sit waiting for that phone to ring, waiting for that letter in the mail? Always watching over my shoulder, because someone could come and handcuff me? Haul me away? No! Instead, what do you do, all of you? You keep secrets, you exclude me from—"

"Shri, shut the fuck up." Paolo was quiet but authoritative. Shri's rant, which had reverberated around the entire restaurant, was suddenly silenced. The hushed pause, however, was equally unnerving, because now, they anticipated a rapid fire round two, more lethal than round one. Shri appeared to be just warming up. By then, people at the other tables were watching them with keen interest. This was like dinner theatre, free entertainment along with the food and drink, and the angsty guy was pretty awesome.

"No one's deliberately hurting you, you know that," Paolo said gently. "So, just sit down and—"

"No! I'm not sitting! I'm *so* done with all this shit. I'm going to go start packing my bags right now! And I'm taking the next flight out!"

"Please!" Shefali pleaded. "I'm sorry. Okay, I know, I should have told you—"

"Well, you didn't." Shri turned to Paolo. "Let's go."

"No." Paolo was emphatic. "We're not going anywhere. And you're not going back to India either."

Everyone turned to stare at Paolo. Did he know something

they didn't? Shri frowned. He had never known Paolo to bullshit. "What d'you mean, not going back."

"I mean you and I—*we*—are going to get married."

There was a huge, collective gasp. All of them, Shri included, stared at Paolo like he'd lost it.

Shri finally found his voice. "Are you crazy? We can't get married!"

"Yes we can. Shri, I'll look after you. I'll love you to eternity . . ." Paolo was down on his knees. "Will you marry me?"

Shri quickly collapsed into sitting position. "You really mean it, don't you?" His voice was an awed whisper.

"Yep." Paolo was still smiling.

By this time, the other diners in the restaurant had got the general drift and had started clapping. Shri was so embarrassed he didn't know whether to take a bow or dive under the table. "Oh my God, I don't believe this. I can't believe . . . and I don't know why I'm—" he broke into a muffled sob "—crying."

The Gang couldn't believe it either. They had just witnessed one guy proposing to another guy. It was the first and probably the last time that they'd ever see such a moment. There, right before their eyes, Shri and Paolo were holding hands, and looking into each other's eyes.

"P, I love you," Shri said to Paolo, mistily.

"Me too," Paolo replied.

Marrying Paolo was certainly the perfect solution to Shri's problems. Once they were married, he would, over time, become a legitimate US citizen. The state of New York had legalised same-sex marriage in 2011, so they could actually get married in New York City itself. Immigration authorities frowned upon marriage under false pretences, but in their case, there was no such issue. Paolo decided to firm up the first available date for the civil ceremony. He wanted to legitimise their union as soon as possible.

Shri's happiness was marred by one spoiler: his parents would not be there for the wedding. Inviting them was clearly not an option, considering that as of now, they didn't even know he was gay! So for him, basically, only the Gang would be attending. In Paolo's case, his half-brother, Pedro, and his wife, Jen, would be the only family members present. His parents were no more.

After the civil ceremony in the morning, Shefali wanted to throw an evening after-party for the newlyweds at her place. Although there was very little time, and very few wedding guests, she still planned to go all out on the celebrations. So despite her hectic work schedule, she got busy with the caterers and florists and musicians and decorators, meticulously coordinating every detail.

Groom-to-be Shri was busy too, getting back on track. He had unrolled his yoga mat again and renewed his lapsed gym membership. But most important of all, he was back in the kitchen—much to Paolo's delight! On that particular day, he was experimenting with an Indian-style Spanish paella, which he called "Dum Paella." It was his own unique culinary invention, a surprise for Paolo, who was expected home soon.

He was so caught up with the intricacies of the recipe that he almost missed his ringing cell phone. He answered absently, stirring the pot of simmering fish stock and throwing some strands of saffron into it. But when he heard the caller at the other end, he almost dropped his cell phone right in with the saffron. It was Morgan Stanley, responding to his interview with them. They wanted to hire him. And he was being asked whether he'd be ready to start in a month? Or did he need more time?

Shri would have no recollection of what he said. All he knew was, at the end of the call, the job was his! When he disconnected, he was too dazed to even finish up his cooking. He simply went into a stupor and stood staring into his gently bubbling paella.

And that was how Paolo found him, a few minutes later. "Shri?" Paolo was concerned about his partner's zoned out expression. He just hoped Shri wasn't regressing into one of his moody blues spells again. But Paolo got the shock of his life when suddenly Shri turned to him with a face-splitting grin.

"Guess what! They just hired me, P! Morgan just hired me! I join in a month!"

For a few seconds, Paolo was speechless. Then, he stepped forward, and put his arms around Shri. He felt Shri return his embrace. It was a moment to savour, to express his love. "I never doubted you, you know that, don't you . . ." Paolo murmured.

Shri was in tears. Till that moment, he hadn't realised just how much he depended on Paolo. And how much he needed him in his life. Shri hesitated. "P, I never wanted you to think I was marrying you for the passport. But now you know it too, right? All this while? All the crap I've put you through? Now I get a chance to show you how much I care . . ." Shri said, and broke out sobbing on Paolo's shoulder.

With the job in place, Shri was all set to have the perfect wedding day. He reflected, gratefully, that he was living his very own American Dream. He was getting married to a man he loved, with full sanction of the state. He couldn't ever imagine making a trip to Mumbai and presenting Paolo as his "husband." Not that homosexuality wasn't common in India, he reflected, but it still had a stigma attached to it. While he wasn't judging, he knew that was the reason he could never go back. India was another world, another planet, not meant for people like him, or Paolo.

On their big day, Shri and Paolo had chosen to wear identical bespoke suits, cut slim and narrow, in the latest Italian style. (Apart from the expense of buying bespoke, they'd also shelled out a hefty premium for speedy delivery!) When the dapper, impeccably dressed bridegrooms arrived at the New York City Clerk's office, half an hour ahead of their appointed time slot, the Gang was already there. And soon, they were joined by Paolo's brother Pedro, and his wife, Jen.

In the normal course, one witness would have sufficed, but they managed to squeeze themselves in, Indian style. The private ceremony was to be conducted by a Marriage Officiant, who appeared to have a busy day ahead. "The grooms both here?" He glanced at Shri and Paolo and leafed through their papers. "All in order. Gentlemen? Witnesses? This way please."

It was a brief and beautiful civil ceremony. The Gang was proud to witness a gay marriage and to be part of a social phenomenon that espoused equality as a basic human right. Shri had needed that acceptance, and here, in the most iconic city in the world, he would have it. Once he was married, he could apply for his green card. Really a case of all's well that ends well.

As Shri and Paolo tied the knot, there was not a dry eye in the room. Neel glanced at Shefali and saw she was busy mopping her eyes. "I'm happy," she informed him, "just getting a bit emotional . . ."

He smiled at her in his usual heart-stopping way. "It's okay, someone has to cry . . . otherwise it wouldn't be an Indian wedding, would it!"

After it was all over, and the newlyweds joined them, they had never seen Shri looking so happy. It was quite a novelty to be congratulating two guys and not seeing a bride around! Everyone, except Shri, had to rush back to work, so the actual celebration would have to wait until the after-party. Although Neel and Shanks had wanted to pool in for the do, Shefali had insisted that she wanted to host this particular bash. "I feel like I orchestrated the whole thing, by getting Shri so hopping mad. So now I have to see it through!"

There had been nothing Indian about the wedding ceremony, so she had been determined, right from the start, to host a full-on *desi* after-party. She'd ordered flowers, and lots of sandalwood incense sticks, and *kandeel*-style lanterns. The menu included an array of fusion cuisine appetisers to go with the drinks, followed by a catered Indian buffet. For those who wanted to dance, she'd arranged a Bollywood-style DJ.

She planned to dress traditional too, in a sari, and managed to persuade Vivian to do the same. "You mean, like, a real sari?" Vivian was nervous about the whole thing unravelling in a puddle around her feet. But Shefali convinced her to come in a little early and get properly pinned up.

So, when Vivian showed up that evening, Shefali had already picked out her ensemble. Vivian would be wearing a beautiful peach-coloured net sari with a silver-gold blouse. The blouse was a stretch viscose, which meant she didn't need an exact fit—it simply moulded to her shape. The look was accessorised with matching jewellery, which Shefali was lending her. "Rachna Ben, pins!" Shefali demanded, as she helped Vivian get draped. Once Shefali got her pleats and *pallu* securely tucked up, and coordinated all the jewellery, Vivian looked like a vision.

Then Shefali got busy with her own dressing up. By the time the guests started arriving, she was at the door, in a rose pink Benarasi tissue creation. She'd set off the pale pink with a spectacular antique-style emerald choker and dangling medallion earrings, in the Umrao Jaan tradition.

"You could be the bride, you look so beautiful!" Vivian exclaimed when she saw her. "And since we don't actually have a bride, you've got to be the eye candy for the occasion!"

Shefali *did* look sensational. Her heart-shaped face and almond eyes were suited to Indian wear. And her elegant, poised demeanour added that touch of class that money couldn't buy.

At the door, she greeted her guests with perfumed water—*attar*—and flowers. When Neel walked in, with Natasha, he did a double take. Shefali in a sari was even more stunning than Shefali in the skimpy bandage dress, and that had to be quite an achievement!

A few minutes later, Shefali did a quick mental headcount. All the guests seemed to have arrived, so she needn't be doing door duty anymore. There were tons of other things that needed her attention. She turned away, and almost shut the door, when suddenly, her eyes widened in disbelief.

Walking towards her, with a smile on his face, was Ryan! What was *he* doing, gate-crashing into her party! He'd worn a kurta, and carried what looked like a gift, so obviously, someone had actually invited him. She tossed her head and pouted. He couldn't just show up at the door behaving like nothing had happened. And how dare he smile so shamelessly after ignoring her for almost a month. Men!

Ryan came up to her, smiling even more broadly. "I know you're pretty mad. And I don't blame you."

Shefali frowned. "What are you doing here and who told you about—"

"I picked up Shri's message when I got back from Zimbabwe yesterday."

"Zimbabwe!"

"Yeah, when I saw his message, we spoke—"

She stared up at him. "So Shri invited you?"

"Yes, but I gotta say, you don't look too happy to see me!"

She wasn't sure about the happy part. Yet. "You know I tried getting in touch, but—"

"Yeah, I know, and I'm sorry." Then he told her that he'd got her messages too, and after talking to Shri, had decided to surprise her, by simply landing up at her doorstep. His trip to

Harare was one of those spontaneous decisions he often made in the line of duty. He'd taken his team to Africa to camp out in the interiors and work on a local project there.

Shefali knew, then, that his work would always come first. He was passionate about making the world a greener place. Renewable energy was his way of life, and renewable love was part of the package. He would disappear into the sunset at frequent intervals, and reappear to a new dawn.

"You know, I can't believe it," Ryan continued, "I've been out for almost a month." He paused. "I missed you."

Shefali knew the emotional yo-yo would have her on tenterhooks, because she'd never know where she stood with him. His casual, free-wheeling ways meant she'd have to cut him slack, lots of slack! So either she could deal with it, by recycling the relationship every time he made a fresh appearance, or bail out right here, right now.

"And in case I didn't mention it, you're looking beautiful!" He deposited the gift down and drew closer. "Can I kiss you in public?"

"It won't be the first time!" The look in his eyes decided it for her. Ryan was a chance she was going to take. Luckily for him, Shefali always believed in making quick decisions.

So the Gang got an action replay of the Ryan and Shefali lip-lock. A long, smouldering kiss that seemed to go on forever. When they finally came unstuck, she was quite embarrassed to see they had a packed audience. Ryan smiled down at her. "We have some serious catching up to do. Meanwhile, I should go congratulate the happy couple."

Soon, the DJ got everyone onto the dance floor, and the party really took off. The spotlight was on the happy couple, who were showing off their synchronised Bollywood dance moves. Shri had spent his idle time well. He'd checked out YouTube for K Jo movie songs with peppy dance tracks. "Desi Girl" from *Dostana* was a particular favourite, so, along with Paolo and Shefali, he'd managed to choreograph a rocking version of his own. While the three of them did an amazing job, it was Shefali, doing the Priyanka bit, who was clearly the belle of the ball.

Neel watched her with mixed emotions. When Ryan had reappeared, and had very publicly demonstrated his feelings for Shefali, he'd felt something like regret. He was witnessing what might have been. But he told himself to stop being selfish, and small-minded. Now, as she danced the night away, without a care in the world, he had to tell himself, yet again, that he had no business to grudge her her happiness.

Shefali *was* very happy. Her personal life seemed to have magically turned around, all in the course of one evening. But romance had to take a back seat, because she was still on hostess mode, mingling with the guests, and making sure that everyone ate well.

She was really surprised, pleasantly so, when Natasha came up to her and held her hand. "Well done, hostess with the mostest! The party's spectacular, as are you! Absolutely stunning!" Shefali sensed that the praise was genuine and couldn't help thinking it was generous of Natasha to be so forthright with the compliments. Maybe that was what had Neel smitten—her sincerity. Certainly, after Layla, she was a refreshing change.

Shanks, the self-appointed "official photographer" was flaunting his new high-end camera at every opportunity. That basically meant he was busy clicking Vivian in her sari, from every possible angle! Whenever he managed to tear his eyes away, his lens focused on the lively goings-on of the Gang. He could feel love in the air. Hopefully, it would be his turn next. Then Vivian appeared by his side, pulled his camera away, and dragged him onto the dance floor.

The new track had a bhangra beat. The mood was electric. The lights changed colour. Shri and Paolo switched to another choreographed act, to showcase their zesty bhangra moves. Their energy levels had the crowd applauding. Soon their friends formed a circle around them and started clapping in sync with the beat. As the tempo picked up to a staccato frenzy, the newlyweds upped the ante too, matching each other step for step.

Their married life had begun.

22

November was upon them. Mrs. Revathi and Tathi Ma were preparing for their long, twenty-seven-hour haul back to Chennai. To make it even more arduous, Mrs. Revathi was lugging back a new eighteen-piece Pyrex set, several yards of lace curtain material, a digital weighing scale, stacks of kitchen wipes, two mock-leather party handbags, and several bunches of plastic flowers that looked almost real. The last item had been purchased for "gifting" to relatives and building friends. Tathi Ma, slightly more circumspect, had bought only a pair of orthotic slippers, her six-month supply of Centrum Silver multivitamin pills, and good quality saffron, because in India, you just couldn't be sure those things weren't adulterated.

Shanks and Vivian had also added several other thoughtful items to the packing list. So, once again, the two ladies were way above their stipulated baggage allowance. Shanks knew he'd have to pay up the fines, but he didn't mind. Ever since his mom had held out her white truce flag, he was feeling expansive about many things in life, including excess baggage.

What had completely blown him away were

his mother's subtle hints about Vivian getting back with him in the apartment. It would have been too much to expect her to endorse a live-in arrangement outright. But clearly, she wasn't against it either. "I'm leaving *sambar* powder in third shelf of the cabinet," she had told Vivian, "when you make for Sankar." Another time, she bought an enormous bottle of coconut oil and planted it in his washroom cabinet. "In case Vivian wants to use, very good for head massage."

That was as good as it got, thought Shanks. He'd never imagined his mom could morph into such an easy-going, indulgent parent in such a short time. Ever since she'd taken the first baby steps, she seemed to be making great strides towards the adjusting process.

The day before they were leaving, the Gang wanted to come by to bid farewell to the two ladies. "Most welcome," Shanks told everyone, "but I'm telling you in advance, gifts not allowed!" He was having a tough time fitting in all the last-minute extras into the jam-packed suitcases.

The Gang now very much included Paolo, so the question was, could he come along too? During the dosa do, he hadn't been a Gang member. Now, he was. Although Mrs. Revathi had mellowed, and mellowed a lot, they decided not to push it. It was decided that Paolo would make his appearance as Shri's colleague, included in the farewell party because they happened to be sharing an apartment. (No subterfuge there, it was the truth on both counts.)

So when Paolo arrived Mrs. Revathi had no idea that she was greeting Shri's new husband. She thought he looked like a nice young man, with very good manners. Upon being told he was a coffee connoisseur, she went out of her way to invite him to Chennai, to sample their exciting array of local brews. The Gang didn't know which way to look when she turned to Shri and said,

"You must bring your friend and both of you come and stay with us, I insist!"

Neel had dropped by solo, without Natasha. She'd been called into ER at the last minute. Mrs. Revathi did not know about Natasha, so she caught hold of Neel at the first available opportunity. "Neel!" she said conspiratorially. He knew exactly what was coming. "So Sankar has Vivian now. What about your turn next, no?"

Neel couldn't wiggle out of it. She was holding onto his hand quite tightly. "Oh, let's hope so!" he said.

"Why hope only? I have very nice girl in mind, she's little bit dark, but otherwise—"

"Oh, no, no, no!" Neel felt he'd better set the record straight before Mrs. Revathi took up his cause in right earnest. "No, what I'm saying is . . . I'm hoping the girl I'm seeing will, umm, agree to, umm, marry me."

Mrs. Revathi was indignant. "Why she will not agree? What is wrong with her that she will not marry *you*? Better you should have mentioned this before. I am happy to talk to her and tell her . . ."

Neel was thanking his lucky stars that she was leaving the very next day, with no time to negotiate a matrimonial alliance on his behalf. It was also fortuitous that she was too preoccupied with Shanks' love story to *really* worry about his friends. Her top priority was her daughter-in-law-to-be, and she was going out of her way to make it up to her. "I am sending some Diwali gift for you, from India," she told Vivian. "My friend Vidya will bring, when she comes to New Jersey next week, but what it is, I will not tell you. It is a surprise!"

Vivian was overwhelmed. From being persona non grata, she'd become the blue-eyed girl, eligible for all kinds of favours. She hoped the warm vibes would continue. Meanwhile, Mrs.

Revathi was already speaking about fixing a wedding date! As soon as she returned to Chennai, and consulted with the family priest, she was all set to send out the invitations for the auspicious event. At that point, Vivian had to remind her, gently but firmly, that *she* still had to inform her parents. Although it was not a huge challenge, it could take some time. The wedding, therefore, could still be several months away.

While the Gang was in full attendance, Shefali was conspicuous by her absence. As it happened, she'd already fixed up to meet Ryan that evening. It was their first legit date, not the make-believe stuff they'd enacted for the benefit of the Gang. So she hadn't wanted to cancel. In any case, he was in the city for such brief spells that every moment was precious.

Not that she'd be missed at Shanks', she told herself. If anything, Mrs. Revathi would be relieved not to see her—after mistaking her for the prospective daughter-in-law, it could have gotten awkward! But despite Shanks' no-gift diktat she *had* sent a gift. She had given Vivian a small blue velvet box to convey to Mrs. Revathi. In it was a gold coin, embossed with the image of Goddess Laxmi. Along with it was a card, saying, "Sorry to miss the farewell party. Please accept this as a small Diwali gift, in advance. Have a safe trip back. God bless."

When Mrs. Revathi saw the gift and read the note, she was completely breathless. What a sweet girl, what a kind gesture! She burst into spontaneous tears and, for the next half hour, was quite incapable of speech. This was quite a novelty for everyone, especially Shanks. Shefali had managed to silence his mom for an entire half hour. Wow!

Shefali, meanwhile, was having a great time with Ryan. They were at a lively Irish pub, and he was thoroughly enjoying Shefali's latest update on the goings-on of the Gang. "So did the Layla gal reappear?" he wanted to know.

Shefali had to tell him that Layla hadn't resurfaced at all. No one knew whether she had reunited with the guy called John. Not that anyone cared. The Gang had had enough of her disruptive presence to last a lifetime. Even Neel had put Layla behind him, and was looking at happier times ahead.

When Ryan had seen Neel with Natasha at Shri's wedding, he'd marvelled at Neel's quick reshuffle on his romantic Rolodex. That guy took serial dating to another level! After Shefali finished her status report, he smiled. "You guys sure had a busy month," he observed. "I mean, think about it. I've been away barely— what?—four weeks? And in that time Shri got a proposal, Shanks got his mom's blessings, and—"

"And Neel got his doctor!"

He smirked. "Yeah. Now that leaves *you*, doesn't it?"

"What *about* me?" Shefali pouted. "You think I'm still pining for him, don't you?"

He looked at her thoughtfully. "No, I don't think so. I think you're over him."

Shefali sipped her drink and looked into his eyes mockingly. "Mind reading, Mr. Odd Jobs Man?"

"Yeah, something like that . . ."

In the month that he'd been away in Zimbabwe, he'd done some serious soul-searching. While he loved his freedom and his unfettered existence, it came with its own handicap—it meant putting his love life on hold. And of late, he was beginning to feel the void. He wondered if Shefali had something to do with this new awakening! Although he barely knew her, he'd felt an emotional connect from the second she'd hurtled into his arms, and into his life, on that fateful day at the Hamptons.

It went beyond the initial physical attraction. They'd started out as strangers, then bonded as co-conspirators, and, finally, become friends. In sharing her dark and duplicitous secret about the make-believe ex, he felt especially close to her. The icing on the cake had been her twenty-fifth birthday celebration. On her special day, he'd been the guy in her life and in her bed. That was a big deal.

He smiled at her. "Remember what you'd said that day at the beach? Life happens?"

She nodded. Surprising he still remembered that little detail!

"So what I'm saying is, life happened to me too. Like I mentioned at the wedding, I was away . . . and I missed you, more than I want to admit."

Shefali was gratified. Unlike Neel, who was always *kanjoos* with the compliments, Ryan was pretty upfront about his admiration. He praised her openly and often. When he told her she looked great, or spoke about missing her, she wanted to believe him! In his easy, laid-back way, he knew how to make her feel special.

After they were through with their drinks, they meandered out onto the frenetic streets of Manhattan. It was a busy Friday night. Although the weather had turned appreciably cooler, the sidewalks were packed. After walking a short distance in companionable silence, Ryan turned to Shefali. "Umm, how about I show you my Manhattan home?"

Her eyes widened. Really, this man was full of surprises! He looked apologetic. "I should have mentioned it earlier . . . I have this pad on the Upper East. Used to be my grandmother's home."

So they made their way to his grandmother's home. *She is no more*, he explained to Shefali. But she'd left it to him in her will. He used it occasionally when he stayed over in the city, but of late, he'd hardly ever visited the place.

When they got out of their taxi and made their way towards the entrance, a white-gloved doorman ushered them in. A liveried concierge greeted Ryan in a formal manner and escorted them towards the elevator. It was a classic white-glove building on the Upper East side, as snooty as you could get. The place exemplified old money, a bygone era, when ostentation was a way of life. Shefali, who wasn't exactly new to any of this, was amazed that despite all the trappings of wealth, Ryan could be so down-to-earth.

What Ryan had modestly called his "pad" turned out to be a large three-bedroom apartment. It was much larger than her place, and far more opulent. "I kept it the way I got it," he said, sounding almost embarrassed, "didn't want to change any of Gran's stuff."

After he'd given her the tour, they settled down with a bottle of cognac. A short while later, the antique four-poster in the master bedroom was put to the test. As they unleashed their passions in bed, their feelings for each other intensified, with each passing moment. Later, the fire in his eyes was still alive, when he held Shefali close and whispered, "I'm not done with us yet. This is only the intermission."

The next morning, they ordered breakfast from a twenty-four-hour deli down the street. And Ryan insisted on serving her breakfast in bed. As Shefali sipped her moccachino, she couldn't help feeling that they were at a turning point in their relationship. Something had changed, overnight.

He appeared to feel the same. "You know, it's kind of weird. I mean, I don't know how this works, but after last night, I feel like I've known you for ever . . ."

She blinked. Was he saying what she *thought* he was saying?

"I have a proposition for you," he continued, smiling. "I'm on offer right now, going cheap. So if you're ready to cut me another one of those cheques, I'm, umm . . . quite available."

"Oh? Really?" She was smiling too. "And the going rate? Negotiable?"

"Your terms."

"My terms! I don't think you know what you're getting into, Mr. Odd Jobs Man. I can drive a pretty hard bargain, you know . . ."

"You're on."

She stared at him, transfixed. He wasn't laughing any more. In fact, he was looking very serious indeed. And waiting for her answer.

"I . . . I'm on," she repeated, shaking her head, like she couldn't believe what she'd just said.

Their eyes locked, and, without taking their gaze off each other, they got under the duvet cover again. "Oh, did I mention, *available with immediate effect?*" He sounded slightly muffled under the cover.

"Now that's what I call a bargain . . ." That was Shefali, equally muffled.

They ended up spending the entire morning in bed. Neither was sure how their situation would translate on the ground. He was still based in the Hamptons. She was in New York City. He travelled all the time, and she had crazy hours on her job. There just wasn't a common meeting point, apart from the occasional rendezvous for dinner, then sex, at his apartment or hers.

However, they'd have to overcome the odds, and find ways to make time for each other. He could come into the city sometimes, and she could manage occasional weekends at the Hamptons. The logistics would be quite a challenge, putting a whole new spin to "meeting each other halfway"!

Interestingly, they had the means to commute by helicopter, a service available to rich and privileged New Yorkers, for a few thousand dollars. They could fly between Manhattan and the Hamptons in a matter of minutes. But Shefali knew, without having to ask, that Ryan would never agree to any such scheme.

Considering how very conscious he was about wasting precious fossil fuel, chopper trips would be a highly avoidable lifestyle choice. If anything, Shefali reflected, *she* might have to cut down on her use of limo services and other such indulgences. Ryan himself was perfectly happy to use public transport.

The next day, when Ryan and Shefali announced that they were dating, it barely created a ripple. The Gang obviously assumed they were dating *again*, after knowing one another for ages, so it hardly seemed like such a big deal! What was astonishing, in their view, was that it hadn't happened sooner.

"So you're official for the Thursday nights now," Shri informed Ryan, smiling. "Join the Gang!" Ryan Giffords was being anointed into the hallowed circle.

From the three original founder-members the Gang had expanded its franchise. Shefali, Vivian, Paolo, Natasha, and, now, Ryan were all part of the core group. Their presence added a whole new dimension to the Gang subculture. It was understood that English would have to be the "official" language. However, that didn't stop the Gang from teaching the new members some choice Hindi swear words, in exchange for similar words in Cantonese, Spanish, and Punjabi. Nothing like sharing some good *gaalis!*

At around the same time as Ryan and Shefali "reunited," Shanks and Vivian were reuniting too, in the real sense. For them, six months of being apart was six months too many! So the minute the two Mrs. Subramanians waved their goodbyes at the airport, and disappeared from view, they headed straight to Vivian's apartment, picked up her bags, and drove back to Shanks' place.

When Vivian stepped into the familiar surroundings, she found some not-so-familiar additions. Stacks of stainless steel vessels were piled in the kitchen, and a plastic shower curtain was lovingly draped over the wall-mounted TV. "To keep the dust out," Shanks told her, with a grin. A pungent smell of asafoetida hung about in the air. And a small washing line had been constructed in the bathroom. It still had a couple of kitchen towels drying over it.

Vivian shook her head, smiling. The love nest would need some work before she could be completely at home.

23

Shri and Paolo were looking at a change of address. While Paolo's studio was great for a single guy, the place was getting too cramped for a couple. Soon, with their double income, they'd be in a position to upsize. The joint budget afforded a really nice one-bedder in an upscale building. With a bit of luck, they might even get a den thrown in.

So they got busy checking out rental condos. Street Easy was a great place to start. And *The New York Times* listings had some great options too. Both Shri and Paolo knew it was going to take time. Their hyper-evolved sense of aesthetic would not allow them to settle for the ordinary. They were going to be demanding tenants!

"I need a kitchen with proper stone counters, preferably granite," Shri told Paolo. "And the flooring's gotta be hardwood, no laminated stuff for me."

Paolo was keen on a rain shower, maybe a jacuzzi in the bathroom, and a good-sized den. In Manhattan, where even basic sleeping space was a stretch, their expectations seemed a little unrealistic. The Gang felt they were getting a little too ambitious.

"Why on earth would you need a den?" Neel wanted to know. "You'll get guests popping up all the time, sponging off you, because you have extra space."

That was when Shri and Paolo glanced at each other. Shri fidgeted. "Umm, well not right away, but, umm, in a year or so, we might think of starting a family, so—" The rest of his words were drowned out by a babble of voices. Everyone wanted to know where that was coming from!

"We'll adopt, of course," Paolo said. "A girl would be nice." Babies were so far from everyone's mind that just the thought of a baby in their midst, in the not-too-distant future, was kind of unnerving. From personal experiences with their own nieces and nephews, babies seemed like a shitload of work. Newborns, at least the ones they'd seen, came with high-decibel vocal chords, 24/7 feeding times, and continuously dirty diapers. Surely Shri and Paolo weren't signing up for all that!

But once again, the newlyweds assured the Gang it wasn't happening anytime soon. Shri reiterated that his top priority was to tell his parents he was married. He planned an Atlanta trip with Paolo to break the news. It made sense to finish that commitment before he took up his job with Morgan Stanley and got consumed with the new work routine.

In the normal course, he'd have stayed with his parents. But introducing a potential daughter-in-law was very different from bringing home a husband! Clearly, courtesies like receiving them at the airport, or welcoming them home, were redundant. Instead, they drove out of the airport in a rented car, and checked into a Holiday Inn.

Before he set out to meet his parents, Shri turned to Paolo for moral support. "P, I'm not sure where all this is going, but regardless, I—"

"Regardless, we're gonna do just fine, right?"

"Right." Shri gave him a lingering hug, and then, reluctantly withdrew. "I love you P."

"Love you too. Drive safe . . ." Paolo smiled tenderly.

As Shri made his way to his parents' home, he was determined to keep it as simple and straightforward as possible. No unnecessary lies, no beating about the bush. He and Paolo had decided that if there was some sort of a positive response from his parents, Paolo could join them later, for a dinner out.

Shri was aware that this was going to be one of the hardest meetings of his life. Far more intimidating than a job interview, or even meeting an "arranged" girl. But it had to be done.

A little earlier, he'd called them to let them know that he was coming. When he drove up, both his parents were out on the front porch, eagerly awaiting his arrival. An unexpected visit from their son was rare indeed. They would have laid out a red carpet if they had one.

Over the past couple of months, they'd often discussed between themselves what a stranger he'd become. Ever since he'd lost his job, their communication with Shri had been stilted and sporadic. They were just grateful that he hadn't cut them off completely. So him showing up like this, at short notice, was like Christmas coming early.

Shri got out of the car and walked up to his parents. "Shri!" He subjected himself, best as he could, to the usual hugging and kissing.

"How's Shefali? Why you didn't bring her?" his mother wanted to know.

Shri made some non-committal noises and shepherded them inside. What he was about to say required them to be sitting down, preferably with a stiff drink in hand. In fact, he could have done with a stiff drink himself! What he got, however, was a cup of his mom's homemade mint tea, made with real mint leaves from the garden. As he sipped his tea, the conversation was desultory, about this and that. He noted that they carefully avoided bringing up his job status.

Through the small talk, the question on his mind was, should he tell them the bad news first? Or the good news?

"I have some news," Shri finally said, taking the easy way out. "I got a job. With Morgan Stanley."

They were all over him, in seconds. His mom draped her arms around him, and his dad thumped his back in jubilation. Their son had come good! They knew he had it in him to succeed! "Shri, such good news, and you never mentioned! Why!" His mom was staring at him in wonder.

By then, Shri was dying a thousand deaths. Served him right, he told himself, for delaying the bad news. Now, after creating this bubble of excitement, how was he going to tell them what he really needed to?

"Umm, *Aai*? *Baba*? I . . . also have some, erm, bad news."

He saw his parents staring at him uncomprehendingly. Bad news? Whatever could he mean? "You don't have proper job, or what," his mom ventured.

"No, no." Shri swallowed. "It's not about the job. I . . . the thing is, I . . . I have to tell you that I don't like girls. I like guys."

His parents turned to each other, quite mystified. What he'd just said made absolutely no sense to them. She reverted to him for clarification. "Means?"

Suddenly, Shri found himself becoming strangely detached. It wasn't *him* saying what he was about to say. Maybe it was his defence mechanism to cope. He turned to his father and looked him in the eye. "*Baba,* I'm gay."

"Gay." His father swallowed. "Gay! Meaning you like to be romantic with another man?"

"Yes."

His mother could scarcely get her next words out. "Shri, do you mean to say you love another *man?*"

Shri was surprised to feel hot tears trickling down his face. He hadn't even known he was crying. "I do."

For the next few minutes they were too shell-shocked to utter a syllable. The bad news cancelled out the good news, several times over. Being jobless was nothing compared to *this!* Their only son was a gay homosexual and he was openly admitting his guilt. Living here, in the US, he had become influenced by all these funny Western ideas. This nonsense about men holding hands on the road, and coming on TV shows like married couples, had turned his head. It was not possible for two men to love—couldn't he see that?

Finally his father looked up. "So . . . you have someone like that? Someone you . . . like?"

Shri hesitated. "Yes, I got married recently, to a very nice . . . partner," he didn't want to say husband, "and he is here in Atlanta with me . . ."

His mother found her voice again. "You are *married?* To a *man?*"

"About two weeks back, we . . ." He couldn't continue. Seeing his parents in their present state of shock and knowing he was responsible for their pain was too much to endure. Even his good news seemed like nothing now—a throwaway bit of information that meant nothing.

"How can we mention this to anyone . . ." It was his father, speaking to his mother, as if he wasn't there. "What will people say?"

It appeared that his parents were going to pretend it never happened. The plan seemed to be to go on as before, ignoring the fact that their son was gay, and had gotten married. The only part they'd skip, figured Shri, was actually showing him any more girls. Tentatively, he asked, "I don't suppose you'll want to meet Paolo?"

Their stony silence was answer enough. Shri rose. There didn't seem to be anything more to say, on either side. By then, his mom was sobbing convulsively into her *pallu*, and his father was staring out of the window, grim-faced. Their brilliant son was now tainted and tarnished beyond redemption. Disowning him was the only face-saver, if they wanted to retain their standing in society.

When the Gang heard about the disastrous Atlanta trip, they consoled Shri best as they could. It sucked having to give parents bad news, especially something as out-of-the-box as Shri's announcement. Not only had he confessed he was gay, he had also told them he'd gotten married to another guy.

"Give them some time to soak it all in," Shefali said soothingly. "Once they internalise the whole thing, they'll accept it too."

But aside from the problem with his parents, Shri was grateful for what he had. A great husband. A kickass job, starting soon. And an amazing group of friends who more than made up for his non-accepting family. So it wasn't all bad, by any means.

Next on his agenda was the big move. He and Paolo had zeroed in on a sensational one-bedroom plus den. When he'd walked into the high end kitchen he'd wanted to start cooking then and there! Paolo, too, had salivated over the library-cum-den, which was ideal for stocking their wines *and* displaying his beloved antique porcelain tea-cup collection. Finally, after some deft negotiations, they managed to seal the deal on a two-year contract.

It called for a party! They timed their move to coincide with the Thanksgiving weekend, so it was going to be a double celebration: a housewarming plus a Thanksgiving bash, all rolled into one happening evening.

"So see you guys at six," Shri informed everyone. "And guys, no Indian Standard Time, please." IST was the accepted time of arrival for all Indian guests. It usually went at least an hour over the actual time of invitation. Sometimes the grace period extended to two hours, or more. Nothing was that urgent, was how the guests looked at it. It was not as if the host was running off somewhere! The main thing was to land up at the right venue, look mildly apologetic, mumble something about the crazy traffic, and head straight for the bar.

The Gang, however, knew better than to land up late for one of Shri's do's. He was perfectly capable of depriving them of the appetisers, or directing late-comers straight towards the dinner table, without allowing them one single drink! His meticulously prepared menus could not be repeatedly warmed up, he'd tell his indignant guests.

But quite apart from Shri's uncompromising stance on tardy arrivals, the Gang had another reason to practice punctuality— they'd finally accepted that Indian Standard Time did not apply to the rest of the universe. The non-Indian Gang members were always on time, often brutally so. That meant everyone else was forced to adhere to some sort of a schedule too. So basically, the host could not be caught in the loo, having a shower, when the doorbell rang. Habitual offenders like Shefali had a really tough time of it, but thanks to the new job, she was getting a little more aligned to the real world.

And, as always, a timely entry into Shri's home came with its own rewards! He had cooked up a chef-worthy storm in his new kitchen, with a menu that offered a cross-cultural tandoori turkey (already slow-roasting in the oven), masala spiced ham, three different salads, and home-smoked salmon. Shefali and Ryan had come with the wines, and Neel and Natasha with two desserts.

"My first attempt at *gajar halwa*," Natasha told Shri, as she unloaded her bags on the kitchen counter.

Shri sampled it and raised his eyebrows. "Umm, Doc, you ever decide to opt out of medicine, you know what to do."

Shanks and Vivian appeared shortly afterwards, bearing an enormous spider palm. It was their house-warming gift for Paolo. He'd spoken about getting in some greenery, and Vivian wanted to inaugurate the garden. The plant was given pride of place in the living room, facing east. It blocked up two whole seating spaces, but plant-lover Paolo was cool with it. Wasn't that why they'd moved into a bigger place to begin with?

That evening, the Gang was celebrating happy endings in many spheres of life, particularly romance. But Neel's situation was still a bit of a question mark. He was dating Natasha, that much wasn't in doubt. But she was still doing more night shifts at the hospital than she was doing with him! As a result, their sex life was getting kind of sporadic.

"I'm tired of having a time limit on you," he said to her. "You come over, and your clock is always ticking!"

"I'm available by the hour," she would joke. "Something like those high-class call girls. Call it my occupational hazard!"

But it wasn't so funny anymore. Her unavailability was beginning to get to him. When he saw Shanks with Vivian, or Shefali getting cosy with Ryan, he was reminded about the inadequacy in his own relationship. Having a partner who was perpetually on call, whether it was Layla earlier, with her boyfriend, or Natasha now, with her emergencies, he seemed to be the one who was missing out.

This Thanksgiving, she'd made a special effort to be with him over the long weekend, which was great. He watched, as she circulated about, very much at home with the Gang. Maybe they'd get the night together, or again, maybe not. With Natasha, he'd have to take things one day at a time—night by night was more like it—and enjoy her company whenever she clocked in.

Neel sipped his non-alcoholic beer and thought about the other little diversion in his life. (As always, he was attracting more female attention than he needed to.) It had happened a week back, quite by accident. He'd been trying to flag down a cab. To his surprise, he found it was occupied, and the occupant was none other than the hot Latina from his building. She had peeped out of the window, smiling. "Great timing, Neel. Are you headed home too?"

He had hopped right in. They'd shared cab rides a few times before too, but this time, she seemed to be smiling more. He already knew that her name was Eva, Eva Lopez, and that she was from Chile. They started the conversation discussing the sucky rules the new building management had enforced. Griping on common problems was, as always, uplifting. The talk soon drifted to more personal matters. Neel discovered she was a banker too, working on the research side of the business.

When they got out of the taxi and walked into the building lobby, she was still smiling. "Great bumping into you," she said. "We should meet up sometime . . . if you're up for it."

Neel could not say no. The following day, they met up at a gourmet burger joint down their street. She hadn't mentioned a boyfriend or any significant other in her life, so he assumed she was single. But he kept telling himself it was only a dinner out, nothing more. True, they *did* live in the same building. She was two floors up, and one phone call away. He tried not to think of the possibilities.

"Hey, last drink before dinner." It was Ryan, holding up a fresh mug of non-alcoholic beer.

Neel reached out for the mug and smiled at Ryan gratefully. "Thanks man. Appreciate your looking out for me."

He rose, and followed Ryan towards the rest of the company. The party was rocking. Paolo was teaching Vivian to salsa. Shefali and Natasha were partners, trying to imitate their moves. Shanks, who was no dancer, was drumming an impromptu salsa beat on the dining table. And Shri, next to him, was accompanying the beat with a high-pitched vocal imitation of an electric guitar. Shefali beckoned Ryan and Neel to join the madness.

"*Aye Ganpat!*" Neel yelled, and jumped in between Shanks and Shri. "*Bajaa na!*"

The three of them went full throttle for the DJ remix version. Everyone else crowded around and waited for their *Aye Ganpat* cue. "*Aye Ganpat*," they yelled when their turn came.

Suddenly, there was a loud ping from the kitchen. "Oh," Shri smiled, "turkey's done, people."

FiNGERPRINT!
DIARIES

Author	Madhuri Iyer
Date of Birth	24th August
Sun sign	Leo/Virgo (I get to choose!)
Hometown	Mumbai Meri Jaan

The Author

Madhuri Iyer completed her O Levels from the London University and graduated in Applied Arts from Sophia Polytech, Mumbai.

She has worked for over twenty years as a copywriter-creative director in Mumbai, Dubai, and Canada, in agencies like FCB-Ulka, Lowe Lintas, Everest Saatchi, Clarion McCann, and Cossette Inc. Currently, she consults for advertising agencies on creative projects.

Madhuri has edited and contributed recipes and case studies to Penguin's *Four-Week Countdown Diet*. She has also edited fitness books for the Times of India Group. Her first book *Pink Champagne* was published by Indireads, an online imprint. *Manhattan Mango* is her second work of fiction.

Favourites:

Authors:	Rohinton Mistry, Hari Kunzru, Vikram Seth, Jane Austen, P. G. Wodehouse, Trevanian.
Movies:	Guru Dutt to Woody Allen, the classics basically.
Singers:	Rafi. What a voice!
Drinks:	Darjeeling tea, any time of the day or night.

In Conversation

Tell us how *Manhattan Mango* took shape.

I had a gorgeous view of the Hudson river from my Manhattan apartment and suddenly, one fine day, the inspiration flowed from there. Okay, just kidding. *Manhattan Mango* made its debut on my MacBook about two years ago. I loved the city's multicultural facets, and the amazing people who've made Manhattan home. Very soon, I found my fictional characters taking over my life and talking me into writing 75,000 words about their shenanigans.

If you were allowed to do only one of these things—reading books, listening to music, watching movies—which one would you choose and why?

Tough! But movies, I think, because the medium showcases every aspect of creativity.

Quotes:	"Life is what happens when you are busy making other plans." - John Lennon
Fictional character:	A toss up between Bertie Wooster, Obelix, Batman, and Poirot. And, oh, Winnie the Pooh!
TV shows:	Right now, *House of Cards* and *Downton Abbey*.

Who introduced you to books? Which were your first books?

The local circulating library. At one book a day (luckily my parents had a monthly membership!), I devoured the Enid Blyton series, Nancy Drew books, and Panchatantra tales.

How did your interest in storytelling originate?

I concocted stories for my little sister. Whenever we got to the climax, I'd ask for a favour before completing the story. It worked every time.

If you could choose any country/city in the world to stay in, which one would it be and why?

I want the people of Mumbai, the buzz of Manhattan, the history of Istanbul, and the beauty of San Francisco. So maybe I'll just settle for the moon.

Ebooks or paperbacks? Why?

Call me old-fashioned but paper any day.

The most blatant lie you have ever told?

Hello, I don't fib!

The best and worst thing about working in advertising?

I love what a great adman once said: "Advertising is the most fun you can have with your clothes on." I loved every moment, even the manic deadlines.

A book that you have wanted to read forever but have not somehow gotten around to reading?
The Lord of the Rings.

If you were stranded on an island, which three things would you want to have with you?
Sunscreen for sure. Food and water optional.

The craziest thing you have ever done?
Driving on black ice.

ACKNOWLEDGEMENTS

Anita Shirodkar, my sister-cum-photographer-cum-sounding board.

My daughters, Disha and Kahini, who read and re-read my drafts and made me delete lots of uncool words among other things.

Friends, for their faith. Shalini Kagal, Rekha Kalekar, Shanti Prakash, Zain Raj, Milena Marques-Zachariah, Manasi Joshi Roy, Jeanne Merchant, Meenakshi Alimchandani, Sanjiv Sharma—thank you!

Sonam Kapoor, Sharman Joshi, Shashanka Ghosh, and Rohit Roy, for such mind-blowing endorsements. I am overwhelmed.

A huge thanks to Kanishka Gupta, my agent, who signed me up with Fingerprint!

Shikha Sabharwal of Fingerprint!, amazing and unflappable, always. My editor, Sankalp Khandelwal, who worked through the line edits with enormous patience.

And to everyone in the Fingerprint! team, thank you.